Challenging the Heart
A MMA Romance
R. Katze

R. Katze

Print ISBN: 979-8-9931528-2-0
e-book ISBN: 979-8-9931528-3-7

Cover design by: Getcovers

Edited by: Wildflower Words Editing

Printed in the United States of America

I would not be writing without the love and support of my friends and my husband. You all mean the world to me.

This story started in High School, with a friend who fought in the underground fighting circuit, who has helped me with making sure I was using the right terminology and mindset for Kane and the fighters. Without him, this story would not have happened, and to him I say thank you, and I truly appreciate you.

Trigger Warnings

This book contains descriptions of fighting scenes, both professional and not. It also has references to injuries and the treatment of the injuries during a match. There are brief mentions of parental abandonment, but they are short comments that explain the personality of one of the characters, and does not feature in a large part of the plot.

Chapter one

The roar of the crowd washed over Kane Mitchell as he stood in the middle of the octagon, his opponent circling him cautiously, bordering on fear. He knew what the man was staring at—6'1" of pure contained power, his short black hair and gray eyes that he had been told shone like coals. He knew he was intimidating, and he had honed that reputation.

Kane felt the familiar anger burning through his blood and let it power his movements. He wasn't studying the movements of the man he was facing; he didn't need to. He had watched enough footage of other fights to know the man's weaknesses, the flaws in his technique.

The referee's voice was a rumble as Kane's focus narrowed, his gaze locked on the drops of perspiration on his opponent's brow. The bell rang out, sharp and demanding, and Kane moved in.

His challenger weighed in at 183 pounds. The man was trying to make a name for himself, but the bleached tips in his dark hair and his many tattoos made it hard to take him seriously. The man launched into the first attack, coming at him with a jab that Kane sidestepped easily.

Kane responded with a gentle hook, not putting weight behind it, just enough to sting. He was bored—he hoped that the fight would help push through that, but given the first few moments, he wasn't sure it would.

"Come on," Kane snarled, his voice muffled by his mouthguard. "Make it worth my time."

The man's eyes narrowed, and he came running, a flurry of punches and blows that Kane blocked. The muscle memory acquired over numerous bouts in the ring had taken over, his body responding to threat before his brain could. No matter the adversary, it was always the same.

A punch grazed Kane's cheek, and he felt a surge of irritation. The guy had power but didn't follow through. Kane retaliated with a knee to the stomach that doubled his opponent in half and concluded with a tight uppercut that sent the man stumbling backward.

It should have knocked the guy out, but Kane held back at the last moment. Taking him out then would have been too simple, too quick. First, the crowd had paid to see a fight, not an execution, and taking the guy down now would have been just that. And second, Kane needed more time to let the rage work through him. Other guys went to therapy, but his therapy had always been his fists. Agitation had been building too long for him to let the fight end quickly.

The round ended with a speck of blood from his opponent's nose spotting the canvas as he backed into his corner. Kane stood in the middle of the octagon for a few seconds longer, barely winded, before slowly turning away with deliberate intent.

"You're playing with him," his coach, Thomas Jackson, said to Kane as he sat on the stool, accepting a squirt of water from the man without once taking his eyes off his opponent.

Kane spat into the bucket. "He's nothing."

"Just finish it in this round. Don't drag it out."

Kane didn't utter a word, but his jaw tightened as he glared across the octagon. There was no way he was doing that. The anger that had been stewing in him had barely been touched in the first round.

The bell for round two sounded, and Kane stepped back into the center with renewed determination. This time, his opponent landed a few more punches, and Kane felt the force of knuckles on his shoulder and ribs as a spark of hope seemed to light up his opponent's eyes. Only they were punches Kane had allowed to hit him. It wasn't that he couldn't block them—it was that he welcomed them, wanting the blows.

As the seconds ticked by, though, his boredom washed over him. This wasn't a challenge. This wasn't worthy of his skill or his training.

His opponent, perhaps sensing a shift, came on with a wild combination. Kane blocked the first two punches, but the third, a looping hook, got past his guard and struck him on the jaw. There was not much force behind it, but the audacity of it sparked something in Kane.

Enough.

With precision that had been developed in thousands of hours of training, Kane pretended to go left, then surged forward with a right hook that connected with his opponent's temple. While the man staggered, Kane followed up with a knee to the gut that forced all the air out of his lungs. And finally, when his opponent's defenses dropped, Kane delivered the final punch, a perfectly timed uppercut that connected on the point of his jaw.

The force of the blow echoed through the arena, silencing the crowd for a moment before they erupted into cheers. His opponent crashed into the canvas, the man's eyes rolled back into his head, and his arms and legs flopped where they landed.

Kane towered over him, his breath ragged from the adrenaline rush, rather than the exertion. The referee pushed him back as he checked the fighter on the ground, but Kane already knew the fight was over. He'd felt the knockout in his hands when he had connected.

As the referee's hand took his to raise in victory, Kane looked out at the screaming crowd with detachment. The rage had ebbed, replaced by an empty feeling of satisfaction that was already fading.

It was another win for his record books. Another night spent proving he was the best.

Yet, as he moved to leave the octagon, Kane could not rid himself of the feeling that none of it mattered. He was 28 years old, the fights should be getting harder with new and younger fighters coming into the league...and yet the fights were growing easier, the victories less satisfying. He required something more, something that would challenge him, push him to his limits.

He needed to feel alive again.

***

The locker room smelled of sweat and antiseptic as he sat alone on a metal bench, removing the tape from his knuckles. Each layer he removed revealed bruised flesh beneath, but Kane ignored the brief bites of pain.

The door groaned open, and Kane's public relations agent, Gavin Richards, stepped into the locker room in a perfectly tailored charcoal three-piece suit. Kane didn't look up, focusing on removing the last of the tape.

"Good finish," Gavin said, his smooth tenor too polished for the locker room. He stood, keeping a wary distance from the bench where Kane's sweat could speck his expensive Italian shoes.

Kane grunted in reply, hurling a wad of used tape into the garbage can beside him.

"I couldn't help but notice you seemed distracted through the first two rounds." Gavin's remark was wrapped in an easy-going tone of someone testing dangerous waters.

Kane's hands paused for a fraction of a second before resuming their work. "Wasn't distracted." The words were short and conclusive.

"No? From where I was sitting, it appeared you were going out of your way to drag out a fight you could have ended in the first round." Gavin crossed his arms, the hints of gray in his dark brown hair glinting in the fluorescent lights. "That's not the Kane Mitchell that fans pay the Elite Combat Federation top dollar to see."

Kane snorted, glancing up finally to meet Gavin's assessing gaze. "You're here to talk about my performance? I thought PR reps only showed up when there was a mess to clean."

"I'm here to check in on my most volatile client." Gavin's smile didn't reach his eyes.

Kane stood up, rolling his shoulders to dislodge the last vestige of tension. He strode across to his locker, pulling out a faded Warrior's Edge sweatshirt, the gym's stylized "WE" logo emblazoned on the back in aggressive red letters.

"I was bored," Kane admitted as he pulled the sweatshirt over his head. "The guy wasn't much of a challenge."

Gavin's eyebrow went up in professional interest. "That 'guy' was the number four-ranked contender in your division."

"Then the rankings don't mean shit." Kane pulled on a pair of black sweatpants with the gym's logo embroidered down the left leg.

"You know what people see when you fight like that?" Gavin's voice dropped into the stern tone Kane mentally called his 'agent voice.' "They see arrogance. They see a fighter who doesn't respect his opponents or the sport."

Kane zipped his gym bag with undue force. "What they see is a fighter who's better than everyone they put in front of him."

"What I'm noticing," Gavin responded, "is a fighter who's getting too close to buying into his own hype." He moved in, lowering his voice despite the two of them being alone in the locker room. "The ECF doesn't care how talented you are if you become a liability, Kane. They're interested in marketability—they want fighters who sell tickets for the right reasons."

Kane returned to his seat on the bench, pulled on his shoes, his movements slow and deliberate. "I won, didn't I? It was a clean knockout, and the crowd went wild. What more do they want?"

"They want consistency, professionalism. Gavin sighed, showing a hint of genuine concern beneath his outward appearance. "This isn't the first time you've done this, and it seems more and more like you are just toying with an opponent because you are 'bored.' It undermines the integrity of the sport."

"What integrity?" Kane snorted. "Half these guys are juicing, the other half are fighting with injuries they should be in rehab for, and you're worried about me not knocking someone out fast enough?"

"I'm worried about you." The simple admission hung in the air between them before Gavin sighed. "This isn't just about tonight. People are noticing a pattern, Kane. Your fighting style, skipped press conferences, and missed promotional events..."

"Those are optional," Kane interrupted, standing up to face off with Gavin. "My contract is to fight. It doesn't say I have to kiss anyone's ass."

Gavin's lips pursed, a warning sign Kane was familiar with from years of their professional relationship. It meant Gavin was biting his tongue, saying something he would later regret.

"Your contract," Gavin said finally, his words chosen with care, "has clauses about professional conduct and upholding the reputation of the organization. Clauses that could be interpreted broadly, or narrowly if the ECF were to decide that you were more trouble than you're worth."

The threat, however thinly veiled, was not lost on Kane. He felt anger begin to churn in his chest, but squashed it. Gavin was not the enemy—at least, not usually.

"Listen," Kane told him, tossing his gym bag onto his shoulder, "I'm the top of my division. I've successfully defended my title three times. If they want some guy who's gonna smile pretty at the cameras and be grateful for the chance to have his brain rattled around, they can find another golden boy."

Gavin's expression eased slightly. "No one's trying to make you be anything other than yourself. But what you are, Kane, is more than what you showed tonight. That's what frustrates me so much. You have the potential to be one of the all-time greats, but you're treating these fights like they're beneath you."

"Perhaps they are." The words escaped before Kane could consider them, and they lingered in the air.

For a moment, there was just the sound of the shower in the distance, an audible reminder of time passing.

"If that's how you feel," Gavin said quietly, "then maybe we need to have a different kind of conversation about your future in this sport."

Kane pushed past him to the door, not wanting to listen to the truth in Gavin's words. "What I need is a challenge. Somebody who isn't going to fold after the first good punch."

"Be careful what you wish for," Gavin cautioned, following Kane to the door. "In this sport, challenges have a way of finding you when you're least expecting them."

Kane pulled the door open and let the sound of the arena—now mostly empty, the crowd having been broken up—wash over them.

"Good," he said, his voice tense with resolve. "I'm counting on it."

Chapter two

T he evening wind hit Kane's face with a slap of chilly truth after the oppressive heat in the locker room. The parking lot lay open before them, half-illuminated now that the bulk of the crowd had dispersed, yellow pools of light from overhead floodlights creating small pockets of light in the darkness. Kane rolled his shoulders to ease the ache spreading into his muscles. Gavin continued beside him with his low-pitched lecture on professionalism and media ethics, words Kane allowed to pass over his head but not through.

"All I'm saying is that a few more interviews wouldn't..." Gavin trailed off in mid-sentence, halted by something before them.

Kane tracked his glance and clamped his jaw involuntarily tight. Propped up against the hood of a shiny black sports car, elbows crossed over his chest in a studied carelessness, was Tony Alvarez, an up-and-coming middleweight fighter in the ECF circuit.

Under the glare of the overhead light, Tony's blond hair glistened in the night. As his head tilted back with a cocky smile, his green eyes glinted with glee. He wore a designer tracksuit that probably cost more than most fighters made in a month, the jacket unzipped to reveal a physique that had clearly been sculpted as much for show as for function.

"Well, if it isn't the great Kane Mitchell," Tony bellowed, his voice ringing across the empty lot like a bad stage actor. "Congratulations on beating another punching bag. Really impressive."

Kane strode on, his eyes locked on Tony's face as the other man smirked.

"Just walk," Gavin breathed alongside him, a hand resting on Kane's elbow in a gesture that was half guidance, half restraint. "He's not worth it."

Tony pushed himself off the car and stepped directly in front of them. "What's wrong, Mitchell? You too chicken to face a real challenge?"

Kane stopped a few feet away, close enough that he could see the taunt in Tony's face. "You consider yourself a real challenge? Don't make me laugh," Kane's tone was low, controlled, despite the heat building in his chest.

"More of a challenge than the cans they've been putting in your lunch." Tony's eyes flicked towards Gavin, then back again. "But your babysitter here is quite well informed about that, isn't he? That's why he keeps you away from fighters who might actually discover that glass jaw of yours."

Gavin stepped forward, his professional mask securely in position. "Mr. Alvarez, this is not a suitable location for—"

"I wasn't talking to you," Tony cut him off without dropping his stare on Kane. "I'm talking to your boy here, who's been ducking real competition for months."

Kane's heart picked up, and he recognized the rhythm as one that always equated to violence in the past. "The only thing I've been ducking are the clowns who talk trash but can't back it up inside the cage."

Tony's so-called laughter was dry. "Is that what you tell yourself? Because where I'm at, you're all anger with no craft. It's a miracle you've had a career as long as yours."

The words strike home, caressing the very insecurity Kane hid behind his layers of confidence and fury. He half-stepped forward before Gavin's hold on his arm tightened.

"He's goading you," Gavin said to him gently. "This is the exact thing we talked about. Leave him alone."

But Kane's attention remained on Tony, on the smug expression on his face. The parking lot lights cast Tony's face into stark relief, heightening the enjoyment in his eyes.

"You know I'm right," Tony continued, his voice sliding into a comfortable, drawling rhythm that somehow stung worse than the sarcasm of his initial cuts. "Your technique's sloppy. Your defense's got more holes than Swiss cheese. The only thing that keeps you on top is your rep and a management team that makes sure you never get up against anybody who could dismantle you."

Kane's jaw spasmed, a tic he'd never quite been able to hold back as anger built inside him.

Tony noticed the spasm and smiled, the grin never quite reaching his eyes. "There it is. That legendary Mitchell temper. The one thing about you that's predictable in the cage."

"Kane," Gavin's voice rose in intensity now. "We're leaving. Now."

But Tony edged closer, stepping into Kane. "You know what the difference between us is, Mitchell? I'm building a career. You're holding onto one that's already peaked."

The words hung there, icy and poisonous, and Kane felt something icy in the pit of his stomach, a counterpoint to the warmth of his fury. This was not just trash talk—this was targeted, personal.

"Your time on top is running short," Tony went on, his voice low, a whisper that made Kane tilt his head forward to catch his words. "Everybody in the division knows it. It's only a matter of time before somebody takes you out for good."

Kane fought to breathe, to resist the tide of anger about to sweep over him. "That's a big mouth for a man who's never been inside a cage with me."

"Whose fault is that?" Tony's eyebrow leapt upwards as he spoke. "I've been calling you on this for months. Your handlers are always making excuses." He shook his head, slowly, the motion infused with feigned sympathy. "No one needs a relic of a fighter, Mitchell. It's time to let go."

Kane felt Gavin's hold on his arm grow tighter, an unspoken threat that he was skating on thin ice. But the fire in his veins had boiled over, drowning out the rational part of his brain that perceived the trap being laid out for him.

"You believe I fear you?" Kane growled, anger brewing.

Tony's lips curled into a smile that lacked warmth, instead being full only of cold malice. "I think you are afraid to know what happens when a person doesn't fall the first time you hit them. I think you are afraid of what happens when fury doesn't work." He flung his hand in the general direction of the arena they had just exited. "What we saw tonight wasn't a champion. It was a bully manipulating a weaker individual."

The parking lot shut in around them, the distant thrum of traffic fading until all Kane could hear was the drumbeat of his own blood and Tony's voice, cutting through his defenses like a surgeon's knife.

"Kane, we're out of here," Gavin repeated, his voice more urgent this time, his fingers digging into Kane's bicep through the sweatshirt. "This is exactly what he wants."

Kane barely registered what he said. All he could think about was Tony's face, the absolute conviction there, the expression of a man who knew exactly which buttons to push and loved pushing them.

"The truth hurts, doesn't it?" Tony sneered, his voice softening in feigned concern. "But don't worry. When I take your place at the top, I'll be sure to thank you in my victory speech. Someone has to remember the has-beens."

Kane's mouth twisted into a humorless smile. Anger in his veins crystallized into something colder as he gazed at the man standing before him. He recognized Tony and recognized that he was eager to scramble his way up. But he also knew Tony had help, at least when it came to piling on the last few months.

"At least I'm not some steroid wannabe hot-air freak," Kane finally said, his tone dropping so that only Tony and Gavin could pick up on the insult. "How long before your pee test comes back hot, Alvarez? Or does the ECF turn a blind eye when it's their new golden boy?"

The response was immediate. Tony's smirk fell away, and an instant flash of rage overtook him, changing his face. His eyes narrowed into menacing slits.

"What did you say?" The words were a hiss, all the mock in them gone. Tony took a step forward, bringing the already narrow distance between them down to where Kane could smell the mint gum he'd been chewing in his mouth on his breath.

Kane stood his ground, eyeing Tony. "You heard me." He let his glance sweep slowly across Tony's physique, taking care to assess him. "Nobody builds that kind of lean muscle in six months without assistance from chemicals. But hey, if you're willing to destroy your body for a couple of wins, that's your decision."

Tony's fists tightened at his waist, knuckles whitening with the strain of not throwing the first punch. "You wanna say that again?" Between gritted teeth, the words issued.

Gavin stepped forward, positioning himself somewhat between the two fighters without actually coming between them. "Gentlemen, this is neither the place nor the time—"

"Who's got the anger issue now?" Kane cut in, disregarding Gavin entirely. He took satisfaction in watching Tony's poise break.

Tony took a deep breath, fighting hard to get a grip on himself. Parking lot lights highlighted the sheen of sweat that had burst across his forehead as he stood there against the chill of the night air. When he finally spoke again, his voice had come back into the previous smooth cadence, though a simmer of rage still lurked beneath.

"Nice deflection, Mitchell." Tony laced his arms across his chest, his attitude a study in contrived nonchalance. "Just what you would expect from a fighter who can't handle the fact that his career is on the slide. Spout off baseless trash instead of doing something about your own shortcomings."

"Baseless?" Kane scowled. "I've seen men come and go in cycles for years. I know the warning signs. The sudden increase, the acne on your back that your high-end designer tops can't hide, the mood swings." He rapped on his forehead. "I don't have your high-end education, but I'm not stupid."

Tony's smile returned, but it was tight on the edges. "Maybe not, but you are still chicken shit." He said his words in a dropped whisper, which was not entirely safe. "Otherwise, why would your manager turn down any actual fights that aren't already rigged?"

The accusation hung in the air, more damning than words yet spoken. Kane felt Gavin stiffen beside him, the PR man's tightly restrained professional grin wavered for a moment, revealing genuine worry.

"My bouts aren't rigged," Kane growled, the icy strategic detachment of moments before lost to the familiar flush of anger. "I win because I'm better."

"Good at what? Playing by the script?" Tony sneered, becoming more confident with the impact of his words. "Everybody knows the ECF spoils its favorites. Gives them favorable matches, the outcome decided beforehand." His gaze flicked to Gavin, then to Kane. "Your agent and your coach see to it that you never get to play someone who might just expose your weakness."

Gavin moved in, all pretense of professional reserve aside. "That's enough, Alvarez. You're throwing around accusations that will harm your career as well as the reputation of the organization." The threat was unmistakable in his voice.

Tony gave the cold shoulder, his whole concentration on Kane. "You'd like to talk about my drug tests? Let's talk then about how your opponents tend to 'run out of steam' if you last the first two rounds."

A red haze was creeping into the edge of Kane's vision. All his battle-hardened instincts screamed at him to shut Tony up with his fists, to show by violence what he couldn't manage to show by words.

"Or how points always seem to be given to you, giving you the win, when everyone can see you didn't have any right to them." Tony continued.

"Kane," Gavin's voice was a long way off, "we're leaving. Now." He tugged Kane's arm with a firm grip, attempting to shove him away from the battle, but Kane shook him free. He moved halfway towards Tony until they were nearly chest to chest.

"You think my fights are on the take?" Kane's tone was deadly in its softness. "Then come at me. Step into the ring and put your money where your mouth is."

Tony's smile grew wider. "I already tried three times. Your team keeps declining, claiming you were 'focusing on higher-ranked opponents.' He quoted with air quotes using his fingers, the movement calculated to insult. His smile faded as his expression grew deadly serious. "They won't play hide the truth, is that it? They are afraid I'll expose you."

"I ain't afraid of any man in there," Kane shot back, the words escaping in a growl. "Especially not some juiced-up poser who's won half his fucking fights."

"Then fight me." Tony snarled. "Stop being a wimp, unless you're also too afraid to take on any match that's not fixed?"

The echo of the accusation snapped within Kane, the last thread of restraint breaking. Kane growled as something feral and uncontrolled substituted.

Kane hit Tony with a rush, ignoring Gavin's shriek of "Kane, don't!" The distance between them was consumed in a moment, and Kane's shoulder was rammed into Tony's chest, and they crashed to the asphalt together.

Tony's back crackled on the sidewalk, his eyes springing wide as he collapsed, and Kane was on him in a rush, pinning Tony's body beneath him with his bulk as he threw back his fist. The initial punch made a satisfying crunch against Tony's jaw, Kane's knuckles splitting open in the impact.

"You bloody liar!" Kane's voice came through barely recognizable. His second punch splatted against Tony's cheek, wrenching his head to the side.

Gavin was shouting behind him, the words indistinguishable through the noise of rushing in his head. Nothing else existed other than the satisfaction of silencing Tony's words with his fists. Fury fueled him, raw, pure, and primal.

Tony parried the third punch to his forearm, shielding his head. Kane shifted his weight, poised to land another blow through Tony's defense, when something in his opponent's face shifted. The look of annoyance and smug smile both vanished, giving way to an air of exaggerated fear.

"Stop!" Tony suddenly bellowed out, his voice shrill to the point of being unnecessarily high-pitched. "Fucking hell, stop!" He threw up his arms in front of his face, assuming a defensive posture that felt curiously theatrical.

Kane stood stock-still, his fist still raised, confusion briefly overwhelming rage. Then it struck him.

Tony wasn't fighting back.

The asshole hadn't even attempted a counter punch, hadn't even endeavored to buck Kane off or roll out. Tony was a professional fighter; he should have been.

That awareness sliced through Kane's anger. He saw things once more and heard Gavin shouting his name with increasing desperation. And something else: the very distinct hum of mutters and electronic shutters snapping.

15

Kane let his fist drop cautiously, turning his head to look over his shoulder, tensing at the view.

There was a crowd of individuals at the edge of the parking area, at least half a dozen folks with phones in the air, capturing it all.

"Jesus," Kane breathed, the name escaping on an exhalation as the full realization hit him.

Beneath him, Tony's expression altered again, the fear dissipating to make way for a smugness Kane wished he could smash off his face. But now he understood. This had never been about trading blows or insults.

This had always been a setup.

"Get off me, you psycho," Tony shouted, still quite loudly for the crowd that had congealed.

The words were accusatory, but his eyes delivered a message meant for Kane alone: I won.

Gradually, Kane rolled off him, his eyes still fixed on Tony. Rising, he saw Gavin standing beside him, the older man's face contorted with his barely restrained anger and panic.

"Are you mad?" Gavin hissed, grabbing Kane's wrist and yanking him back from Tony, who continued to lie on the ground, pretending to examine his jaw for damage.

Kane said nothing, his eyes drawn to the increasing number of on-lookers. All of them had their phones out, snapping every second.

Tony slowly sat up, grimacing at melodramatically exaggerated pain. "You're done, Mitchell," he announced, voice carrying loud enough for the nearest onlookers to hear. "The ECF doesn't have room for fighters who can't keep their heads when they're out of the cage."

A witness walked up, offering his hand to help Tony stand, while looking warily at Kane. "You okay, man? That was crazy. Kane Mitchell just lost his temper on you!"

Tony accepted the help, hamming it up as he stood up. "Yeah, I'm fine. Just surprised, you know? Never thought a champion would be so unstable." Patiently, he dusted himself off, keeping his face prominently visible to the recording phones as he continued to play along with the growing crowd.

Kane moved towards him, but Gavin's grip on him was painful as he held him back.

"Don't," Gavin snapped, his tightly wound rage wrung to within a thread of bursting. "You've done enough damage for tonight."

A sequence of electronic pings shattered the tense quiet, ringing on and on, one after another. Gavin pulled out his phone and pulled it from his pocket, his complexion growing whiter with each succeeding message.

"It's up already," he stated bluntly, holding the screen for Kane to read. "Twitter, Instagram, TikTok—those sites are ablaze."

Kane took in a shattered breath as the screen revealed a viral video clip, all with the same damning headline.

Kane Mitchell, ECF champion, attacks, unprovoked, in a parking lot.

There were further pings, an onslaught of messages that cut like a rebuke.

Tony, surrounded by a tight circle of fans eager to hear his side of the story, caught Kane staring over the top of their heads. He carefully poked his split lip with a flourish, then gave Kane a triumphant smile before it faded behind as he dramatized his wounds for the cluster of onlookers surrounding him.

"Let's go," Gavin told him, his working personality resurfacing as he led Kane to the other side of the parking lot. "We need to get in front of this."

"He was playing me." Kane blustered. "He set the whole thing up."

"Oh, sure he did!" Gavin burst out, his anger at last wearing thin. "And you fell for it! Do you think anyone cares who initiated it? Because they won't. All they'll hear is a trained fighter, someone kneeling on someone, punching a man in the face!"

Kane fell silent, reality's chill seeping in. The adrenaline was fading, being replaced by cold. He had done what Tony wanted him to do, played right into his hands. Kane could hear Tony's voice growing more agitated behind them: "I was talking to him about fighting, and he completely lost it and attacked me. I don't even know what set him off."

Gavin's phone continued to ping away as he walked Kane towards their cars.

Kane caught one last look over his shoulder. Tony stood beneath the glow of a parking lot light, faces of worry around him, his split lip and battered jaw exposed to the cameras.

And in that moment, Kane Mitchell realized his arch-nemesis may have just stripped him of everything.

Chapter Three

The glass and steel skyscraper housing Richards PR Management cast the pale light of February off the windowsill of Gavin's corner office. Kane sat in a chair that probably cost more than his first car, his elbows wedged into his knees as he glared at the buffed floor. The bruises on his knuckles had already begun to turn a yellow-green sick color, a reflection of what he was feeling inside.

Seven days. That was how quickly it had taken for his life to crash and burn.

Gavin leaned against the windows that lined one wall, his arms crossed. His reflection in the glass showed the dark circles under his eyes, revealing his restless nights. He was dressed immaculately as usual, but something in the sag of his shoulders gave away his exhaustion.

"Apex Athletic Wear terminated their contract this morning," Gavin said without glancing around, his voice detached and tone cold. "That's three this week. Apex, Summit Nutrition, and Warrior Performance Systems." Kane did not look up. The names clicked with him, firms that had pursued his partnership at one time now deserted him...and rightfully so, he could only blame himself. "Each one of them alone was a six-figure deal." Gavin finally turned to Kane. "We'd negotiated with Summit to double their first sponsorship, and then..."

Kane's fist curled, the painful flesh above his knuckles tight.

"Get on with it," Kane growled, his voice raw from disuse. "I messed up. Just stop dancing around it."

Gavin exhaled slowly, and the breath was heavy. He crossed over to his desk, a massive walnut slab that dominated the center of the office, and sat down in his ergonomic office chair.

"You want it blunt? Okay." Gavin wrapped his hands around the desk, his wedding ring glinting. "You're losing money, and that's not even the worst part. You still have two other sponsorships that we managed to save, but all of that is dependent on what the ECF does."

"And what are they thinking?" Kane's voice was rough as he breathed. He knew that there had to be more because there always was.

"The board is convening in two weeks to make a ruling," Gavin continued, his fingers tapping once on the desk before dropping into a stillness. "I have had the phone continually ringing, calling in every favor I have to have it as a one-time occurrence, not a whisper of a repeat behavior issue. We will be lucky if they even concur on a six-month suspension."

"What's the worst they can do?" Kane demanded, already knowing.

Gavin stared at him unflinchingly. "They terminate your contract. Make an example of you."

The words are blows to the body, each one landing with precision on the soft, vulnerable places beneath Kane's carefully constructed shell. He fought to sit up straight in the chair, to shift some of the pressure trapped inside his chest away.

"This is rubbish," he growled, pacing to the window and back. "Alvarez set me up. You saw it. He was there, he knew what to do—"

"Kane, of course, he fucking set you up," Gavin interrupted, his professional facade cracking to reveal the anger beneath. "And you took the bait. The ECF doesn't care who started it, Kane. They're interested in the image. They see it as bringing disrepute to the organization and the sport. Do you have any idea how much attention this is getting? The video has seventeen million views. Seventeen million, Kane. Your face is all over the place."

Kane rose to his feet, his rage curling in his jaw.

"His staff is calling for charges of assault." Gavin was quieter now.

Kane turned around, amazement etched on his face. "Charges? He's a professional fighter. Nobody will believe it."

"They don't have to. They simply need to view those tapes. What does that suggest, you on him, him screaming for you to stop."

Gavin leaned forward over the desktop as he braced his elbows. "His injuries are not the problem."

The old fire of anger ignited in Kane's breast. "So that's it? My career's ruined because Alvarez can play a scene?" The words were no more than a whisper. He was not going to lose his mind— he had worked too long, bled too much to get where he was. He wouldn't let it all be taken away now. It was all he had.

Gavin expelled a sigh, raking a hand through his hair. "Not in the least. But we need to change the narrative, and fast. Something for the sponsors and the ECF to hold onto besides 'hothead who can't control his temper.'"

Kane returned to the chair, sinking into it with caution. It wasn't the first time some goon had attempted to rise to the top by using force, and it would not be the last. But this was the first time that it had cut through the wall he tried to keep up, to keep people out. His head fell forward into the chair as he stared upward. Was it because he was scared Tony was right?

Hell, was Tony right?

He shook his head in anger, this time at himself. Now the fucker was in his head, questioning himself.

And that was what the prick had been waiting for.

The cord that had been holding Kane back snapped, torn apart by terror and anger as it consumed him. He jumped out of his chair, crashing it over as he covered the distance between his chair and Gavin's desk in two quick strides.

Kane placed his hands on the desk, leaning forward so that his face was inches from Gavin's. "They didn't hear what he said. They didn't witness how he set it all up. They just saw what he wanted them to. "

Gavin didn't even blink, didn't shift back, didn't give an inch. He just looked back into Kane's furious face. "Again, that's not the way others perceive it. You've seen the video."

"FUCK THE VIDEO!" The yell tore from Kane's throat. He pushed back from the desk so hard that the thick wood inched an inch across the floor.

Kane turned, and without a thought, his leg shot out, his foot catching on the edge of the glass table that resided in the middle of the office, sending it crashing to its side.

The crack of the glass as it shattered resonated through the office, shards flying out in a glittering cascade across the hardwood floor.

For a moment, neither man spoke. Some part of Kane's brain recognized that he should be feeling something—regret, shame, embarrassment—but he just felt numb.

Gavin's chair creaked as he sat back, his eyes taking in the devastation. His eyes moved from the ruined table to Kane, who stood there, breathing heavily, fists clenched at his sides.

"Better?" Gavin asked, his tone level and so reasonable that it cut through Kane's rage more distinctly than any winded scream possibly could.

Kane looked down at the broken glass, at the splintered frame. Slowly, the red haze receded from the edge of his vision, reality creeping back into the burning fury.

"No," he allowed, speaking quietly.

"No," Gavin insisted, rising to his feet and moving around the desk in deliberate steps that avoided most of the glass. "Because breaking things doesn't solve things, Kane. It just makes new ones." He indicated the destruction between them. "Like a seven-thousand-dollar vintage coffee table."

Kane brushed his face. The trail of anger always left him feeling drained and hollow, detached from himself.

"I didn't—" he began, then stopped. Excuses were feeble in the face of the evidence scattered on the floor. "I'll pay for it."

"Yes, you will." There was no hint of sting in Gavin's voice. "Just as you'll pay for what happened to Tony. The issue is whether you want to pay in terms of your career, or if you'd be interested in hearing alternatives."

Kane stared at him, the fight draining from him as quickly as he breathed out. "What else? You've just informed me that the ECF is likely going to suspend me. I have lost most of my sponsors. What do I have left?"

"I think there is a means," Gavin replied, "to keep what's left of your sponsors, show that you've changed your ways, and prove it was a one-off, and maybe get some new sponsors."

Kane looked up, suspicion warring with the first flicker of hope he'd had in a week. "Yeah? What miracle are you going to work?"

Gavin's lips curled up into what might have been a smile on any other day. Now, it made Kane jumpy, and he knew something was about to occur that he wouldn't want, but he didn't see how he could deny it.

"You are going to get a girlfriend."

The words hung in the air between them— he was so stunned that Kane wasn't even sure he had heard correctly. He stared at Gavin, hoping for the joke, but Gavin's face was solemn, his eyes locked on Kane's.

"A girlfriend," Kane repeated flatly. "That's your masterstroke? A woman on my arm is going to make everyone forget I beat the crap out of Alvarez in a parking lot?"

"Not some woman," Gavin chastised, crossing his arms over his chest. "The right one. Someone who exudes a stable, mature presence. Someone who makes you look more settled, stable even."

Kane scoffed in derision, his head shaking at the audacity. "You want me to pretend to date someone to restore my reputation? Who is going to believe that?"

"People will believe what they want to believe," Gavin replied, and Kane knew the words of years spent working on public narratives. "Right now, they'd rather believe you're a wild-eyed hothead that they should lock up, not safe to be around respectable folk. Give them an alternative narrative that's the opposite of that, a man in love, steady, peaceful, and they'll believe that."

Kane leaned back in the chair, trying to take in what Gavin was saying. It was absurd, something out of a bad film.

"You've got to be joking," Kane said, comprehension dawning on him with an edge of fear. "You really think that could happen."

"I know that it could happen," Gavin explained. "I've done it before. Remember Derek Paulson, the NBA player who was videotaped hitting a fan in the stands?"

Kane nodded slowly. Paulson had been on the brink of the end of his career when the incident went viral three years ago. Now he was back on top again, and even in commercials.

"Two months later, he started dating that kindergarten teacher. Sweet, wholesome girl-next-door type." Gavin's fingers tapped out a rhythm on the table beside him. "Six months after that, they were engaged. The story completely changed—he went from being seen as a violent athlete to being a reformed bad boy who had just needed the right woman to guide him down the right path."

"Wait, their relationship wasn't real?" Kane asked, really surprised. He had spotted them together a couple of times at parties they seemed to be head over heels in love with each other. There was no way—.

Gavin's expression did not change. "I didn't say that. I'm saying the timing was...convenient. And it changed public opinion."

Kane rose, having to go again. He crept slowly by the broken glass, stopping at the window to look out over the city far below and the people winding down through the streets.

How simple it must be, he thought, to live beyond the reach of public gaze, to not have any mess up blasted for millions to see and judge.

"Even if I promised to do this lunacy," he growled without looking around, "where in the world am I going to go to locate this miracle woman? I'm not boyfriend material even on a good day, and today I'm toxic."

"You let that be my problem," Gavin said. "I will find her."

Kane spun around him, his eyes hardening. "You're talking about hiring someone."

"I'm talking about an arrangement," Gavin said diplomatically. "A fair relationship that happens to suit our current needs."

The proposition was absurd: paying someone else to be in his life? But after he'd immediately turned it down, Kane started thinking about the possibility that Gavin might be right.

"How in the world would it work?" he insisted, the question in and of itself a small surrender.

Gavin struggled up, entering full-on PR damage control mode. "You'd be photographed in public with her—Restaurants, parties, training exercises. We'd invent a story around how you met, have you two together, smiling, in love. You'd do a couple of staged interviews together, portraying an image of stability and growth."

"And then what? We 'break up' after everybody's forgotten the parking lot?"

"Eventually, yes. A smiling parting of ways when you've demonstrated steady improvement." Gavin nodded. "And by then, the narrative will have shifted. You'll be Kane Mitchell, the fighter who overcame his demons, not Kane Mitchell, the loose cannon who can't seem to stay out of trouble."

Kane smoothed his short hair, trying to envision himself playing at being a boyfriend. It was a betrayal of what he believed about himself —his integrity, his aversion to getting caught up in the PR stunts other fighters fell for.

"This is bullshit," he muttered finally, but his tone was less confident than his earlier tantrums.

"Maybe," Gavin conceded. "But it might save your career. The alternative is to sit around and wait for the ECF to make a lesson of you and wait for your final remaining sponsors to desert you."

The choice hit Kane with cruel clarity: swallow pride and conform to Gavin's scheme or hold out for principle and lose everything he'd built.

For a moment, Kane allowed himself to think about it. Going through the motions, being the rehabilitated bad boy, taking photos with some girl he barely knew on his arm. The sponsors would return. The ECF would reduce his suspension. He could get back to what he did best —competing in the cage —not competing for his reputation.

But something inside him refused. He knew he was many things—unpredictable, tough, angry—but that is what he was, and that was what he showed the world, for better or worse.

"No." The word was with gentle finality as Kane pushed himself up to his feet. "No, I won't."

Gavin's expression hardened. "Kane, come on. This isn't all about your ego. This is about your career, your life."

"A future built on deception isn't one I want." Kane tensed, setting his shoulders as if preparing for a punch. "I'll deal with the suspension. I can even get new sponsors. But I am not paying for some mercenary girlfriend to appease the ECF."

"This has nothing to do with making them happy," Gavin insisted. "This is about giving them what they want to justify keeping you. It's business, Kane. That's all."

"Unfortunately, maybe to you." Kane sidestepped Gavin. "But it's my life. My integrity. And that's not for sale."

He moved towards the door with deliberate slowness, the sound of crunching glass beneath his feet. With each step, he felt the weight of what his decision would cost him settle upon his shoulders: the sponsors he would forfeit, the fights he would miss, the money —Hell, his only money without sponsors —lost. But somehow, he knew that leaving was the thing to do.

"Find another way. Or don't. But I won't do this."

He did not wait for Gavin to speak, did not need to witness the respect and frustration that fleetingly crossed his face. Kane departed the office, the broken glass, the broken career, and the broken faith in the one individual he'd trusted who had actually understood him.

Kane stalked along the marble hall of Richards PR Management, his footsteps echoing down the corridor. Workers scrambled from out of his path, either perceiving the barely contained anger in the lines of his shoulders or in fear after that damn video.

A girlfriend. A fucking girlfriend. The thought reverberated through his mind, every return igniting the flame of his rage back into a burning inferno. Did Gavin actually think that of him? That he was something that could be shelved, his rough edges buffed off for the masses to view?

The idea itself revolted him. Kane Mitchell didn't pretend. Not in the cage, not anywhere. You got what you saw—hard, fierce, unrelenting. If that made him unsellable, fine. At least he could look in a mirror and be certain that he was exactly who he was.

He made his way to the revolving door and shoved with more force than necessary. The bitter February air slapped him, the cold dispelling some of the anger-induced fog from his mind. Downtown Philadelphia towered around him, oblivious to his personal crisis. The ordinariness of it was surreal after the frantic action that had just passed in Gavin's office.

Kane breathed in deeply, letting the cold air fill his chest, his racing heart slowing.

He had done it.

Now he would have to live with the consequences, whatever they might be. Suspension, lost endorsements, and financial hardship—any of them pale in comparison to the cost of becoming something other than himself.

He had taken three paces towards the parking garage when a woman approached him on his right, eyes focused on the building directory rather than the road ahead, an armload of papers clutched in one hand. Kane didn't notice her until their bodies collided with enough force to scatter the papers she held onto the sidewalk.

"Shit!" The curse poured out as Kane involuntarily stepped back. His fists came up, his fighter's reflexes overriding his brain before it could comprehend what was occurring.

The woman wasn't as lucky. The impact jolted her off balance, and she would have stumbled were it not for Kane catching instinctively at her arm, his hand closing more tightly than he had intended around her wrist. Their gazes locked for a brief moment—hers wide and shocked, his pinched in lingering anger—before she looked down at where his hand rested on her arm.

Kane pushed her away, stepping back as if burned. Great. Just what he needed. Another viral hit: "ECF Fighter Attacking Woman Outside Office Building." He could already see the headlines, could picture Gavin's frustrated breath when he tried to explain that apprehending someone in the act of falling wasn't assault.

"Watch where the fuck you're going," he growled, the words emerging gruffer than he'd intended. He wasn't angry at her, not that precisely, but she was there, and for that unfortunate reason, in his path.

" I-I'm sorry," she stammered, dropping to her knees to gather up the papers scattered on the floor, her cheeks aflame with embarrassment or rage—Kane couldn't quite decide which. "I was just looking for—"

But Kane was already turning his back on her, not even stopping to take a look at what she had been looking for. He didn't need another complication today, couldn't afford another meeting that might go awry.

He felt a stab of guilt as he walked to the parking garage, letting her pick up her papers alone. Usually, he would have pulled over to help or at least grunted a curt apology for his part in the collision. But these were not usual times, and Kane was not in a place where he could be trusted with even the most minor social exchanges.

What in the world was Gavin thinking?

The notion spun round and round in Kane's mind as he reached his car, a gleaming black Range Rover that now seemed a luxury he could no longer afford. A girlfriend would not fix what was lacking in Kane's life—Gavin was mad to think it would. It would just add another layer of dishonesty to an already complicated public-private life.

Kane slid into the driver's seat, chill leather against his back even in February sunlight. He sat there for an instant without starting the engine, hands gripping the steering wheel, forehead dipping momentarily to touch his knuckles.

He wasn't the boyfriend type. Never was. His relationships, if one could even refer to them as such, were fleeting and simple deals—bodily encounters with women who knew going in that fighting preceded, and emotional involvement was not in the bargain. If he was being truthful, none lasted longer than two or three times, tops, before he tired of them.

The concept of strolling around with some PR-approved date, posing for pictures, spinning a line about household bliss—it was so distant from his own existence that it came close to being ludicrous.

No, Kane decided not to entertain the notion as he finally activated the engine, the powerful machine roaring into life under him. There had to be another way to fix this fiasco. He would find out.

Without Gavin's schemes, without the approval of the ECF, without the funding of the sponsors, if necessary.

Kane Mitchell had not reached the pinnacle by fighting his way there; he had not taken the easy route, following the roadmap to success created by somebody else. He had succeeded on his terms, rough and true and uncompromising.

And if his career went up in flames as a consequence? Then he would be standing among the ashes, unfazed. He would rather that than live a deceit, grinning through clenched teeth as some woman he had only just met became his redemption.

Chapter four

Daphne Wilson stood on the sidewalk outside Richards PR Management as she took a deep breath to ease her nerves. The February wind tugged at her carefully styled brown hair, completely undoing her attempts to tame it.

This was her dream opportunity.

Daphne's fingers tightened around her leather portfolio. When she'd first graduated from her marketing program, she'd believed that doors would quickly open and that she would find her place in a traditional marketing job.

Reality had proven harsher, something she had quickly learned.

Her thoughts shifted to the man who had bumped into her three days before. She had been doing a trial run to get to the office when someone had slammed into her with the force of a linebacker.

Her papers had scattered across the sidewalk, the hand around her wrist the only thing that stopped her from falling. The man who had caught her had the darkest eyes she'd ever seen, yet they had blazed with fury.

For a moment, those eyes had locked with hers, and Daphne had felt something electric and dangerous pass between them before his expression had hardened further. But even that hadn't stopped the flash of heat that coursed through her with that one look.

Daphne shook off the memory, refusing to let one unpleasant encounter dim her enthusiasm.

She was ready for this.

She'd researched Gavin Richards extensively, reading every interview, studying the lives he had turned around. She had skimmed a new article about him from earlier that week about his latest mess, some MMA fighter involved in some controversy about...something.

Crap, maybe she should have read that again, just to be prepared, but she had focused on Gavin Richards' methods, hoping to impress him.

If she met him, that is.

"You can do this," Daphne whispered to herself. "You are qualified, you are exactly what they're looking for."

Drawing herself up to her full 5'5" height, Daphne took one final, steadying breath and pushed through the revolving door.

The lobby was pleasantly warm, with a subtle lemon scent, and a security guard nodded at her from behind a marble desk.

"Daphne Wilson for Richards PR Management," she said, pleased at how steady her voice sounded. "I have a ten a.m. appointment."

As the guard checked his computer and prepared a visitor's badge, Daphne let herself look around. This was where she belonged—all she needed was the chance to prove it.

As she stood in silence in the elevator, Daphne took a moment to center herself. By the time the doors slid open with a soft chime, she was ready—or as ready as she would ever be—for this interview.

God, she hoped she could impress whoever she was meeting with.

The waiting receptionist led Daphne through a maze of sleek corridors towards the interview room. Her heart raced the further they got into the office until they came to a stop outside an office.

A corner office.

She was going to be sick.

When the door swung open to reveal Gavin Richards himself sitting behind an imposing walnut desk, she felt her stomach clench.

"Ms. Wilson for you, Mr. Richards," the receptionist announced, seemingly unfazed by Daphne's sudden stop.

Gavin rose from his chair with an easy smile. Daphne swallowed as she took him in, tall and lean with his salt-and-pepper hair meticulously styled. She was not ready for this. Not at all.

"Ms. Wilson, please come in." His voice was warm, even as she caught a calculating look in his eyes. "Thank you, Jessica," he added to the receptionist, who nodded and withdrew, closing the door behind her.

Daphne remained frozen in the doorway, her mind going blank. She'd expected days, perhaps weeks, of preliminary screenings before meeting this man. Yet here he was, extending his hand to her, only she hadn't moved to take it.

"Is something wrong?" Gavin asked, his eyebrow arching slightly.

"No, I'm sorry." Daphne forced herself forward, her hand extending automatically to meet his. "I just wasn't expecting...I mean, I thought I'd be meeting with HR first."

A smile lifted the corners of Gavin's mouth. "I prefer to meet promising candidates personally. Saves time in the long run." He gestured to a leather chair positioned across from his desk. "Please, have a seat."

Daphne settled into the chair, her fingers pressing into the leather portfolio hard enough to leave marks.

"Your resume is impressive," Gavin began, glancing down at a tablet on his desk. "Top ten percent of your class, competitive debate team, marketing degree with a minor in psychology, and three internships during your undergraduate years."

"Thank you," Daphne responded, her voice softer than she intended. She cleared her throat and tried again. "I believe in maximizing opportunities."

Gavin studied her for a moment, his expression unreadable. "Tell me, Ms. Wilson, why do you want to go into public relations? With your credentials, you could have gone into any number of marketing fields, many with higher starting salaries."

It was a question Daphne had answered in a dozen interviews, yet something about Gavin's direct gaze had her pausing. She took a breath and decided to give him an honest answer.

"I tried that," she admitted, a hint of frustration coloring her tone, "and for about a month after graduation, I worked in a short-term position in traditional marketing. I've written copy for products, designed email campaigns, and analyzed metrics for engagement." She paused as she thought about the monotony of the tasks and shook her head slightly. "They were all...distant. Impersonal."

A flicker of interest crossed Gavin's face. "So do you prefer direct communication to metrics?"

"I prefer working with people," Daphne answered. "Marketing reduces consumers to demographics to be targeted. PR recognizes that behind every story, every crisis, there are actual people involved."

The corner of Gavin's mouth twitched upward, and this time the hint of a smile seemed more genuine. "That is an idealistic view of an industry that is often criticized for being nothing more than manipulation and spin."

Daphne met his gaze with determination in her eyes. "Every form of communication involves some degree of spin."

Gavin gave a small laugh. "Well said, Ms. Wilson." He leaned back in his chair, his posture relaxing slightly. "Though I suspect that line of thinking might be tested if you were to join us. Our clients aren't always easy to present in the best light."

"That's why I'm interested in sports representation, if I'm honest." Daphne shrugged. "Athletes are human beings who have to perform at extraordinary levels under intense scrutiny. What people don't want to see is that they make mistakes, they have flaws, we all do. The challenge isn't hiding who they are, it's helping the public see the person behind the name."

Gavin's brows rose in consideration. "And if that complete picture includes behaviors that some would say are difficult to defend?"

Daphne took a moment to consider the question. "Then you start with helping them understand how those behaviors affect their image. PR can't manufacture authenticity, and someone who tries to fake it will be busted. What you can do is try to help them make change for themselves and show it in the way that most humanizes them."

For a moment, she would have sworn Gavin was shocked by her statement, but it was only for that moment. "You have a fascinating perspective for someone so fresh out of college."

"I watched my brother struggle with it in high school," Daphne smiled. "He played lacrosse, thought he could do no wrong until everything blew up in his face. When he pretended to make changes, it just got worse until he started to make the changes." She grinned at the thought. "It also helped that his 13-year-old sister was his hype man, so you could say I've had training."

This time, Gavin's laugh seemed genuine. "Fair enough. Let's talk specifics then. What do you know about our client roster?"

The interview shifted as they discussed the agency's work. Daphne found herself relaxing, her responses becoming more natural as her nerves settled.

Gavin nodded slowly as she spoke through the rest of the interview, his expression thoughtful. Eventually, he fell silent as his gaze lingered on her, his fingers steepled beneath his chin. The sudden change sent a ripple of unease through Daphne.

The silence stretched between them.

Daphne felt her nerves rise as she met his gaze, fighting the urge to fill the void. As the seconds ticked by, she couldn't help but fidget.

What was he looking for? Had she said something wrong?

Daphne thought through everything she had said, trying to figure out what had caught his attention so deeply.

She couldn't think of anything. And suddenly, she felt her chances of working there fly out the high-rise window.

Was this some kind of test? A power play designed to see how she handled uncomfortable silences? If so, she was failing spectacularly.

She cleared her throat, and Gavin's gaze sharpened at the sound, his eyes narrowing slightly. The corner of his mouth twitched as if he had reached a conclusion.

"I'm sorry, is something wrong?" Daphne's question was harsher than she'd intended.

Gavin startled slightly, almost as if he'd forgotten they were in the middle of an interview.

"No, no," he said, as a smile curved his lips. "I think something is very right."

"Right?" Daphne echoed, unable to keep hope out of her voice. Maybe it wasn't a bad sign, it...

"Ms. Wilson—Daphne, if I may—you have a rather unique combination of skills." Gavin leaned forward slightly, his elbows coming to rest on the desk. "You have marketing knowledge as well as a strong sense of emotional intelligence."

"Thank you," she replied cautiously, unsure where this was heading. Part of her wanted to preen at his words, but his behavior was concerning.

Gavin tapped his index finger against his desk. "Tell me, how do you describe your problem-solving approach? Do you tend to follow traditional approaches, or do you seek creative solutions?"

Daphne felt slightly relaxed, but there was still something off about how pointed his expression was.

"I believe that you need to understand the problem first." Her words were slow as she watched his expression. "If you don't understand, you can't figure out an effective plan. Sometimes you can't rely on most traditional approaches."

Something flickered in Gavin's eyes—approval. "And where do you draw the line between creative problem-solving and your ethical beliefs?"

These were no longer standard questions, and the thought had her speaking hesitantly.

"I don't believe in sacrificing integrity for expediency," she responded, "but I also recognize that sometimes there are no clear-cut choices between right and wrong. The world isn't that cut and dry."

Gavin nodded slowly. "Daphne, I'm going to be direct with you. The position you applied for is certainly available, and based on this conversation, I believe you would be an excellent fit here."

The unspoken "but" hung in the air between them, and it had Daphne's breath catching.

"However," Gavin continued, "I wonder if you might be interested in hearing about another opportunity within our organization. Something more...immediate."

Daphne's pulse quickened, both intrigued and a little wary.

"I'm certainly open to hearing about other opportunities," she replied carefully. She would do almost anything to get her foot in the door there.

Gavin's smile widened, and for a moment, Daphne was reminded of documentaries she'd seen about sharks.

"Excellent," he said, "because I believe you may be the solution to a rather tricky situation we have with one of our highest-profile clients."

Daphne frowned, her mind slipping through the most recent articles she had read. "A tricky situation?"

"There was a...public incident that damaged our client's image and brand significantly. He's lost significant sponsorships, is temporarily suspended from competing, and is currently drowning in negative media coverage." Gavin's voice was tinged with irritation, but Daphne couldn't tell if it was for the situation or the client. "This is definitely a 'hands-on' matter, as this client brings in, or brought in, significant revenue. So, this will require day-to-day focus and attention."

"Doing what, exactly?" she asked, unable to keep her concern out of her voice.

Gavin met her eyes directly. "Acting as his girlfriend."

For a moment, Daphne was sure she had misheard.

"Wait..." she began, her voice higher than usual. "What? Is this a joke?" A flush of heat crept up her neck as it dawned on her what he must think...and she was going to end that right there.

"I'm sorry," she continued, not waiting for his response, "I am not here to be part of an escort service and..."

"No, I swear that's all it is, acting like his girlfriend." Gavin interrupted, raising both hands in a placating gesture. "I swear, it's a PR strategy, not a—" He broke off as he cleared his throat, his cheeks flushing as he realized how it must have sounded. "I promise you, this would be entirely professional. We need someone to act as his girlfriend in public for a year. Living accommodations would be provided—there are spare rooms at his apartment...."

"A YEAR?" Daphne's voice rose sharply as she pushed herself to her feet. That was the craziest thing she had ever heard. A year of pretending to be someone's girlfriend? Of living in their home? And for what? To be able to show she deserves a position at their firm? Why would anyone work somewhere that saw female employees as mere props, deployed for client convenience?

"I'm sorry," she said as she rose from her chair. "I am not the girl you are looking for. Thank you for your time."

Daphne turned toward the door, crossing as quickly as her legs would carry her. Her hand had just touched the doorknob when Gavin's voice cut through the tension-filled room.

"The pay is $2,000,000 for the year, paid monthly, with benefits."

Daphne's fingers froze on the cool metal of the doorknob. For a moment, she was certain she had misheard again. Slowly, she turned back to face Gavin.

"Two million dollars?" she repeated, the words feeling foreign on her tongue.

"As I said, he is a very lucrative client, or was, and it is our job to get him there again. The position comes with full health insurance, retirement contributions, and a guaranteed position with the agency as a full PR agent when you are done, should you want it."

Daphne's mind was spinning. That was more than most people made in a decade. More than enough to pay off her student loans, with enough left over to buy a home wherever she wanted.

For pretending to date someone.

"This can't be real," she murmured, more to herself than to Gavin. "This has to be a joke."

"I wish this were a joke." Gavin gave a slight grimace before he gestured for her to return to her seat. "Let me explain the full situation before you decide."

"I can't believe I am considering this," she said, questioning her sanity, as well as his, as she moved to the chair.

"It is entirely above board," Gavin continued. "We have a client whose ability in the ring, paired with his temper, has caused his reputation to implode. This would be a true trial by fire in helping change his image and public perception, which is why, at the end of the year, you would be guaranteed a position here if you wanted. As you said, the public doesn't see the person behind the name."

Daphne paused, first at the irritation he had used her own words against her, and second to honestly think about the situation. Fake relationships weren't unheard of in the entertainment industry; she had studied plenty of similar cases.

She had just never expected to be part of one...

"Who is it for?"

"One of our MMA fighters," Gavin replied, watching her reaction carefully.

Daphne's eyes narrowed as pieces began to click into place. A fighter with image problems serious enough to warrant this kind of approach. Recent enough that the damage was still fresh and in the public eye. Why did that ring a bell?

"Who?" she pressed, needing a name. Her thoughts went through everyone she could remember who was attached to Richards PR Management.

Gavin hesitated for just a moment. "Kane Mitchell."

The name meant nothing to Daphne.

"What happened that he needs this level of intervention?"

"Kane has had some...challenges recently," Gavin replied carefully. "An altercation outside the arena that was captured on video and went viral. Sponsors pulling out, the ECF considering suspension."

"What kind of altercation?" she asked, needing more.

Gavin sighed. "He had a physical confrontation with another fighter in a parking lot after an event. Bystanders recorded it, and it went viral."

"Wait, he attacked someone?" Daphne's concern was increasing.

"It was more complicated than that," Gavin countered. "Kane was provoked—deliberately, we believe. The other fighter said things specifically designed to trigger Kane's temper, knowing cameras were present."

"So, this Kane has anger management issues, and your solution is to give him a girlfriend?" She couldn't keep the doubt from her voice. "How exactly is that supposed to help?"

"Public perception is driven by image, and right now, Kane is seen as an uncontrolled hothead. We want to create a different image for people to latch onto."

The PR logic wasn't entirely unsound.

"And Kane is on board with this plan?" Daphne was surprised that anyone would agree to it unless they already had a girlfriend.

A flicker of frustration crossed Gavin's face. "Kane understands the severity of his situation. The...details of how we fix it are still being finalized."

Translation: Kane either doesn't know or has already refused.

"I'd want to meet him before making any decision," her voice firm. "And I'd need to understand exactly what this arrangement would entail."

"Of course," Gavin agreed readily, sensing he'd gotten as far as he would today. "Let me set it up. Are you available tomorrow?"

Daphne nodded mutely, already wondering what she was getting herself into.

Gavin reached for his phone.

"Kane," he said after a moment. "I need you in my office tomorrow at ten. There's a situation we need to discuss." He paused, listening to whatever response came through the phone. "No, this can't wait. It's about your current situation." Another pause. "Yes, I'm aware of your feelings on the matter, but ...Fine then, I'll meet you at the gym since you can't be bothered to get here. Ten o'clock."

He ended the call without waiting for agreement, his smile reminding Daphne of the Cheshire Cat.

"Wonderful, I have an address for the meeting tomorrow." Gavin said calmly, "Once you two meet, things will be clearer.'

Daphne wasn't so sure. Yet she found herself nodding, agreeing to meet a man to discuss pretending to be his girlfriend for a year—she owed it to her future to give it a chance, because the salary offered would transform her life.

"Tomorrow at ten, then," she confirmed, her voice steadier than she felt.

As she shook Gavin's hand, Daphne wondered what kind of man Kane Mitchell was beyond the anger issues Gavin had tried to downplay.

More importantly, what kind of situation was she walking into tomorrow morning at ten o'clock?

Chapter five

The thud of fists echoed through Warrior's Edge gym. The fluorescent lights flickered overhead as sweat dripped from Kane's brow, stinging his eyes.

He didn't bother to wipe it away.

Instead, his wrapped knuckles fell with fury into a heavy bag, grunting with each impact as he thought back over the conversation with Gavin.

"Fucking Gavin," Kane muttered, punctuating the name with a vicious right hook.

"Easy there," Jackson grunted, his salt-and-pepper beard glistening with perspiration in the warmth of the gym. "You're gonna tear something if you keep hitting like that."

Kane ignored him, launching into another combination—jab, cross, uppercut. The methodical movements did little to calm his anger.

"Gavin wants me to get a girlfriend," Kane spat, the words bitter on his tongue as he shifted back into his stance, his feet hip-width apart, fists ready to launch at the bag again. "A fucking fake girlfriend."

Jackson's eyes narrowed beneath his perpetual furrow. "Is that what Richards called about yesterday?"

Kane stepped back, chest heaving, and reached for the nearest chalk bag. He dipped his hands into the powdery substance, ignoring the sting as it settled into the small splits in his hands from the pounding he had given the bag.

"His brilliant solution to my 'image problem.'" Kane said with a sneer. "Find some woman willing to pretend she's tamed the wild beast. Wants me to fucking play house, make nice with the big wigs, all so everyone can pretend I'm someone, anyone, other than me."

"You gonna hear him out at least?" Jackson asked, his voice gruff with frustration as he grabbed the Muay Thai pads that lay near the bag.

"Again? Fuck that." Kane resumed his position, focusing his gaze on the pads. "He's going to tell me that I need to lie to save my career. How I need to convince everyone I'm a changed man, a 'tamed' man."

The jab-cross combination that followed landed with enough force that Jackson grunted. His expression remained carefully neutral, but Kane could see the calculation behind his eyes.

"Richards has gotten you out of worse spots than this." Jackson reminded him.

Kane snorted. "Yeah, well, this time he's asking me to sell out." His next punch landed with particular venom. "They want a performing monkey, not a fighter."

"They want a professional," Jackson countered, his voice lowering to keep his words from reaching others in the gym. "Someone who understands that fighting in the cage and fighting in parking lots are different things."

The reminder of the incident with Tony Alvarez sent a fresh surge of anger through Kane's system.

"Tony deserved it," Kane said, the words automatic, a mantra he'd repeated to himself over the past ten days.

"Maybe he did." Jackson acknowledged, which surprised Kane. "But it doesn't matter when you're on the verge of losing everything you've worked for. "

Kane stepped back with a look of disdain before he turned from Jackson. He made short work of unwrapping his hands before reaching for a towel to wipe the blood and chalk from them. It was several moments before he was able to rein in his irritation and respond.

"So you're on his fucking side?" Kane's voice was sharp with irritation. "You think I should just pretend I'm dating some random woman Gavin found to make people, what, like me? They never liked me."

Jackson shot Kane an annoyed glare. "What I think," he said, "is that you should consider it before throwing your entire career away because of one stupid prick. Don't just say no just out of principle."

Kane's head snapped up. "Fuck that, principles are all I've got left." He shot back. "My sponsors are gone, the ECF is making an example out of me, fuck I can't even walk down the street without someone glaring at me or turning their back to me—what the hell do you want me to have other than my principles?"

"Your future," Jackson replied simply. "This suspension, if they give it, it's temporary if you play it smart. But if you keep digging in your heels, it becomes permanent."

Kane turned away, unwilling to let Jackson see the uncertainty that flickered beneath his anger. He grabbed a water bottle from the cooler and took a giant gulp.

"So you are asking me to pretend to be something I'm not, just to make others happy?" Kane asked, crushing the bottle in his fist as he spoke, uncaring of the water that splashed out and to the floor.

"I'm asking you to consider what's more important to you." Jackson's tone was gentle, and that unnerved Kane more than his anger would have: "your career or your pride."

Kane stared at the crushed bottle in his hand and the pink tint of blood that snaked down his hand. The question hung in the air between them. What was more important?

Sticking to his principles and being authentic, or losing the thing that had defined him since he was a punk kid on the streets?

The creak from the gym's front door echoed through the room, and Kane tensed, a glance at the clock telling him who it would be.

Gavin was never late.

The man stood framed in the doorway, dressed in a crisply tailored navy suit that looked as out of place as Kane knew Gavin likely felt.

But it was the figure who stepped in behind him, though, that caught and held Kane's attention. The woman was slim but curvy in all the best places, dressed professionally in a crisp blouse and pencil skirt that almost reminded him of a librarian. Still, he didn't remember any librarian looking like her.

As he took in the waves of her brown hair and saw her face, his brow furrowed.

He recognized her, but from where?

"Right on time." Jackson muttered as he began to cross to meet the pair inside the door.

The woman hesitated just inside the door, her eyes scanning the space. When her gaze landed on Kane, something flickered across her expression that he couldn't quite identify. Was it recognition, concern?

His gaze dragged over her, certain he'd seen her before, but he couldn't recall where. He was sure he would have remembered someone who looked like her. She wasn't a past hookup, that he knew; he would have remembered those curves.

Gavin spotted Kane and moved toward him, navigating around equipment with unexpected ease for a man who had only been at the gym a handful of times. The woman followed more cautiously, her heels loud when they struck the bare concrete floor.

"Kane," Gavin called, "Glad to see you're getting in some training."

Kane didn't respond to him; all his attention was fixed on the woman.

Her movements were graceful, if a little self-conscious, as if she knew everyone in the gym was watching her. Her dark brown eyes met his directly, assessing him.

And then it hit him. The collision on the sidewalk outside Richards PR Management. Her wrist in his grip, those same brown eyes wide with surprise before narrowing in anger when he had turned his back on her.

Fuck.

Of all the women in Philadelphia, Gavin had found the one Kane had already managed pissed off before even meeting her.

"Kane Mitchell," Gavin said as they reached him, "I'd like you to meet Daphne Wilson."

Daphne extended her hand; her eyes held both wariness and irritation. "Mr. Mitchell."

Her voice slid around him like honey, something he hadn't noticed in his irritation the first time they...could he really say met if they had knocked into each other?

Kane looked at her outstretched hand, then back to her face, but made no move to take her hand. As much as he wanted to feel her skin against his, more than just her hand if he was being honest, he wasn't going to do that, not when she was being hired to help him.

And that thought pissed him off. He turned to Gavin, his jaw clenched tight.

"Didn't I tell you no fucking way on this?" He didn't miss the way Daphne flinched at his tone, but better she realized that this was just how he is, so she could walk away.

Even if he wanted to know what her lips tasted like.

Gavin's brow raised as he responded. "Daphne has an impressive background in marketing and public relations. She's exactly the kind of person you need to help you through this mess you created."

The not-so-subtle reminder made Kane want to put his fist through the nearest wall.

He turned his attention back to Daphne, unable to stop his gaze from traveling over her.

She was different from any of the other women he had been linked with, mostly because they were only there for one night and then gone. But he knew she would be the kind to stay, and that strangely made him uneasy.

She was beautiful in a subtle, composed manner that he hadn't thought he would be attracted to, but fuck if he wasn't. Her lips were unpainted but full. He watched as they pressed together under his gaze, her cheeks flushing even as her eyes stayed locked with his.

Kane knew how he looked—shirtless, sweat-slicked, wearing nothing but gym shorts that hung low on his hips. He looked like what he was—a fighter. He wasn't some pretty boy in a three-piece suit, and he never would be.

How long had it been since he'd been with a woman? Two months? Three? He had gotten tired of the meaningless hookups, the women seeking to grab attention on social media by posting private moments. He just hadn't bothered, but he had never met a woman who tempted him as much as Daphne.

"Kane," Jackson's voice broke through his thoughts, "why don't we all step into the office to continue this conversation?" The man's tone said he expected to be obeyed.

Yet Kane ignored him.

"Seriously, what part of 'no' was unclear to you?"

"I would say the part that's the six-month suspension that you are facing," Gavin replied evenly. "Or where you know every sponsor that you had either walked away from you or is about to walk away."

Daphne's expression was shifting from being neutral to something that almost looked like concern. And for some reason, that pissed Kane off even more.

"I don't care," Kane said, his words harsh. "I already fucking told you; I am not doing this—"

"Mr. Mitchell," Daphne interrupted, her honey voice wrapped around steel as her chin lifted. "Should we talk about this privately first?"

Kane shot a glare at her. Unfortunately for him, it was just as the light from the window shone from her hair, highlighting strands of amber among the brown.

For a moment—just a moment—he allowed himself to imagine what it might be like to run his fingers through those waves, to discover if they felt as soft as they looked.

But this situation wasn't one where he could have those lines of thought. Not when she was there to try and what, fix him? No, that wasn't happening.

"The public responds to narrative, Kane," Gavin interjected. "Right now, the narrative is that you're volatile, unpredictable, unsafe outside the controlled environment of the cage. We need to counter that with evidence of stability, of growth."

"Evidence," Kane echoed, the word bitter on his tongue. "You mean window dressing." He ran his hand over his short hair with a curse. "I'm not a fucking redemption arc for your resume."

"No," Daphne agreed, her dark eyes meeting without flinching. "But from what it sounds like, you're a professional athlete whose career is in jeopardy because of a PR crisis."

"Kane," Jackson's gruff voice cut through the tension, "step into my office. Now. You can continue this fight where others can't overhear."

The unnatural silence from the gym finally dawned on Kane. He glanced around to find every eye on them as he cursed. Great. More fodder for the rumor mill.

"Fine," he bit out, gesturing sharply toward the small office at the back of the gym. "After you."

As Gavin and Daphne moved in the direction he'd indicated, he used the moment to draw a deep breath. That was exactly what he didn't need right now, especially in a group of fighters that, while he respected them, he didn't trust them, not when they all wanted to be where he was...or had been.

As Daphne passed him, Kane caught the slight tremble in her hand as she tucked a strand of hair behind her ear. The gesture was small, but it told him she was more nervous than she was letting on.

Kane ran a hand through his sweat-dampened hair, frustration building with each passing moment. This was ridiculous. All of it. Most of all, the fact that he hadn't already told them both to go to Hell.

Yet he found himself reluctantly following them toward the office. Was it the knowledge that his career hung by a thread, and that without fighting, he had nothing?

Or maybe it was the way Daphne had looked at him when she thought he wasn't watching. A look that had nothing to do with PR strategies, and everything to do with awareness of him as a man.

Kane shoved the thought aside as he reached the office door. Who the fuck was he kidding? This was just a farce. And despite what Gavin seemed to think, Kane Mitchell was not for sale.

Chapter six

Daphne took a deep breath as she pushed down her irritation as she heard the door close behind them. She had prepared herself since yesterday, had researched Kane's career, and run a pros and cons list of what was being suggested.

What she hadn't prepared for was the impact that Kane had in person. Even his glare did nothing to diminish his appeal, not when he was wearing nothing but a pair of dark gray gym shorts that hung low on his hips.

Because good god, the man was ripped.

She couldn't stop her gaze from traveling over his torso as his jaw clenched.

His shoulders were broader—she hadn't realized quite how broad when he had knocked into her, and that now seemed a shame. She had seen fit men before. Hell, she had been friends with the guys on the college football team, but she had never seen an eight-pack. Her eyes trailed down to the cut of muscles that formed a V leading to the waist of his shorts.

It was a body honed as a weapon.

Daphne turned to face Kane and Jackson and saw Gavin do the same.

"Let's be completely honest here, Kane," Gavin said, his tone going flat. "You are desperate, whether you want to admit it or not. The ECF board will meet soon to determine your suspension. Rumor is they are considering a minimum of 6 months, potentially longer. Every major sponsor has already walked. You do *not* have a choice."

Daphne watched Kane's reaction closely, taking in the muscle ticking in his jaw, the slight flare of his nostrils, the way his fingers flexed at his sides before he deliberately crossed his arms over his chest.

"You think I don't know that?" Kane scoffed, his voice harsh. "You think I need a reminder of how thoroughly they're screwing me over the bullshit that Alvarez engineered?"

There it was—the defensive posture.

Daphne had seen this pattern before, had grown up with it. Her brother Aaron, five years her senior, had displayed the same resistance to admitting to any perceived vulnerability. And all that had accomplished was to keep making things worse.

"Kane, I am here to offer a solution." Gavin's eyes narrowed at the anger on Kane's face.

Kane's eyes flicked briefly to Daphne before returning to Gavin. "What, turning my life into a reality show? Acting like I'm the 'Bachelor' or something?"

"By showing the public a side of you they don't normally see," Gavin corrected. "Let's be honest, the ECF doesn't want to lose you as a draw—they make too much money off of ticket sales. Same with the sponsors —they make too much money off your ads. But they want to know that you can control yourself outside the cage as well as you do inside it."

Jackson, who had been leaning against the wall in silence, straightened slightly. "Kane," he said, his gruff voice cutting through the tension, "you know I've always been straight with you. You need to consider this. It's not about selling out. It's about playing the game long enough to stay in it." He took a deep sigh before his hand came to Kane's shoulder. "And sometimes you gotta take a step back to move forward."

Kane's shoulders tensed, clearly torn between his instinctive rejection of the plan and his respect for the older man's opinion.

Daphne tilted her head slightly as she watched the silent conversation between the two men. It was clear that Jackson held influence that even Gavin didn't possess. If she agreed to this arrangement, that could prove useful.

And the fact that she hadn't already said 'no, thank you,' and walked out was a little surprising. But there was something that drew her to Kane; she just wished it was more professional interest than personal, but the heat curling in her abdomen told her that wasn't the case.

But she could ignore it. She was a professional.

"Mr. Mitchell," she said, her voice soft in the office. "We can work out something that doesn't require you to change who you are, but maybe softens you a bit for the public, changes the perspective without changing you."

Kane's gray eyes locked onto hers, his gaze intense enough to make her heart rate quicken.

"You don't know anything about me," he bit out, "you don't know who I am, or what I am like."

"I know you're stubborn." She replied. "I know honesty is preferred over convenience. And I know you're willing to risk your career rather than compromise anything of your values."

His eyebrows rose slightly, genuine surprise flickering across his features. "You got all that from a five-minute conversation?"

"And from watching you with Gavin and Jackson," she added. "People reveal themselves through the way they behave, especially when they are acting under stress."

The assessing look he gave her was more curious than antagonizing. Once again, he reminded her of Aaron during high school, that moment when her brother realized someone had seen past his carefully constructed facade to the person beneath.

"My brother's the same way." She found herself saying. "He was a Lacrosse player, not a fighter, but you both have similar personalities.

He's very driven, and I swear he is allergic to any suggestion that he might need to change, rather than have things change around him."

Kane's eyes held a mixture of offense and curiosity as his brow rose.

"Your brother sounds like an asshole," he said finally.

"Oh, he definitely can be." Daphne smiled. "But he's also loyal, determined, and occasionally right about the world needing to meet his expectations rather than change to fit in."

Something in Kane's posture eased at her response, and his gaze shifted from hostile to calculating. Daphne took in a deep breath as she met his gaze, wanting to show him that she was seeing him, not just assessing him as if he didn't matter.

Gavin, ever sensitive to shifts in interpersonal dynamics, seized the opening. "Kane, all we're asking is that you consider the possibility. Meet with Daphne a few times, see if there's enough common ground to make this work. If not, we'll explore other options."

The way Gavin said "other options" made it clear there weren't any—at least, none that offered the chance to save his career.

Kane seemed to understand this, too; his jaw set as he realized he had been backed into a corner.

"Fine," he finally snarled. "But I make no promises beyond that."

Daphne studied him, noting the rigid set of his shoulders, the careful control of his breathing, and the tension in his crossed arms. She knew he was only agreeing because the threats to everything he had were unavoidable.

If she took on this assignment, she would have to try to focus on that stubborn resistance. She could already imagine how hard it would be; Kane was a man who defied categorization.

Gavin shifted his attention to her, his question clear in his eyes. Kane's eyes narrowed as he watched Gavin before he shot a look at Jackson for a moment before turning his gaze to meet hers.

For a moment, Daphne was quiet as she considered him and everything Gavin had told her the day before. Was the challenge worth $2 million?

She saw Kane's eyes close as his head dropped. He must have just realized that it wasn't a sure thing, that she could still walk away. With a sigh, he turned and grabbed the handle of the door.

"I'll do it."

The three words, spoken with quiet certainty, froze Kane mid-motion. He turned slowly; disbelief etched into every line of his face.

"What?" The question emerged as barely more than a whisper, as if Kane couldn't quite process what he'd heard.

"I said I'll do it," Daphne repeated as she nodded to Gavin. "One year."

Kane's expression shifted from confusion to something approaching contempt.

"Why?" He growled. "So, you can add 'tamed a fighter' to your resume?"

His words stung a little, but Daphne kept her expression neutral. "No. There are several reasons, but I think it could work."

"You think it could work." Kane echoed, his tone making it clear he found the idea absurd. "You think anyone is going to believe that someone like you, someone who clearly doesn't belong anywhere near my life, wants anything to do with me?"

"That's actually the point," Gavin interrupted. "It's the contrast between you two that makes it compelling. It's exactly the narrative shift we need."

Kane shot him a look of pure venom. "This isn't one of your scripts, Gavin. This is my life."

"A life that's hanging by a thread professionally," Jackson reminded him, his gruff voice softening the harsh reality of the words. "You want to keep fighting? This might be your only path back to the cage."

"And you don't think it's going to get out that she has a fucking degree in what, marketing? That's not going to give everything away the moment they realize?"

"Not necessarily." Gavin shrugged. "A lot of people graduate each year with marketing degrees. And you have done fights at college arenas before; we could spin it that you met after one of your fights and sparks flew."

"Why are you really doing this?" Kane asked, his attention returning to Daphne.

Daphne paused for a moment, wondering how honest to be, but his gaze was raw, and that told her he needed the whole, unvarnished truth.

"Two million dollars," she said simply. "A chance to clear my student loans, build financial security, and gain experience that would normally take years to accumulate. And helping the world see the person behind the image, behind the name. To help them see you, not just the fighter."

Kane's eyebrows rose. "Two million," he repeated, the tick in his cheek deepening. "That's what Gavin thinks saving my career is worth." He ran his hand over his face as he slumped against the wall. "You have got to be shitting me."

"To be fair," Gavin leaned against Jackson's desk as he spoke, "your career is worth considerably more to the ECF, my firm, and your sponsors. So don't act like it's an exorbitant amount. Last year alone, you made what, eight million just from your fights, not even including your income from sponsors. That added another five million, so you easily make over 13 million a year."

Kane's gaze shifted to Daphne. She met his scrutiny steadily, holding his eyes with hers for several moments.

"Fine," Kane sighed as he let his head drop back against the wall. "If you're willing to sign up for this circus, that's your choice. But don't expect me to play the devoted boyfriend when the cameras are off. This is a business arrangement, nothing more."

55

"Agreed," Daphne replied, extending her hand to him. "Business only."

Kane looked at her outstretched hand for a moment before taking it. His skin against hers caused a spark of awareness to flood through her as she drew in a breath. When his fingers closed over hers, she was keenly aware of the calluses on his palm and the warmth of his skin.

"Excellent," Gavin said, his smile widening. "Kane, please meet your new girlfriend."

Kane dropped her hand immediately, taking a step back as he curled his fingers into his palm and slipped his hand to his side.

"This is going to be Hell," he muttered, running his other hand through his short dark hair.

"It doesn't have to be," Daphne shrugged.

"Do you really believe that we can fake a relationship that will change how people see me? What happens when it's over?" Kane challenged. "When the year is up and the 'relationship' conveniently ends? What then?"

The question caught Daphne off guard. She hadn't expected Kane to look that far ahead with how resistant he had been to the idea. But she quickly realized there was a lot more to him than he showed.

"Then," she said after a moment's consideration, "we part amicably, having both benefited from the arrangement. We'll arrange a breakup, say it just didn't work out, say we are parting as friends."

Kane's gray eyes studied her, his expression unreadable.

"We'll see," he said finally.

As Gavin began outlining next steps—living arrangements, public appearances, the narrative they would craft—Daphne maintained eye contact with Kane. She knew one thing: this was going to be complicated.

Two million dollars, one year, and one very angry, *very* attractive fighter.

What had she gotten herself into?

Chapter seven

T he limo glided to a stop outside the Arts Ballroom, its engine
purring softly beneath the clamor of Philadelphia's evening traffic.
Daphne Wilson sat rigidly on the leather seat, her fingers twisting together in her lap as she tried to control the flutter of anxiety in her chest.
Through the tinted window, she could see the flash of cameras already
aimed at them, reporters and photographers clustered near the red carpet
like predators sensing fresh prey. This was their debut as a couple, the
first public test of the elaborate lie she'd agreed to for two million dollars.

It had taken Gavin only one week to orchestrate this moment—and
Daphne had spent all seven days of preparation, coaching sessions on
Kane's public history, cramming a crash course in MMA terminology.
Kane had reluctantly been pulled into endless discussions about their
"relationship narrative." Now they were here, about to step into the
spotlight at the ECF's annual charity gala, where Kane was scheduled to
present an award despite his precarious standing with the organization.

Daphne smoothed a nervous hand down the front of her dress, a
midnight blue beaded halter gown that caught the dim light of the
limo's interior and scattered it like stars. The dress was gorgeous, it really
was. But it was so far beyond anything she had ever owned. She had
stammered that when Gavin had given her the directions to the couture
store, but the man had been adamant about it.

Silver shoes sparkled on her feet as she shifted her legs. Her sable hair was drawn up off her face, the delicate curls the stylist had spent hours creating brushed softly against her cheeks and the back of her neck.

"You look fine." Kane rolled his eyes as his arms crossed, and she adjusted the skirt for the umpteenth time since getting into the limo.

She frowned and barely suppressed the urge to stick her tongue out at him. It wasn't fair how she needed hours of preparation, makeup, hair, and the perfect dress to try and look presentable, and all he had to do was shrug into a tuxedo, probably one of many in his closet.

And damn him for looking like the million-dollar draw that he was.

The black jacket accented his shoulders, the cut highlighting the lean power of his body. When his eyes cut to hers, the gray reflected the lights from outside, and damned if the look didn't take her breath away.

His gaze turned back to the window as they started to slow. After a moment, he scoffed before his head fell back against the seat. "Fucking vultures out there." He jerked his chin toward the window. "They'll be dissecting our every move before we even make it inside."

She knew he was right, which only amplified her discomfort.

Outside, a reporter pointed toward their limo, and several cameras swiveled toward them. It was showtime. From the moment she stepped outside, she wouldn't just be Daphne Wilson anymore. It was time to become "Kane Mitchell's girlfriend."

"I don't know if I can do this," she whispered, the words escaping before she could stop them.

Kane's eyes snapped to her face, his expression unreadable in the dim light. For a moment, she thought she saw something flicker there—but then his features hardened in irritation.

"Too late now," he said, his voice flat. "Unless you want to give back the money."

The mention of the money had her take a deep breath, a reminder of what was at stake. Financial freedom. The end of debt.

She straightened her spine, lifting her chin slightly. "No. I'm ready."

Kane studied her for a moment longer, then nodded once. Outside, the driver had circled the car and was approaching the door on Kane's side.

"Let's get this shit over with," Kane groaned, uncrossing his arms and shifting forward in his seat as the driver opened the door.

Cool evening air rushed in, carrying with it the murmur of the waiting crowd. Kane hesitated for just a fraction of a second, then slid across the leather seat and stepped out, his movements fluid even as they showed his coiled strength. He turned immediately, extending his hand back toward the limo's interior.

Daphne stared at that outstretched hand—strong and scarred, the knuckles still bearing the faint yellowish marks of recent bruising—the hand of a man who resented this arrangement.

She took a deep breath, remembering Gavin's coaching: Look at him like he's the only man in the world. Touch him whenever possible. Laugh at his jokes, even when they aren't funny. Sell the illusion with every glance, every gesture, every smile.

Daphne placed her hand in Kane's, feeling the warmth of his palm against hers. The cameras began to flash in earnest as she emerged, the beaded dress catching the light, her stilettos finding purchase on the red carpet.

Kane's hand tightened almost imperceptibly around hers as the first questions hit them. Microphones were extended like weapons, the reporters hungry for anything on Kane Mitchell, the fighter who couldn't control his temper.

"Kane, how does it feel to know your career is in jeopardy?"

"Kane, do you want to apologize to Tony Alvarez for the assault?"

"Kane, sources say the ECF is considering terminating your contract entirely. Any comment?"

The questions kept coming, relentless and accusatory, each one striking like a body blow. Daphne felt Kane stiffen beside her. His fingers flexed against hers, the careful restraint in his grip beginning to slip.

They had prepared for this, but the reality was more intense than any simulation. These people didn't want answers; they wanted blood.

A reporter with a sports magazine logo on his microphone stepped into their path. "Is it true that Tony Alvarez is still suffering from injuries sustained during your attack? His team says he might not be cleared to fight for months."

Kane's face darkened, his eyes narrowing to dangerous slits. Daphne could feel the anger radiating from him in waves and knew.

She needed to intervene—now.

Daphne slid her hand from Kane's grip and placed it against his chest, shifting until she was between him and the reporter. The touch was deliberate, selling their relationship while simultaneously preventing Kane from lunging forward.

"I'm so sorry." She said as she watched Kane. When she felt him take a deep breath and his chest relax, even though it was only a little, she turned to the reporter with a bright smile. "We're running a bit late for the ceremony. But I'd be happy to answer a few questions about our work with the children's foundation while we walk."

The reporter blinked, momentarily thrown. His eyes flickered between Daphne's smile and the lingering hostility in Kane's gaze.

"Actually," the reporter said, recovering quickly, "I am curious about who you are. This is the first time we have seen Kane with anyone."

Daphne's smile widened as she slid her hand down to reclaim Kane's hand. She gave it a gentle squeeze, hoping he would interpret it as both a warning and an encouragement.

"Me? Oh, I'm Daphne." She gave another smile to the reporters as the flash of lights flickered around them.

"How do you know Kane, Daphne?" Another reporter's microphone was shoved towards her face. "Are you a probation officer or someone who is monitoring him?"

"The fuck are you talking about?" Kane sneered. "A probation officer? She's my..." his jaw tightened as his eyes met hers, and she hoped the reporters couldn't see the anger that reflected in them with what he was about to say. "She's my girlfriend."

The reporters froze for a moment before a cacophony of voices threatened to deafen her as they all started clamoring for more information.

Daphne looked up at Kane, her hand on his arm, and his posture gradually relaxed under her touch as his eyes shifted away from the shouting crowd to meet hers. It was exactly the picture Gavin had wanted—the volatile fighter visibly calmed by the presence of his new girlfriend.

After a moment, Kane's hand dropped to her lower back as he made his way up the carpet, ignoring the shouts and questions of the reporters.

Gradually, the questions began to shift.

"Daphne, when did you meet Kane?"

"How does it feel dating a professional fighter?"

"Kane, has Daphne been a stabilizing influence in your life?"

This last question made Kane stop, and he turned to look at the female reporter at the back of the crowd who had asked it.

"She's certainly changed my perspective," he said, the words emerging stiffly but without the hostility that had colored his earlier silence. Daphne felt a flash of surprise, but she recovered quickly and beamed up at him as he raised a brow in amusement.

The reporters ate it up, their pens scribbling frantically as they called out questions, not about the fight with Tony Alvarez or Kane's reputation, but about their meeting, and about her.

Exactly as they had planned.

Chapter eight

K ane stood with his hand on Daphne's back, slowly trying to make their way to the door. He watched through narrowed eyes as Daphne laughed at something one of the reporters said, her head tilted back slightly, the sound genuine enough that even he almost believed it. Almost.

The woman was good—better than he wanted to admit.

When Gavin had first talked about this harebrained idea, Kane had imagined a stiff, awkward performance that would fool no one. But he had to admit, Daphne was not what he'd expected.

She leaned against him, her head resting against his shoulder as she answered a question from a sports blogger that had been particularly nasty with him in the aftermath. The man was smiling now and laughed at what Daphne had said. It was the friendliest Kane had ever seen the man.

The constant touching was part of their strategy; fuck, Gavin had drilled it into them during their preparation sessions. Kane had expected to hate the touching—he generally disliked physical contact outside of fighting or sex, but strangely, it wasn't bothering him.

Daphne's touch was light, almost casual, even though it was always present. Each contact was brief, yet apparently enough to create the impression of intimacy.

A reporter from one of the major sports networks approached, her cameraman in tow, and Kane felt his muscles tense automatically. Fuck, this man had a lot of followers with his network; if he fucked up, there wouldn't be enough charm in the world to undo it.

"Kane, Daphne," the reporter greeted them with a practiced smile on his face, "would you mind answering a few questions for our viewers?"

Before Kane could respond, Daphne stepped slightly forward, her hand catching his in a way that looked natural but kept him from clenching his fist.

"Sure, if it won't be too long," she said as she glanced back at the line of people behind them. "It already looks as though we are blocking the line." She squeezed Kane's hand in warning when he shifted beside her.

The reporter nodded as his cameraman set the shot. Once the man gave the thumbs up, the reporter's eyes sharpened. "Kane, there's been a lot of speculation about your future with the ECF following the incident with Tony Alvarez. Can you tell us where things stand?"

Kane felt his jaw tighten. He knew someone would probably ask that, but had hoped it would have been a small reporter, not someone from ESPN.

Daphne's fingers squeezed his as she rested her other hand on his elbow, forcing his attention away from the man and to her. When his gaze met hers, she took a deep breath. He unconsciously mimicked her, and the tension coursing through him eased marginally.

"The ECF is reviewing the situation," he said, the words coming out slowly as he turned to face the reporter again. "I'm cooperating fully with them and will abide by whatever they decide."

The reporter's brow rose as he stayed still with his mic out, and Daphne smoothly interjected.

"Kane's been focusing on working with the community while things get sorted out," she said, her voice warm with what sounded like pride. "He's been helping with the Philadelphia Children's Foundation, organizing self-defense classes for the kids at his gym. It's a really important project for him."

Kane blinked, surprised by that. The Foundation was real—and yeah, he'd done the appearances that Gavin had arranged. But usually, he was standing awkwardly in the background while others worked with the kids. If he was honest, it was something he did, but he'd never considered it important. But Daphne made it sound like his life's passion.

The reporter's expression softened as he shifted his focus to Daphne. "That's right, you're here supporting the Foundation tonight. How did you get involved, Daphne?"

"Through Kane, actually." She replied, glancing up at him with a smile that made something strange flutter in his chest. "It was one of the first things he shared with me when we started dating, and then I saw how much it meant to him. It says a lot about a person where they choose to give their time."

The reporter nodded, his focus now entirely on Daphne. "And how are you finding the spotlight, being with someone so high profile?"

"It has its challenges," Daphne admitted with a small laugh, "but Kane's worth it." She looked up at him again, and Kane was startled by the warmth in her eyes. If he didn't know better, he would almost think it was genuine. "I like that I get to know the real Kane, not just the public image. Would you believe he's quite private? I know a lot of people think that he's a fighter all the time, but that's his profession, not his personality."

Kane watched the reporter, someone who had no problems tearing Kane apart after a brutal match, nodding.

How the fuck was this working?

As they made their way through the door into the ballroom, Kane found himself watching Daphne. She smiled and charmed everyone they encountered. She never moved too far from his side, her presence a buffer between him and the curious attendees.

When they finally made it to their assigned table, Kane was relieved to sit down. He hated crowds—dealing with them often left him more drained than a five-round fight. Daphne took the seat beside him, her shoulder brushing his as she arranged her skirt.

"You're good at this," he said quietly, the words emerging before he could consider them.

Daphne glanced at him, surprise flickering on her face as her eyes darted around. "It's just PR," she replied, her voice equally low as she gave a small shrug.

"No," Kane disagreed. "It's more than that. These people would have torn me apart; Hell, they have torn me apart in the past. But they are all entranced by you."

A faint flush colored her cheeks. "That's the goal, isn't it? Make them forget about the fight, focus on us...I mean, on the relationship."

Kane nodded slowly, his eyes scanning the room. Every person he saw was watching them with open curiosity. There were no hostile looks, no side eye glances followed by an eye roll.

Could this work? For the first time since Gavin had proposed it, he found himself considering that it may not be completely insane.

Daphne's hand rested on his forearm again as she leaned in and whispered about one of the officials across the room. The touch was light—yet Kane found himself oddly conscious of the warmth of her palm through the fabric of his suit.

It was just an act, he reminded himself.

But as he watched her charm the table with the same effortless grace she'd displayed with the reporters, Kane felt his dislike of her giving way to something new...

Respect.

*　*　*

Kane felt himself relax as dinner was served, and there had been no further questions about Tony fucking Alvarez. He sat back in his chair and watched Daphne chat with the ECF executive seated to her right. With the program about to begin, it seemed that the worst was over.

Then he saw the man approaching from across the room—short, balding, with the hungry eyes of a scavenger who had just spotted wounded prey—and something in Kane's gut tightened.

Martin Sheer was a reporter for one of the more sensationalist sports sites, known for baiting fighters into making controversial statements. After the fight with Alvarez, he had written a scathing article, peppered with anonymous "sources," that claimed Kane had a history of unprovoked violence outside the cage.

The article had led two sponsors to drop him, which Kane hadn't forgotten.

"Shit," Kane muttered under his breath.

Daphne turned at the sound, following his gaze to the approaching reporter. A flicker of recognition crossed her face; he was one of the reporters Gavin had made sure she knew.

"Let me handle him," she said quietly as her hand came to rest on Kane's, but Sheer had already reached them, positioning himself to deliberately block Daphne from participating.

"Kane Mitchell," Sheer said as he raised his voice, the sound drawing attention from nearby tables. "Martin Sheer, Sports Central. I'm hoping to get your exclusive comment on some new developments in the Alvarez situation."

"No comment," Kane said flatly, even though he knew it wouldn't end with that.

Sheer smiled, the expression never reaching his eyes. "So, you have no comment on the medical reports? Tony's team has been quite open about the extent of his injuries, the concussion that he's still recovering from, and his ongoing physical therapy. They are speculating he may not be able to fight for six months or more."

Kane's hands clenched into fists beneath the table, his knuckles whitening with the effort of restraint as he felt anger coil through his body. This was why he hated events like this.

"I find that interesting, considering he never went to the hospital," Kane said slowly, fighting to keep his temper under control. Every muscle in his body had tensed, and he knew he was slowly clenching and unclenching his hand.

"That's not what his medical team is reporting." Sheer gasped his voice, taking on a performative innocence that made Kane's blood boil. "In fact, they've documented quite extensive injuries. Are you calling the medical experts liars, Kane?"

Daphne shifted beside him, clearly preparing to intervene, but Sheer pressed on, deliberately ignoring her.

"I'm curious how your fans are supposed to feel about a hothead who can't control his temper," Sheer continued, his tone slipping from faux innocent to openly provocative. "Do you think that fans should continue supporting someone who puts other fighters in the hospital when the cameras aren't rolling? Someone who"

"You fucking—" Kane started, beginning to rise from his chair, the rage he'd been trying to fight all evening rushing to the surface. His vision narrowed until all he could see was Sheer's smug face.

Then Daphne's hand was on his arm, her fingers curling around his bicep with surprising strength. The touch cut through his anger, but he wasn't sure he wanted it to. He tried to pull from her grip, but her other hand came up to his face, and she firmly turned his head toward her.

"Kane," she said, her voice soft. "Look at me."

He did, reluctantly dragging his gaze from Sheer to meet her dark eyes. What he saw there wasn't fear or judgment, but steady calm. Her thumb moved slightly against his cheekbone, the gesture intimate enough to momentarily short-circuit his anger.

"He's not worth it," she said quietly. "Don't fall for his game."

Kane held her gaze, his breathing gradually slowing from its rage-fueled pace. As his head cleared, he realized how close he'd come to giving the reporter exactly the story he'd been gunning for.

Daphne held his gaze for a moment longer, watching him until he gave a slight nod. She then turned to Sheer, her smile both polite and a bit threatening.

"You'll have to forgive him," she said, her voice carrying just enough to be heard by the nearby tables that had fallen silent. "It's irritating how Tony manufactured the entire incident, and somehow Kane is the only one being punished for it." She kept her hand on Kane's face for a moment longer, then let it slide down to rest on his shoulder, maintaining the physical connection while addressing Sheer. "I am with him more than anyone, and I haven't seen any signs of a temper outside of the ring when he's in a match."

It should have sounded ridiculous. Hell, everyone in the nearby vicinity had just seen him start to lose it. But somehow Daphne made it strangely plausible, as if he were different in private.

"Is that so?" Sheer sneered, unwilling to abandon his attack entirely. "And yet we all just saw—"

"A normal reaction to someone deliberately provoking him with lies," Daphne interrupted. "I think you'd be upset too if someone falsely claimed you'd sent someone to the hospital when there's no record of any such visit."

A murmur ran through the onlookers, and Kane realized with a jolt that Daphne had just publicly challenged the extent of Tony's injuries. That was something neither he nor Gavin had dared to do.

"Are you suggesting Tony Alvarez is lying about his injuries?" another reporter asked, pushing forward to join the conversation, effectively crowding Sheer out.

Daphne's smile remained even as she turned to the new reporter. "I'm suggesting that the timeline and severity of any injuries may have been exaggerated. Kane has been nothing but cooperative with the ECF's investigation. Meanwhile, Tony has been enthusiastic about his media appearances." She squeezed Kane's shoulder gently. "I just think it's unfortunate that only one side of this story is being told."

And just like that, the mood shifted. Kane could only stand, watching in awe as other reporters pressed close. He had expected them to keep asking about Tony, but their questions had changed, focusing on Daphne's perspective and on what he was like in private rather than in public.

"As I said," her voice was warm, "he's sweet, thoughtful, and I've never once felt unsafe with him. What happened with Tony was an isolated incident involving very specific provocation and attacks—that is not who Kane is day to day."

The rage that had nearly consumed Kane moments before had faded, replaced by something he couldn't quite name—a mixture of gratitude, surprise, and grudging admiration for how skillfully she'd turned a potential disaster into an opportunity.

She'd done exactly what Gavin had hired her to do—she controlled the narrative, shifted focus from his mistakes to their relationship, and made him more human.

But something about the instinctive way she'd reached for him when he was on the verge of losing control felt different. It hadn't felt like a performance; it had felt real. And for the first time since this charade began, Kane Mitchell allowed himself to consider that perhaps—just perhaps—this arrangement might not be the complete disaster he'd anticipated.

***

The limo hummed quietly as it pulled away from Daphne's apartment building after the event. Kane loosened his tie with a rough jerk, as she sat back with a sigh. Through the tinted window, he watched the modest brick building until the car turned. Who was she...and why was he wondering? He groaned as he felt the vibration from his phone-again-grimacing when he looked at the display.

He had missed 200 notifications.

He ignored the social media alerts—he wanted nothing to do with those—he had told Gavin that and returned the five calls...all from Gavin.

The phone barely rang once before it was answered.

"Kane! I was just about to call you."

Kane leaned his head back against the seat, exhaustion settling into his bones, the roller coaster of the evening suddenly hitting him.

"Yeah, well, we survived." He grunted, the words coming out more roughly than he'd intended.

"Survived?" Gavin let out a short laugh. "Kane, you did a hell of a lot more than that. Have you seen social media?

"#KaneAndDaphne is trending, and not a single major outlet has led with the Alvarez fight. Everything is about your relationship, curiosity about who Daphne is, and how good you two looked together."

Kane frowned. He'd expected some positive spin, but not to that extent. "There's no way everyone just forgets about what happened with Tony." He said flatly.

"Not forgot, no," Gavin conceded, but Kane could hear the satisfaction in his voice, "the headlines aren't about your temper—they're about your 'reformed bad boy' image, about how Daphne seems to have a 'calming influence' on you. One blog even called you two 'The Beauty and the Beast of MMA.'"

Kane grimaced. "Fantastic. I'm a fairy tale monster."

"Who gets redeemed through love," Gavin countered smoothly. "That's the whole point of that story, Kane. Transformation. It's exactly what we're going for."

The limo turned onto the expressway; the city lights streaked past the window. Kane rubbed a hand over his face, fighting the urge to be both irritated and overwhelmed.

"How did Daphne do?" Gavin asked. "From what I can see, she handled herself beautifully, but I want to hear from you, and if today helped change your mind on this whole thing."

Kane hesitated, not wanting to admit Gavin had been right. But the truth was undeniable. "She was...good," he admitted slowly. "Fuck, she was better than good. She knew exactly what to say, made people focus on the relationship, and the work I supposedly do in the community."

"Work you will be doing," Gavin stated, and his tone told Kane there was no room for negotiation. "I'm particularly interested in how she handled the situation with Sheer. That could have gone very badly."

Kane's jaw tightened at the memory of Sheer's attack and how close he'd come to proving Sheer correct. "She stepped in before I could deck the guy," he said bluntly, "made me look at her instead of him."

"And it worked," Gavin noted, not a question but a confirmation.

"Yeah," Kane admitted, still somewhat surprised by his own reaction. "It worked. She said something about him not being worth it, about how he was trying to provoke exactly that response." He paused, remembering the steadiness in Daphne's eyes, and a small smile twitched his lips. "Then she turned the whole thing around, made it sound like Tony was the one lying."

"Brilliant," Gavin murmured. "That's exactly what we need. And coming from her, it has credibility—the girlfriend defending her man against lies."

Kane frowned as he pushed himself up. "I'm not 'her man,'" he corrected sharply. "This is business, remember?"

"Of course," Gavin replied, but Kane didn't buy it. "Did you know the ECF president was watching the whole exchange? He texted me afterward, seemed impressed by how you handled yourself."

"How I handled myself?" Kane let out a harsh laugh. "I was about two seconds from grabbing Sheer by his throat. Daphne's the one who handled the situation."

"And that's exactly the point," Gavin chuckled. "In public, you're a team. Her strengths complement yours. She has the charm, the narrative control. You have the athletic credibility. Together, it becomes a fighter channeling his intensity more productively."

Kane stared out the window, not even seeing the scenery as it passed by. He was still amazed. It had just been one night; was that really a good enough test?

"This will work, Kane," Gavin's voice softened over the phone.

For once, Kane didn't immediately reject Gavin's statement. The evidence was hard to deny.

Maybe—just maybe—this ridiculous scheme wasn't doomed to failure after all.

"We'll see," he said finally, unwilling to concede too much ground too quickly.

Gavin chuckled, clearly recognizing the grudging acceptance in Kane's tone. " Get some rest. I'll call you tomorrow with the media round-up and our next steps."

Kane ended the call as the limo turned into his condo complex. He was exhausted, his head slightly aching from the tension he'd carried throughout the evening.

As he made his way to the top floor, Kane found his thoughts returning not to the relief of being home, but to the moment Daphne had placed her hand against his cheek, turning his face away from conflict and toward her steady gaze. Her touch had grounded him, and that made him nervous.

For now, it was enough to acknowledge that tonight hadn't been the disaster he'd anticipated.

It wasn't trust, not yet. But it was a beginning.

Chapter nine

The door to her apartment had barely closed behind her before Daphne was kicking off the borrowed heels, a groan of relief escaping her lips as her bare feet met the cool hardwood floor. The glamour of the evening fell away as she moved. This, her one-bedroom apartment with its mismatched furniture, was her reality, even with the payment she had been offered. That wouldn't change.

Daphne's fingers dialed her best friend, Melissa Anderson, before she even reached the bedroom. She tucked the phone between her ear and shoulder as she carefully shimmied out of the dress, hanging it carefully on the back of her closet door.

The phone rang three times before Melissa answered, her voice carrying the slight rasp that indicated she'd already been asleep despite the relatively early hour.

"This better be good," she mumbled. "I have a presentation at eight tomorrow."

"I don't know if I can do this anymore," Daphne blurted without preamble, as she yanked a worn Northwestern University t-shirt over her head. "The man is a grouch."

There was a rustling sound as Melissa presumably sat up in bed, sleep fading from her voice as interest took its place. "Well, hello to you, too. I take it the big debut didn't go as planned?"

Daphne groaned as she moved to the bathroom to remove her makeup, setting the phone on speaker. "It went exactly as I thought it would.

That's the problem. I knew he'd be difficult—Gavin warned me repeatedly—but I wasn't prepared for just how..." She paused, searching for the right word. "...resistant he would be. To everything. To me."

Melissa laughed. "You always did like a challenge. Remember that marketing project junior year? The professor said it was impossible to rebrand that awful campus cafeteria, and you took it as a personal mission."

"This is different," Daphne insisted, though she couldn't help the small smile that tugged at her lips at the memory. "That was a project. This is a year of my life tied to a man who looks at me like I'm some corporate spy sent to steal his soul."

"Geez, drama queen much?" Melissa teased. "Come on, tell me everything. What was he wearing? How did he act? Did he at least pretend to be into you for the cameras?"

Daphne sighed, setting down her makeup remover and leaning against the bathroom counter. "He wore a suit that looked like it was borrowed from someone twice his size—all baggy and rumpled. Every smile looked physically painful, like it might crack his face. And he spent the entire night either glowering at reporters or staring into space like he was plotting someone's murder."

"Sounds dreamy," Melissa deadpanned. "No wonder you agreed to date him."

"I didn't agree to date him," Daphne corrected automatically, "I agreed to help rehabilitate his image. There's a difference."

"For two million dollars, you'd rehabilitate Satan himself," Melissa pointed out pragmatically. "So aside from his charming personality, how did it go? Did the press buy it?"

Daphne fell back onto her bed as she thought. "They were hostile at first—all questions about the fight with Tony, about Kane's career being in jeopardy. But then their focus turned to me once they realized I was *with* him, not just next to him."

"What did you expect?" Melissa questioned. "Bad boy fighter with a squeaky-clean girlfriend? That's catnip to the press. Did he at least play along when you needed him to?"

"Barely," Daphne groaned. "He let me do most of the talking, which was probably for the best. But there was this one moment..."

She paused, remembering the last confrontation with Sheer, the way Kane had tensed beside her. How he'd responded when she'd touched his face, turned his attention to her instead of the provocation.

"One moment, what?" Melissa prompted.

"There was this reporter who bypassed me completely, went straight for Kane. He claimed Tony was still in physical therapy, might not fight for months because of his injuries, but just kept, I don't know, almost attacking Kane with it. The entire thing just seemed designed to provoke a reaction."

"And did it?" Melissa asked.

"Almost." Daphne's eyes drifted closed, suddenly exhausted. "Kane was about two seconds from completely losing it. I could see it happening."

"Were you able to stop it?"

"Yeah." Daphne pursed her lips as she remembered the moment. "I made him look at me instead of the reporter." Daphne's voice softened as she spoke. "I told him the guy wasn't worth it, and Kane...well, he listened. He backed down."

There was a moment of silence on the other end of the line. "You put your hand on his face?" Melissa finally asked, a note in her voice, but Daphne chose to ignore it.

"I needed to break his focus on the reporter," she said defensively, "redirect his attention. It worked, that's what matters."

"Smooth," Melissa acknowledged. "So, despite being a grouch, he at least responded to your intervention. That's something, right?"

Daphne frowned. "I guess. But it doesn't change the fact that I'm committed to a year with someone who clearly resents every minute he has to spend with me."

"Does he?" Melissa asked. "Resent you specifically, I mean. Or does he just resent the situation?"

The question gave Daphne pause. She'd been so focused on Kane's hostility that she hadn't really considered whether it was directed at her personally. He'd been equally cold to Gavin, to the reporters, to pretty much everyone except his coach, really.

"I don't know," she admitted finally. "Either way, it doesn't make it any easier."

"At least he's hot," Melissa offered helpfully. "I googled him after you signed the contract. Those shoulders? That jaw? The man is walking testosterone."

Despite her exhaustion, Daphne felt heat rise to her cheeks. She couldn't deny Kane's physical appeal. But acknowledging it felt dangerous somehow and was a complication she did not need.

"His looks aren't relevant," she said firmly, hoping to convince herself as much as Melissa. "This is a job; I'm not actually dating him."

Melissa laughed. "Keep telling yourself that. Meanwhile, you've spent the last ten minutes ranting about him, and you know what you didn't say once in all that ranting?"

Daphne's brow furrowed as she thought back over the conversation. "What?"

"That you don't like him."

The observation landed with unexpected weight. Daphne opened her mouth to protest, but the words didn't come.

"That's different," Daphne stammered finally, her voice less certain than she would have liked. "Not actively disliking someone isn't the same as liking them."

"Mm-hmm," Melissa hummed, skepticism evident in the sound. " Just remember the cardinal rule of PR: don't fall for your own press."

"Believe me, I know," Daphne said, even as she felt something twist in her stomach. "It's one year of my life for two million dollars, then back to reality."

"Speaking of reality, I need to sleep if I'm going to be conscious for my presentation tomorrow," Melissa said through a yawn. "Call me this weekend with a full debrief."

"Thanks for letting me vent." Daphne sighed

"That's what friends are for," Melissa replied warmly. "Calling you out on your bullshit. Goodnight, superstar."

After they hung up, Daphne lay in the darkness of her bedroom, staring at the ceiling as Melissa's words echoed in her thoughts. She didn't dislike Kane Mitchell, well, not after the event. Even though his general demeanor was barely contained hostility, something was compelling about him. Something that had made her reach for his face when he was on the verge of losing control.

That wasn't part of the contract. Her job was to shift the narrative and clean up his image, not to develop actual concern for the man.

Daphne pulled her comforter up to her chin as she closed her eyes, determined to put the evening out of her mind until morning. It was business, she reminded herself firmly.

Nothing more.

But as sleep finally claimed her, Daphne couldn't quite silence the small voice in the back of her mind that whispered a dangerous truth: the most convincing performances always contained elements of reality.

Chapter ten

Daphne stood in the doorway of what would be her bedroom for the next year. The guest room in Kane's condo was impeccably clean, stylishly furnished with mid-century modern pieces that she suspected he hadn't chosen himself, and utterly devoid of personality.

It had only taken Gavin three days to orchestrate this new phase. "We need to capitalize on the momentum." He'd insisted.

Kane had objected, of course. Vehemently. But even he couldn't argue with the points Gavin presented—Kane's social media engagement was up 300%, new sponsors were contacting Gavin, and the ECF board suspension meeting had been postponed for "further assessment of the situation." His career was clawing its way back from the brink.

And so here she was, unpacking her clothes into drawers that smelled faintly of cedar, arranging her toiletries in a bathroom larger than her entire apartment kitchen. The condo itself was a showcase of wealth but lacked the warmth of a home. True, it was beautiful with its soaring ceilings, floor-to-ceiling windows overlooking the Philadelphia skyline, and sleek leather furniture. But it was cold. Everything was various shades of gray, black, and white, no color, no life.

The front door opening pulled Daphne from her thoughts. Kane had been at the gym when she arrived, which had given her time to settle in without his glare. That small reprieve had ended. She smoothed her hands down the front of her jeans, took a steadying breath, and stepped out into the hallway.

"Oh, good, you're here," Kane said, his voice carrying a false pleasantness that she'd come to recognize. "Make yourself at home." The words were polite, but his tone conveyed the exact opposite of welcome.

He stood in the kitchen area, his hair still damp. His black t-shirt stretched across his shoulders, while the gray sweatpants he had on rode low on his hips. Everything about his posture screamed territorial animal finding an intruder in its den.

"Thank you," Daphne replied, forcing politeness into her tone when she wanted to just roll her eyes. "I appreciate the welcome."

Kane's eyes narrowed slightly at her calm response. "Gavin's idea, not mine," he bit out, "but whatever gets me back in the cage faster."

"Of course," Daphne agreed smoothly.

Kane studied her for a moment longer, then turned away, pulling open the refrigerator door with more force than necessary. He grabbed a protein shake from the door and drank half of it in one long swallow.

"I'll need to go grocery shopping," Daphne said, forcing her gaze away from the movement of his throat.

Kane shrugged, the motion deliberately casual. "Whatever. Mi casa es su casa and all that bullshit." His lips curved into what might have been a smile if it contained any warmth. "For now."

Irritation stirred in Daphne's chest. She was well aware of the artificiality of their arrangement. She didn't need Kane rubbing it in at every opportunity.

"I'll keep that in mind," she replied, her voice carefully neutral.

An hour later, Daphne sat on one of the kitchen barstools, her laptop open before her as she drafted a schedule of potential public appearances. Gavin had been insistent about maintaining their momentum, emphasizing community events where Kane could interact with children or support charitable causes. Gavin wanted to focus on settings that would soften Kane's image and highlight the "reformed bad boy" narrative they were cultivating.

She was so engrossed in her work that she didn't immediately notice Kane stepping into the kitchen. When she looked up, the words she'd been about to type evaporated from her mind.

He'd changed—if one could call it that. The t-shirt and sweatpants were replaced by nothing but a pair of black boxer briefs that left very little to the imagination. She couldn't help it; her eyes drank him in. Every angle and muscle of his body was defined. He reminded her of a Greek statue.

Before Daphne could restart her brain, Kane sprawled himself across the leather sofa, his legs spread wide, with one arm flung along the back of the couch, the other resting casually across his taut abdomen. The pose managed to both take up the entire couch and display his physique to maximum effect.

It was so obviously calculated to make her uncomfortable that Daphne almost laughed. Instead, she let her gaze slide over him once, clinically, before returning to her laptop screen with a small, dismissive roll of her eyes.

Kane's brow furrowed slightly at her lack of reaction. He shifted his position, somehow taking up even more space on the couch.

"Is the temperature in here okay for you?" he asked, his voice dripping with false concern. "I tend to run hot."

"I'm fine, thank you," Daphne replied without looking up from her screen. "Though if it changed, I'd be happy to adjust the thermostat for you."

A muscle ticked in Kane's jaw, the only sign that her composed response had irritated him. Good. Two could play this game.

"Just making sure my guest is comfortable," he said, stretching his arms overhead in a movement that highlighted every ripple of muscle across his torso. "Since we're going to be roommates for a while."

Daphne glanced up briefly, her expression professionally blank. "Very considerate of you."

Kane's eyes narrowed almost imperceptibly. He wasn't getting the reaction he wanted, and Daphne could see him calculating his next move. She returned her attention to her laptop, refusing to give him the satisfaction of appearing flustered by his display.

"I usually walk around naked," he announced casually. "But I figured I'd ease you into the house rules."

This time, Daphne didn't bother looking up at all. "How thoughtful," she murmured, typing a sentence she'd have to delete later because her focus was shot. "Though I should warn you, I'm remarkably difficult to shock."

She could feel his gaze on her, his annoyance filling the space between them. When she finally risked another glance in his direction, his expression had settled into something harder.

Daphne suppressed a sigh as she saved her document and closed her laptop. It was going to be a very long year if this was how Kane intended to approach their situation. She'd expected resistance, even hostility, but was juvenile.

As she gathered her things to retreat to the guest room, she allowed herself one final look. Despite his childish behavior, there was something almost vulnerable in his attempt to regain control of a situation that had spiraled beyond his grasp.

Perhaps that was the key to surviving this arrangement—remembering that beneath the rage was a man deeply uncomfortable with losing control of his narrative.

Daphne tucked that observation away as she turned toward the hallway, feeling Kane's eyes follow her retreat. Round one might have ended in a stalemate, but the match had only just begun.

***

The kitchen smelled of coffee when Daphne emerged from her room the following morning. Kane sat at the island counter, shirtless again—of course—a mug clutched in one hand and his phone in the other. He didn't look up when she entered, but his posture shifted slightly, muscles tensing as if preparing for battle. Daphne bit back a smile as she headed for the coffee maker. If he thought a display of morning testosterone would send her fleeing back to her room, he clearly had no idea what growing up with her brother Aaron had entailed.

She poured herself a cup, aware of Kane watching her from the corner of his eye, as if waiting for some reaction to his bare-chested breakfast routine. When she turned, leaning casually against the counter to face him, he made a show of stretching, the movement rippling across his torso in a way that would have been impressive if it weren't so transparently calculated.

"Sleep well?" he asked, his voice smug.

"Like a rock," Daphne replied cheerfully. There was no way she was telling him she'd spent half the night staring at the unfamiliar ceiling, hyperaware of his presence in the apartment. "Your guest bed is surprisingly comfortable."

Kane's eyes narrowed slightly. "Good to know," he said, taking a slow sip of his coffee. "Though I should warn you, I have training early most mornings. I'm not exactly quiet when I get up."

"That's fine," she said with a shrug. "I'm a heavy sleeper. Growing up with an older brother who thought 6 AM lacrosse practice in the hallway was acceptable weekend behavior tends to teach you to sleep through anything."

Something flickered across Kane's expression, but whatever it was, it vanished quickly as he scowled.

"Your brother plays lacrosse?" His voice was dismissive, and Daphne fought down her irritation.

Daphne took another sip of coffee, hiding her amusement behind the rim of the mug. "Played," she corrected. "Division I at Princeton. Now he uses that competitive energy into corporate takeovers and making junior executives cry during presentations."

Kane snorted, the sound almost resembling genuine amusement, before he caught himself. "Sounds like a real charmer."

"Oh, he's delightful," Daphne agreed with a small smile. "Especially when he was seventeen and I was twelve, and he decided that proper sibling bonding meant seeing how many times he could flush the toilet while I was in the shower before I would break down in tears."

This time Kane didn't quite manage to suppress his surprised laugh. "And did you?"

Daphne raised an eyebrow. "I filled his lacrosse helmet with maple syrup and left it in the sun for three hours. He didn't try the shower trick again."

Kane studied her with new interest, as if reassessing her. "So, you fight back," he said, the words more statement than question.

"Always," Daphne confirmed, her eyes meeting his with a raised brow. "Aaron spent eighteen years trying to break me. No offense, but you're," she gestured vaguely at his shirtless form, "amateur hour in comparison."

"Amateur hour," Kane repeated, amusement in his voice. "You think this is me trying to break you?"

"I think," Daphne said carefully as she set her mug down, "this is you trying to reassert control over a situation where you feel powerless. The same way Aaron used to mess with me whenever he felt threatened. It's textbook older sibling behavior."

Kane's expression darkened. "I'm not your brother," he said, his voice low and edged with warning.

"Thank god for that," Daphne replied without missing a beat. "One Aaron in my life is quite enough, and at least he owns more than one shirt."

There it was again—that flash of amusement in Kane's eyes before he could mask it with irritation. "I own shirts," he said, rising from his stool to take his empty mug to the sink. His shoulder brushed her as he moved, and she was proud of herself for not reacting. "I just don't see the point of wearing them in my own home."

"Of course not," Daphne quipped back. "Fabric is so restrictive for the professionally intimidating."

Kane turned to face her fully, close enough now that she could feel the heat radiating from his skin. Annoyance warred with reluctant amusement in his eyes.

"You're not intimidated," he stated after a long moment.

"Should I be?" Daphne countered, "The shirtless brooding routine is impressive for Instagram, I'm sure, but I grew up with the master of psychological warfare. Aaron once convinced me our parents were sending me to boarding school in Switzerland because they found me 'too ordinary' for the family legacy. I was nine and spent three weeks trying to develop a personality interesting enough to keep."

Kane's lips twitched, the ghost of a genuine smile threatening to break through. "Did it work?"

"I tried to learn conversational French and perfected twirling flaming batons," Daphne shrugged. "Neither skill proved particularly useful when I discovered he'd made the whole thing up."

A short laugh escaped before Kane could catch it. "Your brother sounds like an asshole," he said, as his lips twitched, fighting a smile.

"I told you then he could be," Daphne agreed, "but he's my asshole brother. And living with him prepared me for pretty much anything, including half-naked fighters who think lounging around in their underwear constitutes psychological warfare."

Kane's eyes widened slightly. For a moment, he seemed unsure how to respond, and Daphne felt a small surge of victory.

"So, nothing I do is going to bother you," he said finally.

"Oh, I'm sure you could find ways to annoy me if you really applied yourself," Daphne replied, allowing a smile to curve her lips. "But is that really how you want to spend the next year? Trying to out-Aaron Aaron? Because I should warn you, he once replaced all my makeup with identical-looking products containing hot pepper oil before my senior prom. The bar is quite high."

Kane studied her for a long moment, then, to Daphne's surprise, the corner of his mouth quirked upward.

"You know," he said, stepping back and giving her space, "you're not what I expected."

"I'll take that as a compliment," Daphne replied, picking up her coffee again.

"You should," Kane said, and for the first time since their arrangement began, there was no edge to his voice.

As he turned away to retrieve his phone from the counter, Daphne caught the hint of a genuine smile. It transformed his face, softening the hard angles into something unexpectedly appealing.

Chapter eleven

K ane let out a groan as his phone began to ring and Gavin's name appeared on the screen.

"It's too early for this." He growled as Daphne laughed softly.

"Better answer it anyway," she cautioned, "otherwise he will just keep calling."

Kane shook his head even as he hit accept.

"Kane, is Daphne with you? I want to firm up your next few outings." Gavin started rather than greeting them.

"Considering you had her moved into my condo, where else would she be?" Kane snarled.

"Knowing you, she may have already run screaming."

"No such luck," Kane muttered as Daphne shot him a glare.

"I'm still here, Gavin; he wasn't able to chase me away in one day." Irritation laced her voice as she crossed her arms and let out a small huff.

Why the hell was that cute? He had no idea, but damned if it wasn't.

"Good," Gavin acknowledged, "I wanted to see if we could add some appearances."

"What kind of appearances?" Daphne asked, drawing Gavin's focus and giving Kane a moment to compose himself.

"I've lined up several options," Gavin advised. "There's a children's hospital visit next Tuesday—the pediatric cancer ward has several young fans who've been asking to meet Kane. Then, on Thursday, there's a career day at a local high school in one of Philadelphia's underserved neighborhoods. The following weekend, there's a charity 5K for veterans' services."

With each item on the list, Kane's mood darkened further, his fingers digging into his biceps where his arms remained tightly crossed.

"All of those sound perfect," Daphne said smoothly, her eyes locked on his. "We'll need to coordinate with Kane's training schedule, of course."

"Already done," Gavin assured her. "I spoke with Jackson yesterday. He's adjusted Kane's sessions to accommodate these appearances."

That revelation was to be the final straw for Kane. His head dropped back, eyes fixed on the ceiling as a low groan escaped him.

"Fantastic," he muttered, the word dripping with sarcasm.

"Kane's thrilled," Daphne translated, and the glare he shot her was resignation rather than genuine anger. "We'll review the details and make any necessary preparations."

"Perfect," Gavin exclaimed. "I'll send over the complete schedule and briefing materials this afternoon. The hospital visit is particularly important—there will be media present, but we're positioning it as a 'private' visit that the press happened to learn about. Creates a more authentic narrative."

Kane's eyes rolled hard. "Because nothing says 'authentic' like a pre-planned 'spontaneous' visit with photographers on standby," he muttered.

"We'll make it work, Gavin," Daphne assured, "anything else we should know?"

"Just keep doing what you're doing," Gavin replied.

When the call finally ended, Kane remained motionless for several seconds, his head still tilted back, eyes closed as if searching for patience.

"Well," Daphne said finally, "at least we know the strategy is working."

Kane lowered his head to look at her, his expression a complex mixture of resignation, irritation, and something that might almost be grudging respect. "Yeah," he agreed, his voice rough around the edges. "But at what cost?"

Kane turned to pace the length of his living room. The call had left him wound tight, but for once, he wasn't sure how to react.

Daphne remained by the kitchen island, giving him space while she watched him.

"Why do you hate these events so much?" she asked finally, her voice quiet but clear enough to carry across the space between them.

Kane stopped pacing, pausing for a moment before he turned, his eyes narrowed with suspicion. "What?"

"The community events," Daphne clarified. "It's not just that they're taking time from your training. There's something else about them that bothers you specifically."

Kane's jaw tightened. "They're bullshit," he said finally, the words clipped and harsh. "Manufactured photo ops that don't mean anything. Just one more fake performance."

Daphne nodded, which surprised him. "They are performances," she agreed. "But that doesn't explain why you hate them more than, say, media interviews or sponsor appearances. Those are performances too."

Kane moved to the couch and sat down. He scrubbed a hand over his face as he thought how to respond...how much to reveal. Fuck, he would need to be honest if she was going to actually be of any use. Maybe she could shoulder most of them and take the pressure off him.

Decision made, he finally responded.

"I'm not good at them," he admitted, his voice low. "The smiling, the small talk, the pretending to be...whatever it is they want me to be. Some inspirational figure or role model." His lips twisted in a humorless smile. "I'm a fighter. That's what I'm good at. That's all I've ever been good at."

His statement was raw. It wasn't something he liked admitting. In response, Daphne moved carefully to sit at the end of the couch, her attention focused on him.

"You're clearly very good at fighting," she acknowledged. "But I doubt that's all you're good at."

Kane's eyes flicked to her face, searching for any sigh of mockery. When he didn't see any, he leaned forward, his elbows resting on his knees as his gaze slid to the floor.

"I want people to respect me for my abilities," he said after a long pause. "Not how well I can smile and bullshit people." He paused and took a deep breath. "I don't know, I was always told I would never amount to much, and people always told me to sit down and shut up, so I learned to let my fists do the talking."

Daphne remained quiet, as if she could sense there was more.

"When Coach found me and started training me, people started paying attention, praising me, but only when I am in the ring." Kane's fingers laced together, his knuckles whitening as he continued. "I don't know how to talk to the people at the events, and it frustrates me how they always just talk down to me or something."

He saw Daphne shift from the corner of his eye but kept his gaze on the floor.

"How did Jackson find you?" she asked gently, and he could tell the question was honest.

"Bar fight," he responded, his lips quirking slightly. "I was nineteen, working construction during the day and bouncing at night to make ends meet. I was on my own after my eighteenth birthday. Some guy thought it would be funny to try to rush the door with his buddies. I handled it." He shrugged. "Coach was there, saw how I moved. Said I was wasting natural talent throwing drunks out of dive bars."

"And you believed him?"

"Not at first," Kane admitted. "Thought he was full of shit, to be honest. But he kept showing up, kept talking about potential and discipline and all that motivational crap." He darted his eyes to meet hers. "Eventually, I figured I had nothing to lose by trying it his way."

"And the rest is history," Daphne supplied when he fell silent.

Kane nodded, then leaned back against the couch. "The first time I won a real match—not some underground thing in a warehouse, but an actual sanctioned fight—it was like...I don't know. Like finally proving everyone wrong who said I'd never be anything."

"What about your parents?" Daphne frowned as she watched him.

Kane let out a wry laugh. "Yeah...they aren't part of my life anymore, let's leave it at that."

Daphne paused at that and the pain she thought she heard in his voice. She knew she should probably stop before he got annoyed, but her curiosity won out. "Is that why fighting means so much?"

Her expression was troubled as his eyes met hers. "I don't know, I guess it's really just...proving them wrong or something," he said softly. "But it's also the only place where everything makes sense. There's no bullshit, no pretending. Everything is decided based on skill." He gestured vaguely toward the world outside the window. "Out there, I'm always waiting to say the wrong thing, to be that kid again who everyone expected to fail."

Daphne nodded slowly, understanding dawning in her gaze. "So, when people say you are just a fighter," she said, connecting the dots, "it's frustrating because it's reductive, but it's also safer than having them expect more from you."

Kane's eyebrows rose slightly. "Something like that," he acknowledged.

"For what it's worth," Daphne said softly, "I think people underestimate you. You're more well-spoken than you let on, and more perceptive than most people. But it's like you don't trust that those qualities will be valued the way your fighting skills are."

Kane stared at her, thrown by her assessment.

"You don't know me."

"I'm starting to," Daphne countered quietly.

Kane held her gaze for a moment longer, then looked away, uncomfortable with all he had revealed. "Yeah, well," he muttered, pushing himself to his feet, "don't get too attached to the idea. I'm still the same asshole who's making your life difficult for the next year."

He knew the statement was more self-deprecating than hostile, but he couldn't find it in himself to be angry. He moved toward the kitchen, aware that Daphne watched him go.

"I think I can handle it," she said to his retreating back. "After all, I survived eighteen years with Aaron. You're practically a teddy bear in comparison."

Kane snorted. "Don't push it, Wilson."

Chapter twelve

D aphne closed the door to her bedroom with a soft click, leaning back against it as she processed everything she had just learned. She felt like an intruder on his true self. He had revealed things that honestly surprised her. The vulnerability he'd shown lingered, reshaping her understanding of him.

As she moved through the room, she tried to reconcile the Kane she'd just spoken with and the man she had met in the gym. He was the angry fighter, the reluctant 'boyfriend,' who tried to make her uncomfortable with childish antics...all versions of Kane, yet each seemed like simplified sketches compared to the more complex man she was starting to see.

I was always told I would never amount to much, and people always told me to sit down and shut up, so I learned to let my fists do the talking.

The words kept repeating through her thoughts. How many times had she misread his hostility as just anger issues when it was armor forged through years of dismissal and underestimation? His resistance to her and the entire façade suddenly made sense.

Daphne ran a hand through her hair, disturbed by how quickly her professional assessment was shifting into something more personal. She'd been hired to help fix Kane's image, not to understand the man behind it.

Yet she couldn't deny the effect his admissions had. The image of a young Kane—someone who was constantly dismissed, someone told repeatedly he would never amount to anything— God, that hit more deeply than she wanted to admit.

She thought back to the night of the charity gala, to the moment between Kane and Sheer. At the time, she'd seen his hostility as just part of his anger issues that had landed him in this predicament. Now, with the context she now had, she saw something different—a man conditioned to expect attacks, one who had to prove his worth through physical dominance when words had failed him.

When she'd placed her hand on his face, she'd acted on instinct. But his response, the shift in focus, the way his eyes had locked onto hers, suggested something beyond simple distraction techniques. He had trusted her in that moment, however briefly. The thought had warmth surging through her chest.

Daphne moved to the window and looked out at the Philadelphia skyline. Kane wasn't the one-dimensional character she'd expected. He was complicated, a fighter who valued respect above victory, a man who projected strength when he had deep-seated insecurities, and was some-one who fought because no one would hear him.

Something about him, the whole him, drew her. And that surprised her.

It was more than how he looked, though she couldn't deny the impact of that. What drew her most was the vulnerability he tried so carefully to conceal.

'This isn't part of the arrangement.' She reminded herself firmly. She was supposed to pretend to be his girlfriend, to help change public opinion. Nowhere was there room for genuine attraction.

Two million dollars, she reminded herself. It was only for one year—a performance, not a relationship.

Yet she found herself wondering what other depths lurked beneath Kane's carefully maintained exterior. Did he have any other vulnera-bilities that he hid behind gruffness and physical intimidation? What would it be like to be trusted, truly trusted, with those parts of himself? Someone to help shield him, to support him.

"Stop it," she commanded herself. This was precisely the kind of thinking she needed to avoid. If his behaviors told her anything, it was that Kane wasn't looking for understanding; he only agreed to the whole thing because it was the only way to salvage his career. His vulnerability was born of frustration, not any desire for real connection.

With that thought, Daphne turned from the window and moved to her laptop, opening it to focus on the work ahead. Work was safe. Work had defined parameters.

Unlike the feelings Kane increasingly caused her to feel.

After an hour where she could barely focus, Daphne finally conceded that she needed a break. She saved her progress, mentally preparing herself to see Kane again after he had revealed so much.

The living room was quiet when she emerged. Kane sat on the couch, his attention focused on something on his phone, and she was surprised to see that his posture was more relaxed than she'd seen since she met him. He'd put on a shirt at some point, the simple gray t-shirt stretched across his shoulders with his basketball shorts, his bare feet propped on the coffee table. The domesticity of the scene struck her.

She hesitated in the hallway. Before she could decide to retreat or proceed, Kane looked up, as if he had sensed her presence.

His eyes met hers across the room, the gray unexpectedly clear. Something passed between them in that moment, not quite understanding, but an acknowledgment of the shift that had occurred during their earlier conversation.

Daphne felt her pulse jump, a flutter of awareness that had nothing to do with professionalism and everything to do with the man watching her. His vulnerability from earlier was gone, hidden once again by his control, but now that she'd glimpsed what lay beneath, she couldn't unsee it.

And God help her; she found that disturbingly attractive.

This wasn't part of the plan; it wasn't part of the arrangement that had brought her into Kane's life. It complicated everything.

Yet as Kane continued to hold her gaze, his expression unreadable, Daphne couldn't deny the truth: when Kane angered her, frustrated her, pushed against her carefully maintained boundaries, it didn't drive her away. Instead, it seemed to draw her closer.

And that attraction was the most dangerous element of all in their precarious arrangement.

Chapter thirteen

D aphne followed Kane through the doors of Warrior's Edge, and the gym's atmosphere enveloped her immediately. There had been three weeks of accompanying Kane to charity events and appearances Gavin had insisted on; many times she had stood at his side, but there was something about this place that felt different. Here, his stress fell away, and she got to see more of *him*, not just the public face.

"You can sit over there," Kane said, gesturing toward a weathered bench against the brick wall as if she hadn't sat there numerous times over the past weeks. His voice carried none of the defensiveness of their early interactions. Over the weeks, they had settled into a grudging acceptance of each other's presence.

Daphne nodded and made her way across the worn blue mats on the floor while Kane headed toward the locker room. As she settled onto the bench, her gaze traveled around the converted warehouse space. High, wire-reinforced windows filtered morning light across the training equipment—heavy bags hanging from steel beams, weight racks lined against the far wall, and finally drifted to the octagon stage in the center.

The past few weeks had transformed them in ways neither of them had anticipated. Their appearances had evolved from painfully awkward to something resembling a comfortable routine. Kane no longer tensed when she took his hand in public. She'd stopped overthinking every casual touch designed for the cameras. They'd developed a rhythm, almost a language in and of itself, with subtle touches and changes in pressure.

They had even come to a truce of sorts at his condo. Kane had abandoned his juvenile displays of underwear after their conversation, though he still rarely wore shirts at home. Daphne had stopped retreating to her room when she was home. They'd found common ground over terrible reality television, which Kane watched while interjecting with scathing commentary that made Daphne laugh despite herself.

But this—watching him emerge from the locker room in training shorts, his hand wrapped, his focus already narrowing to the work ahead—this felt like she was watching a different man. Here, he was in his element, moving with purpose and dedication.

Jackson met him near the center mat, and the older man's greeting was brusque, no-nonsense, and Kane responded with a nod. They began a series of warm-ups, and Kane began moving through a series of dynamic stretches.

Daphne found herself watching his face more than his technique. The furrow of his brows had gone, replaced by concentrated focus that seemed to quiet his restlessness. His breathing was controlled, each exhale measured.

When Jackson pulled on focus mitts and positioned himself across from Kane, the energy in the room shifted perceptibly. Kane's stance changed, his weight balanced perfectly between his feet, as his hands rose to guard position, eyes locked on his target with predatory intensity.

"Jab-cross-hook, then drive through," Jackson commanded, his voice echoing against the high ceilings.

Kane unleashed the combination with controlled precision—a sharp jab that cracked against the left mitt, immediately followed by a cross that carried the full rotation of his hips, then a hook that seemed to materialize from nowhere, connecting with a loud thud. Without pausing, he dropped his level and drove forward into a perfect double-leg takedown simulation, stopping just short of lifting the older man from the ground.

"Again," Jackson said, resetting his position. "Faster transition."

Kane repeated the sequence, this time with barely perceptible space between the strikes and the level change. The sound of his knuckles against leather echoed through the quiet gym. Daphne watched his jaw clench after each strike, the determined exhale he forced through flared nostrils, and the tight control he kept over his movements.

It was poetry in motion. Each movement had been refined through thousands of repetitions, his technique honed through failure and correction. She'd seen him fight in videos Gavin had shown her during her preparation, but those had captured only the spectacle, not this quiet craftsmanship.

"Good," Jackson said after Kane completed the sequence again. "Now give me the spinning elbow to that same combination."

Kane nodded, barely catching his breath before launching into the expanded sequence. His feet pivoted with surprising grace for someone his size, as he shifted into a back elbow that stopped just shy of Jackson's raised mitt. The older man nodded approval, and Daphne caught the flicker of satisfaction in Kane's gray eyes.

That struck her. Kane, the man who approached charity events with the enthusiasm of someone headed for root canal surgery, found genuine satisfaction in his coach's nod.

'He's fighting for more than wins,' she realized.

Kane continued the drill, sweat beginning to drip down his back, his breathing controlled despite the increasing intensity. The moments weren't for show, weren't for cameras. This was just Kane—disciplined, focused, and fiercely committed to a craft that demanded everything from him.

Daphne found herself transfixed. Fighting wasn't simply an outlet for aggression or a path to fame—it was the language through which Kane had learned to express himself.

And perhaps for the first time since their arrangement began, Daphne felt she was seeing the real Kane Mitchell.

Over the weeks they'd lived together, she'd learned to read his subtle tells, the tightness around his eyes when Gavin called with new PR opportunities, the slight relaxation of his shoulders when he stepped into the privacy of his home, the rare smile that sometimes emerged during their late-night television critiques.

But watching him now, she knew there was still something more for her to learn. His training wasn't fueled by anger, as she'd initially assumed from the reports she'd read about him. It was something more fundamental; this was a space where he could communicate through action rather than words.

"Pivot faster on the second elbow," Jackson instructed, his face impassive but his eyes tracking every detail of Kane's technique. "You're telegraphing it."

Kane absorbed the criticism and immediately adjusted his approach for the next repetition. The correction was subtle, she swore it was no more than a fraction of a second shaved from his rotation, but the improvement was obvious. The resulting impact was cleaner, sharper.

The tension eased further from Kane's shoulders as he found his rhythm. His expression shifted, his eyes softening as he released the pressure that normally kept his features locked in a perpetual scowl. It made him appear younger than the twenty-eight she knew he was.

Daphne felt something change inside her as she watched. The man before her was a person who had found his purpose and pursued it with single-minded dedication.

'His dedication isn't anger,' she thought, the realization spreading through her like warmth. 'It's everything.'

The knowledge settled in her chest. Her attraction to Kane had begun as something she could try to rationalize. But this was different. This was seeing him beyond both who the public thought he was and how Kane saw himself.

And she found herself drawn to him.

As she watched Kane pivot into another perfect spinning back elbow, the doubt in his eyes vanishing as Jackson nodded approval, Daphne couldn't deny what was happening. She was no longer just playing the role of Kane Mitchell's girlfriend.

She was starting to wish it were real.

Chapter fourteen

J ackson called a break after forty minutes of increasingly complex combinations. Kane grabbed a water bottle, pouring some of it over his face before taking a long drink. He exchanged a few quiet words with Jackson, nodding as he gave Kane feedback. Every bit helped keep him focused and sharp. Then the heavy door to the gym swung open, and the atmosphere in the gym changed.

Kane's head snapped up, his body tensing mid-sentence. Jackson turned more slowly, his face frowning as he placed a restraining hand on Kane's forearm. Kane swallowed as he glowered at the man who stood silhouetted against the morning light.

"Well, well," Tony called, his voice carrying across the gym with practiced projection. "Look who's back in training. Heard you may be squirming your way out of a suspension."

"Tony," Jackson acknowledged, his tone carrying a warning rather. "Didn't realize you had booked Warrior's Edge today."

Tony shrugged, moving further into the gym with easy confidence. "Just thought I'd stop by, see who was around." His dark eyes fixed on Kane with predatory focus. "Heard through the grapevine that the ECF ethics committee had a change of heart about your situation. It must be nice having friends in high places."

The implication hung in the air, and Kane saw Tony smirk. He glanced briefly at Daphne and found her eyes on him, not Tony. The glance settled him. He took a deep breath, trying to let his irritation go.

"Just finishing up here, Tony," he finally replied, careful to keep his voice neutral. "Gym's all yours in ten."

Tony's eyebrows rose in mock surprise. "What, no angry comeback? No threats? Man, who are you and what have you done with Kane Mitchell?" His gaze shifted to Daphne, and Kane stiffened as the man made a show of looking her over. "Although I guess I can see why you might be in a better mood these days."

Kane's eyes flicked briefly to Daphne before returning to Tony with renewed focus.

"It's a shame the Committee chose not to suspend me," Kane taunted. "You're probably wondering who I had to fuck to get that?"

Tony's eyes narrowed, clearly thrown by Kane's unexpected composure. Kane's gaze met Daphne's again for a moment before he smiled, but there was no humor in the expression. "No one," he answered his own question as he turned his attention back to Tony. "They realized it was all a setup in the first place, and that I'm not the man you tried to get them to picture me as."

Tony's composure slipped for an instant, and irritation flashed across his face before his smirk reasserted itself. "Right, the big redemption story," he drawled, moving closer to Kane. "I've heard all about it. The dangerous hothead saved by love." His gaze slid to Daphne again, lingering with a sick smile. "You and your bullshit PR girlfriend. I gotta say, she's fucking hot for a trick. Maybe she will appreciate a real man when she learns you are hopeless."

Kane saw Daphne's cheeks flush, but her expression told him it was anger, not embarrassment. Kane's hands curled into fists at his sides. For a moment, rage flowed through him. Tony was always a fucking thorn in his side, but he had finally found the right button to push. Kane took a small step forward before darting his eyes to hers again. His eyes asked if she was ok, checking in on her, and hers responded that she was, that she was irritated but ok.

The fact that he needed to know surprised him, but over the weeks, she had become less of an irritant and someone he was coming to respect.

Tony grew irritated at the silent exchange between them. "What, no response? The great Kane Mitchell letting someone talk about his girl like that?" He stepped closer, voice dropping to a stage whisper that still carried. "Or maybe you all know it's fake."

Jackson moved forward, positioning himself between the two fighters. "That's enough, Tony," he said gruffly. "If you're here to train, go change. If not, the door's right where you left it."

Tony held his ground for a moment longer; his eyes locked on Kane in challenge. The tension in the gym thickened until it felt almost difficult to breathe. Kane felt himself slipping into the controlled breathing he did while training, letting the technique calm him. He knew his control was being tested, but he would be damned if he let the fucker win.

The feel of Daphne's soft hand on his cheek sent another wave of calm through him as he dragged his eyes off Tony to her. The moment their eyes met, everything else in the gym faded. Her hand drifted from his cheek to his chest, his own raising to cover hers to keep her from stepping away. Her eyes widened slightly, showing the flecks of gold deep in their depths as his breathing began to match hers.

"Don't," she whispered, her voice carrying no further than the space between them. "He's not worth it. He's just being an ass."

Kane swallowed. "Yeah," he agreed, his voice low.

Time stretched between them, as something shifted between them. All the contact they'd had for the benefit of cameras suddenly seemed hollow compared to this moment. Behind them, Tony made a sound of disgust, but they ignored him. Kane tensed beneath Daphne's hand, but his focus remained on her rather than shifting back to Tony. The anger that had been flaring had faded, replaced by an awareness of her, and only her.

"You good?" she asked softly.

Kane's thumb moved in a small circle against the back of her hand, where it still rested on his chest. "Yeah," he nodded. "I'm good."

And he realized...he was. His anger at Tony was gone, thanks to the feeling of her skin against his.

The moment stretched between them, neither wanting to be the first to break the connection. It was different. She was different. For the first time, Kane believed that someone saw *him*, not just the fighter.

Eventually, it was Jackson who broke the spell, his gruff voice carrying across the dead-quiet gym. "Kane, let's finish up that last combination sequence before we call it a day."

Kane's eyes lingered on hers for a moment longer before he nodded, his hand finally releasing hers. Daphne's fingers trailed across his skin as she slowly withdrew, the touch simple, but somehow it meant more to him than the others that had come before.

"Gotta hand it to you, Mitchell," Tony called as Kane moved back toward the training area. "You've got everyone buying this whole 're-formed bad boy' routine." He made air quotes with his fingers, his smirk widening as Kane's shoulders tensed. "Brilliant move, I gotta say. Almost had me convinced for a second there. You are a better liar than I thought."

Kane continued walking, shutting Tony out as he joined Jackson back on the mat.

"Oh, please," Tony sneered, raising his voice to ensure it carried across the gym. "Don't try to make me think this is real. You were single, then suddenly in a committed relationship with the perfect girl?" He shook his head as he stalked to the ring. "Give me a break. You aren't man enough to catch any real woman you aren't paying."

Kane froze mid-movement, his body going rigid. Tony had inadvertently struck the truth: Daphne was being paid handsomely, and everything he had imagined was just pretend. For a moment, he had forgotten that.

Jackson stepped closer to Kane, his voice low as he gave the sequence he wanted run, but Kane only half heard him. He nodded once in response, his jaw clenched tight.

"What's the matter, Mitchell?" Tony continued his taunts. "Hit a nerve?" His gaze shifted to Daphne, assessing her with renewed interest. "Or maybe she doesn't know she's just a publicity stunt? Is that it?"

Kane kept his composure with effort, keeping his expression neutral despite the echo of his own doubts that had crept in. Had the moment been real, or was it just another fake moment, something scripted? All the doubts he had about the entire thing came back.

"You know," Tony continued as he turned to face Daphne directly, "you should ask yourself why Kane Mitchell, who's been seen to models and industry insiders for years but never for more than one night, suddenly settles down with someone completely outside his world right when his career is imploding." He spread his hands in mock innocence. "You can't deny that the timing is interesting."

Kane felt his jaw tick. "You don't know what you're talking about," he said, the words emerging with controlled precision.

Tony's smile widened, as if satisfied at getting a reaction. "Don't I? Come on, man. Everyone in the industry is talking about it. The sudden girlfriend who appears just when your reputation is shit? Who magically knows exactly what to say to reporters? " He shook his head. "Did you honestly expect people to buy that? Come on, no one's ever seen you two kiss." Tony laughed. "I've checked your coverage. I've seen you smile, hold hands, hold each other, but that's it." He tapped his temple with one finger. "You expect anyone to believe that you are okay with a relationship that looks like it should be in a junior high school yard? Stop the bullshit."

Kane's fists tightened at his sides as he went cold inside. "Stop the bullshit, huh?" he echoed, his voice dropping. "Yeah, you're right," he smirked, "but you have to fuck your hand tonight. I don't."

Tony's expression faltered as Kane moved with fluid grace toward Daphne. His arm snaked around her waist in a single motion as he pulled her against him, leaving no space between them.

He barely had time to register the heat of her before his free hand cupped her cheek. His eyes met hers for a fraction of a second, enough time for her to see determination there, but also to check that she understood what was happening.

Then his lips claimed hers.

The first touch was firm but controlled; his mouth pressed against hers with purpose rather than passion, but heat coursed through him at the contact. Daphne gasped against his lips, and the sound created an opening that he immediately exploited, his tongue brushing against her lower lip in a tentative exploration that transformed the performative kiss into something more intimate. The taste of her as his tongue brushed hers made him groan as Daphne's hands grasped his arms.

Daphne let out a small whimper, the sound igniting them into an inferno. Her hands slid up his arms to wind around his neck. Her fingers threaded through the short hair at his nape, and the feeling sent a shudder of need through him.

The kiss deepened, Kane's initial restraint dissolving as Daphne responded. His tongue teased hers, the contact sending sparks of sensation cascading through him. Kane's hand shifted from her cheek to cradle the back of her head, his fingers tangling in her hair as he angled her face to deepen the kiss further. His other hand spread wide against her lower back, holding her tight against the hard planes of his body. His pulse began to pound as he felt himself tighten, his blood moving south as his body responded to the desire that surged through him.

She was addicting.

A small sound escaped her throat—half sigh, half moan—as Kane's teeth grazed her lower lip in a gentle nip that sent another surge of heat through his body. The unexpected edge of aggression should have startled her, but instead she pressed closer, her fingers wrapped through his hair.

Somewhere in the periphery of his consciousness, Kane registered Tony's scoff of disgust and the sound of his footsteps retreating. Yet neither he nor Daphne made any move to separate.

He gentled the kiss as it turned from pure heat to something more tender. As Kane's grip softened, his hand moved from her hair to trace the line of her jaw with surprising delicacy. He finally drew back slightly; his forehead rested against hers as they both struggled to regain equilibrium.

Daphne's eyes fluttered open, meeting Kane's gaze, her brown irises darkened to the color of molten chocolate, pupils dilated with desire. Something vulnerable flickered in their depths.

They remained there for a moment, bodies pressed together from chest to thigh, faces close enough that the slightest movement would bring their lips together again.

"He's gone," Daphne whispered, the words barely audible despite the silence surrounding them.

Kane nodded slightly, his forehead still resting against hers, but made no move to release her. "Yeah," his voice rough. His eyes searched hers. "You okay?"

Hers fluttered shut as she nodded. "I'm okay," she confirmed softly, her fingers still resting in his hair, unwilling to break the connection between them.

Kane's thumb traced the outline of her lower lip, and he held back a groan as her lips opened in response. "Good," he whispered.

Around them, the gym remained silent. What had begun as a performance for Tony's benefit had revealed a truth they could no longer ignore. The line between pretense and reality had not merely blurred; it had been irrevocably crossed.

Chapter fifteen

D aphne stared at the spreadsheet on her laptop screen, the numbers and formulas blurring together as her mind drifted yet again to the memory of the kiss. It had been distracting her for the past two days. Her fingers hovered motionless over the keyboard, her mind on the feel of Kane's lips pressed against hers, his arms pulling her against the solid wall of his chest. She had managed to avoid being alone with him, unsure how to act near him.

Her eyes drifted closed as she tried to will herself to focus, but it was hopeless. With a frustrated sigh, she pushed back from the small desk in her room.

Their attempts at avoidance had been almost comical. Kane had taken to training at odd hours, leaving before she woke and returning late. When their paths crossed, conversations were stunted. There was no mention of Tony and no acknowledgment of what had happened. Now it was just...awkward between them.

Daphne stretched her arms that had stiffened from hunching over her laptop. She glanced at herself in the mirror and shook her head. She was a mess, her hair pulled back in a messy bun, oversized Northwestern sweatshirt hanging off one shoulder. She'd retreated into comfort to hide.

Her fingers rose to her lips, tracing their outline in an unconscious echo of Kane's thumb when he'd drawn back from the kiss. The sensation came rushing back—the heat that had coursed through her body, the racing of her heart when his tongue had touched hers, the small sound that had escaped her throat unbidden.

"This is ridiculous," she muttered to her reflection, dropping her hand as if caught in something shameful. "It was just a kiss."

But the lie fell flat even in the empty room. It hadn't been just a kiss. The sound of Melissa's ringtone broke her out of her thoughts. Daphne hesitated; she knew what Melissa would ask...but if she didn't answer, her friend would just keep calling. With a groan, she answered the call.

"Finally!" Melissa's voice exploded through the speaker before Daphne could even offer a greeting. "I've been trying to get you alone for two days! When were you going to tell me about that kiss? It's everywhere online!"

Daphne winced as she sat on the bed. "Hello to you, too, Mel."

"Don't 'hello' me," Melissa cried. "Someone posted a video, and it's got more views than those kittens that learned to high-five. Spill. Everything. Now."

Heat crawled up Daphne's neck at the realization that their moment had been captured and shared. Realistically, she had expected it, but it still seemed...invasive in a way. "It wasn't a big deal," she tried to brush it off, but even to her it sounded fake. "Tony Alvarez was being an ass, insinuating our relationship was fake because we hadn't been photographed kissing. Kane was just...responding to that."

"Responding to—" Melissa sputtered. "Daph, I've seen people 'respond' to things with a quick peck. That was not a response. That was a statement. A very hot, very thorough statement that has convinced the entire internet that Mr. Kane Mitchell is madly in love with you."

Daphne squeezed her eyes shut as the memory of Kane's arms around her waist, his hand cradling her head, the gentle brush of his thumb across her cheek, the warmth of his lips against hers, all flooded back. "It's complicated," she managed, her voice smaller than intended.

"Complicated like the calculus final we crammed for junior year, or complicated like you're actually developing feelings for the man you're being paid to pretend to love?" Melissa's tone softened.

"I don't know," Daphne admitted, the truth slipping out before she could filter it. "I'm in way over my head, Mel. This was supposed to be straightforward, just an extended job interview, I guess. But he's not who I thought he was, and when he kissed me..." She trailed off, unable to articulate the confusion of emotions that had overwhelmed her in that moment.

"When he kissed you...?" Melissa prompted gently.

"When he kissed me, I forgot it was supposed to be pretend," Daphne confessed as panic rose in her chest. "And that terrifies me, because in eight months it ends. One year, then back to reality, that was the deal. Feelings weren't supposed to be part of it."

Melissa hummed thoughtfully. "But feelings rarely listen, do they?"

"They have to," Daphne insisted, rising to pace the limited confines of her room. "I can't afford to—"

The sound of the front door opening halted her mid-sentence, followed by the soft sound of Kane's footsteps. Daphne froze.

"He's home," she whispered into the phone, panic edging her voice. "I have to go."

"This conversation isn't over," Melissa warned. "I want details. All of them."

"I'll call you tomorrow," Daphne promised hurriedly, ending the call as Kane's footsteps moved toward the kitchen.

She stood motionless in the center of her room, listening to the faint sound of him moving around the kitchen. She took a deep breath, reminding herself she was a professional. Whatever happened in the gym, she could manage it.

Even if the memory of his kiss continued to haunt her every waking moment...and a few of her dreams as well.

***

The corner table at Hideaway Café, the coffee shop Daphne frequented with Melissa, was thankfully tucked behind a decorative bookshelf. She had purposefully chosen a seat far enough from other patrons that Daphne could talk to her friend without worrying about being overheard. She curled her fingers around her latte, the ceramic mug warm against her palms as she avoided Melissa's expectant gaze. Her friend's green eyes were locked onto her, an auburn brow arched as Melissa ran a hand through her short auburn hair. Two days after their interrupted phone call, her friend's patience had clearly reached its limit.

"You've been fidgeting with that mug for ten minutes," Melissa finally said, leaning forward. "Are you planning to drink it or just use it as a hand warmer while avoiding eye contact?"

Daphne managed a weak smile. "Both?"

"Nope. Not acceptable." Melissa pushed her own coffee aside. "I've given you forty-eight hours to process, and now I want details. " That kiss..." she lowered her voice slightly, though her eyes still gleamed with excitement, "was not the kiss of two people in a fake relationship. That was..."

"I know what it was," Daphne interrupted, her cheeks warming at the memory. She glanced around to make doubly sure no one was in earshot before leaning closer. "It's been haunting me, Mel. I can't stop thinking about it."

"Haunting?" Melissa echoed, eyebrows raised. "That's a strong word."

Daphne took a deep breath. She needed someone to tell...even if she knew Melissa would freak. "I can't sleep. When I do, I dream about it and my mind takes it...further." The admission sent a fresh wave of heat across her skin. "It's like my brain is determined to extrapolate from that one kiss to..." She trailed off, her cheeks burning.

Melissa's expression softened into understanding. "Oh, honey."

"It's ridiculous," Daphne muttered, dropping her gaze to the untouched latte before her. "I'm a professional. This is a job. I'm literally being paid to be with him. But I'm struggling to keep it just professional, so what the hell does that say about me that I am lusting over someone who is essentially a client."

Melissa reached across the table, covering Daphne's hand with her own. "Okay, but in your defense, the man is hot as hell. What woman wouldn't dream of being with him?"

"The woman who is paid to be with him." Daphne pulled her hand back to drop it into her lap. "And that's the problem, Mel. He was supposed to be a client. Now granted, this is more hands-on than anything ever discussed in school, but still...part of me wonders if wanting more while I'm being paid to be there is like a 'Pretty Woman' thing."

Melissa studied her friend for a moment. "Daphne, tell me straight. Do you still feel like it's all pretend?"

The question hung between them as Melissa arched a brow. Daphne opened her mouth to respond, only to close it. "Yes," she began, then shook her head. "No." She groaned, burying her face in her hands. "God, I don't know."

Melissa waited patiently, giving Daphne the time she needed.

"When we started this, he was exactly what I expected—surly, difficult, resistant to everything." She paused, remembering his deliberate attempts to make her uncomfortable. "But there's so much more to him than I initially thought."

A small smile tugged at her lips as she continued. "In a way, he's like Shrek, he's got these layers, and I'm being drawn in the more layers that get revealed to me. There are times that I get to see this whole other person that nobody else seems to notice."

"And that person appeals to you," Melissa stated simply.

Daphne nodded. "And it's not just physically, though obviously tha t's..." She trailed off, her cheeks warming again. "But it's more than that. I respect him, appreciate his dedication, his focus. And when he kissed me, it felt..."

"Real," Melissa finished for her.

"Yeah." Daphne's voice dropped to almost a whisper.

Melissa reached across the table again, this time wrapping both hands around Daphne's, her touch warm and grounding. "Is it such a bad thing, though?" she asked.

"It is when it's one-sided." Daphne sighed. "This ends in eight months, Mel. That's the contract. If I'm the only one developing feelings here, I'm setting myself up for heartbreak."

"Are you sure it's only one-sided?" Melissa questioned, her head tilting slightly as she studied Daphne's expression. "You said the kiss felt real. Maybe it wasn't just you who crossed the line."

Daphne went quiet as she remembered the gentle brush of his thumb against her cheek, the way he'd continued to hold her close even after Tony had left. "I don't know," she admitted finally. "There was a moment after Tony left, when we were still..." She gestured, unsure how to describe it, "something felt different. But it could have been adrenaline, or the heat of the moment, or—"

"Or he could be just as confused as you are," Melissa interjected.

Daphne frowned, pushing the hope that was rising down. "Even if he was, that doesn't change things. I'm being paid to be there, and that has an expiration date."

"Contracts can be renegotiated," Melissa said with a small smile. "Terms can be amended when circumstances change."

Daphne shook her head, though the analogy resonated more than she wanted to admit. "This isn't a business deal we're talking about."

"Isn't it, though?" Melissa countered, squeezing Daphne's hands before releasing them. "I get it, that's how it started, maybe. The question is whether you want to see where it leads or if you would rather hide behind the job."

Daphne picked up her latte, finally taking a sip of the now-lukewarm liquid. "I don't know," she confessed. "Keeping it purely professional was safe. This...isn't."

"The best things rarely are," Melissa replied, her eyes soft with understanding. "Just promise me you won't shut down what you're feeling because you are trying to just stick to the original plan."

Daphne managed a small smile. "When did you get so wise about relationships?"

"Oh, I'm not," Melissa laughed. "I'm terrible at my own. But I'm excellent at managing other people's emotional crises. It's my superpower."

The teasing broke the tension, and Daphne let out a laugh. She still had no clear answer about how to proceed, but acknowledging the truth had lifted some of the weight she'd been carrying.

Whether Kane shared her confusion remained to be seen. But pretending it didn't exist was no longer an option she could maintain, even with herself.

Chapter sixteen

D aphne stood in the doorway, half hidden by the shadows in the room. She moved toward him, and each step revealed more as his eyes adjusted. He couldn't help but take in the loose waves of her hair falling past her shoulders, the thin cotton of her sleep shirt, the curves he'd forced himself not to fixate on. He remained motionless on the bed, afraid that any sudden movement might shatter the moment and have her hiding away again.

"Kane," she whispered.

He extended his hand, palm up—an invitation rather than a demand. When her fingers met his, the contact sent electricity racing through him. She sank onto the mattress beside him, her eyes bright as she bit her lip.

"I can't stop thinking about you," she whispered.

His restraint crumbled at her words, and he reached for her. His hand found her cheek, cradling it with a gentleness that contradicted the hunger that burned in him for her. His thumb traced the curve of her cheek, and he let out a groan as her lips opened on a soft sigh.

"Kane," she whimpered as he placed a kiss on her neck. He let his tongue tease her skin, tasting her unique sweetness. The small shudder that passed through her body made him smile, curious to know what else she would react to.

His hands slid up her sides, his fingers trailing across the thin fabric of her shirt. When his thumb brushed the side of her breast, the hitched breath that escaped her sent heat pooling low in his abdomen.

She shifted against him restlessly, her body seeking closer contact even as her eyes remained locked on his. Kane responded to the unspoken plea, his hands moving to her hips to shift her over him, her legs falling to either side of his.

"Is this okay?" he asked, his voice rougher than intended, but the feel of her warmth against him was fraying his control.

Her response was a shift of her hips against his rapidly swelling length. The heat of her through the barriers of their clothing seared, and all he wanted was to burn with her. They both moaned at the contact, and her head fell back slightly as a soft cry escaped her lips. Kane fought the urge to rush, to claim, to consume, instead making himself focus on memorizing each reaction she gave.

His hands returned to their exploration, sliding beneath the hem of her shirt to find bare skin, warm and impossibly soft beneath his calloused palms. He'd spent years training his body, teaching himself control, yet her gentle curves shattered it entirely.

Her hips continued their maddening movement against his, and he bit back a groan at how good she felt in his arms. His hand slid back down her side, his finger briefly brushing against her swollen nipple as it traced a path toward her hips. The small gasp this elicited made him want to linger, but the growing urgency in her movements drove him to seek more intimate contact.

He reached the edge of her panties, letting his fingers trace the edge. Her breath grew more ragged as he moved his hand. Her eyes were dark with want, and it made his chest tighten with his own need.

Kane slid his hand beneath the fabric, fingers seeking the heat that was consuming him. Her head fell forward, forehead pressing against his as her breathing quickened in anticipation—

The sharp ring of his cell phone shattered the moment. Kane jerked awake, disoriented and achingly hard, his cock still clutched in his own hand beneath the sheets.

"Fuck," he swore, drawing his hand down his face as awareness returned fully. The dream had felt so real—the weight of Daphne in his lap, the softness of her skin beneath his fingers, the small sounds of pleasure she'd made as he'd touched her.

Kane stared at the ceiling, trying to regain control of his breathing and his thoughts. This wasn't the first dream he'd had about Daphne since their kiss in the gym, but it had been the most vivid. It wasn't just her body he wanted; both her humor and her mind drew him just as much. He groaned, throwing an arm over his eyes. Daphne Wilson was the one woman entirely off-limits for him. But fuck if she wasn't the one he wanted.

The phone continued its persistent ringing, and Kane grimaced as he saw Gavin's name flashing. Kane was tempted to ignore it entirely, but years of discipline overrode his personal irritation. With a growl of frustration, he snatched the phone from the nightstand, swiping to answer with more force than necessary.

"The hell do you want?" he snarled into the receiver, free hand rubbing roughly at his face as he tried to dispel the lingering images from his dream.

"Well, good morning to you, too, sunshine," Gavin chuckled. "Someone woke up on the wrong side of the bed, I take it?"

Kane's brow lowered as he pushed himself upright with a sharp exhale. "Fuck off, Gavin. Someone always wakes up grumpy." He glanced at the digital clock beside his bed—6:43 AM. "You're also calling at the ass crack of dawn."

"This is sadly true," Gavin conceded, "but I was hoping that with a beautiful woman in the house, it would have improved your morning disposition somewhat."

Kane's jaw tightened at the casual mention of Daphne, fragments of his dream flashing unbidden through his mind. "Why are you calling?" He gritted out as he tried to push the images from his mind.

There was a brief pause on the other end. "I'm calling because you've been scheduled for a new fight."

The words cut through Kane's lingering frustration, instantly refocusing his attention. "For real?"

"For real," Gavin confirmed. "In six weeks at the Camden venue. The ECF board finally met about the incident with Alvarez and voted yesterday against suspending you due to, and I quote, 'his demonstrated commitment to personal growth.'"

Under normal circumstances, Kane would have scoffed at the corporate doublespeak, but right now he couldn't bring himself to care about the phrasing. After months of uncertainty and the carefully orchestrated rehabilitation of his image, he was finally getting back in the cage. The relief was intense.

"Who am I fighting?" he asked, already mentally calculating how to adjust his training schedule. He would need to tell Jackson right away.

"Elijah Carter," Gavin replied. "Relatively new to the ECF roster but making waves. Five and one record, with three TKOs. He's aggressive, technically solid, and particularly strong ground game."

Kane nodded. He'd seen Carter fight once and had been impressed by the younger fighter. He wouldn't be an easy opponent, but he wasn't unbeatable either, and more importantly, he was a legitimate contender rather than some sacrificial lamb being thrown in for an easy win.

"They're not giving you a softball for your return," Gavin continued, echoing Kane's thoughts. "The board was clear, this isn't just a formality. They want to see if you've really got your head on straight."

"Good," Kane said firmly. "I don't want special treatment. I just want to fight."

He felt calmer than he had in months. This was what he understood, not the tangle of emotions that had been consuming him since Daphne had entered his life.

"That's the right attitude," Gavin approved. "Jackson already has the footage and is working on a strategy. You'll start prep tomorrow." There was a brief pause before he added. "Kane, I don't need to remind you how crucial this is. Their choice is conditional on continued good behavior. One slip, one hint of the issues that led to the Alvarez situation, and the board will insist on the six months they had originally considered, potentially with additional penalties."

Kane's jaw tightened, but he nodded. Then he realized Gavin couldn't see him. "I understand."

"I know you do," Gavin's voice softened slightly. "You've been making real progress. But this fight is the real test. Every eye in the industry will be watching to see if you have really changed."

"I'll keep it together," Kane promised, as he began to pace, energy now running through him.

"I know you will," Gavin agreed. "Just make sure Daphne will be there."

Kane's stride faltered at the mention of her name. "Daphne," he repeated.

"Yes, Daphne," Gavin emphasized. "Your girlfriend, remember? The woman whose presence has been instrumental in convincing the board you're stable enough to compete again? You need her in the front row. This only works if she's part of it."

Kane closed his eyes, suddenly tense. The fight represented everything he'd been working toward. But Daphne complicated everything.

In the past, fighting had been his sanctuary. The ring was the only place where distractions fell away. Now, knowing she would be watching added a layer he wasn't sure how to handle.

"Kane? You still there?" Gavin's voice cut through his thoughts.

"Yeah," Kane managed, his voice rougher than before. "She'll be there."

"Good." Gavin paused before Kane heard him clear his throat. "This is the turning point we've been working toward. I'll send over the contract details and media schedule later today. In the meantime, celebrate a little. You earned this."

When the call ended, Kane stood motionless in the center of his bedroom, phone still clutched in his hand. His path forward had always seemed straightforward. He needed to fight, win, and advance his career. Now there was Daphne, and he wasn't sure whether she was a bump in the path or a different one.

He had two weeks to prepare for his return to the cage. Two weeks to figure out how to focus on his opponent when all he could think about was the woman who would be watching.

Kane exhaled slowly. The fight came first. It had to. Everything else, including the feelings Daphne caused, had to wait.

But as he headed toward the shower, the memory of Daphne's lips against his, of her body responding to his touch in his dream, followed him.

Chapter Seventeen

K ane gripped the edges of the podium as camera flashes flickered around the crowded room. The ECF logo stretched across the wall behind him, and its image was a reminder of everything he'd nearly lost. Reporters filled every seat, their expressions hungry. They wanted drama, wanted to pick apart the changes in the man they'd written off as an uncontrollable liability. He could feel Daphne behind him, and her presence calmed his nerves.

He cleared his throat; the sound amplified through the microphone system. "I appreciate everyone coming out today," he began, the rehearsed words feeling stiff on his tongue. "I'm grateful to the ECF board for giving me the opportunity to return to competition earlier than expected."

A rush of relief coursed through him as he said the words. Two more weeks. After months of PR appearances and charity events, he was finally getting back to what he understood, the honest simplicity of the cage.

Behind him, Daphne shifted slightly, the subtle movement drawing his attention. He hadn't told her about the press conference until this morning, their first real conversation since Gavin's call had awakened him from that dream. She'd taken the news with professional composure, slipping seamlessly into her role despite the tension that had hovered between them since the kiss in the gym.

"Kane, how do you feel about facing Elijah Carter for your return bout?" called out a reporter from the second row, and Kane recognized

Brian Carter, a veteran MMA journalist. He was grateful Brian was the first question; he knew the reporter would be fair and focused on the fight, unlike some of the others who just wanted their new clickbait headline.

"Carter's a solid opponent; he's aggressive, technically sound, with an impressive ground game," Kane said honestly. "I respect what he's accomplished, but I'm ready for the challenge. My coach and I have been studying his previous matches, and we're developing a strategy that plays to my strengths."

"Is it true the board was divided on choosing not to suspend you?" another reporter called out. "Sources suggest the vote wasn't unanimous."

Kane tensed slightly. It was the kind of question that would have likely triggered him months ago. He knew what the reporter was trying to ask: had he earned it, or were politics what had influenced the decision?

"I can't speak to the board's internal discussions," he replied, keeping his voice level. "All I can control is my own behavior and preparation. I've worked hard to demonstrate that I deserve this opportunity, and I plan to prove that in the cage on fight night."

He sensed Daphne's approval in the slight relaxation of her posture behind him. Her presence and reactions had become something he could feel without even seeing them. He just knew how she would respond. The thought sent an unwelcome surge of heat as thoughts of his dream flashed through his mind.

A woman in the front row raised her hand, one Kane didn't recognize. Her press badge identified her as being from one of the glossier sports and lifestyle magazines that had begun covering MMA when it gained mainstream acceptance, and he braced himself for what would surely follow. "Kane, many are attributing your personal growth to your relationship with Daphne. Has she helped you channel your energy in more positive directions?"

And there it was, the pivot he'd been expecting. Kane's jaw tightened almost imperceptibly as his hand gripped the podium edge with renewed force.

"Daphne has been..." he began, then paused, searching for words that wouldn't sound fake. The truth was too complicated, especially when he could still taste her if he thought about the kiss. "She's been a steadying influence," he finished, even though he knew that it was drastically downplaying just how much of an influence she had already been.

The reporter smiled, clearly sensing blood in the water. "Would you say she's changed you as a person, not just as a fighter?"

Kane swallowed, aware of Daphne standing just feet away, hearing every word. "I think any meaningful relationship changes you," he said carefully. "Daphne sees parts of me that others don't. She..." He trailed off, suddenly uncertain how to complete the thought without revealing too much. He felt exposed, and it had nothing to do with the cameras and everything to do with the woman behind him.

"Will we see Daphne at the fight?" asked another reporter, shifting attention directly to her for the first time.

Kane shifted to meet Daphne's gaze, including her in his response. Their eyes met briefly, and he was struck again by how easily she maintained her composed exterior despite whatever turmoil lay beneath the surface.

"Of course," Daphne answered smoothly, her voice carrying clearly without approaching the microphone. "I wouldn't miss it."

Something twisted in Kane's chest at her words, though he didn't know if it was pride, possession, or something deeper, an emotion that he wasn't ready to name. He turned back to the podium quickly, hoping the heat he felt rising in his face wasn't visible to the cameras.

"Kane," called a voice from the back of the room, "your reputation before meeting Daphne wasn't exactly that of a settled man. There were different women at different events, nothing serious. What makes this relationship different?"

Kane's throat tightened, the question hitting closer to the complicated truth than the reporter could know. "It's not something I can really explain." He said after a moment. "Sometimes you meet someone who changes your perspective," the words emerged with sincerity, "who makes you want to be better."

A murmur rippled through the assembled press, and Kane suddenly worried that he'd revealed more than intended.

"So, when are you going to propose?" called out a voice from the middle of the room.

Kane froze, his mind suddenly blank as the question echoed through the now-silent room. He turned instinctively toward Daphne, finding her eyes already fixed on his, her composure momentarily shattered by the unexpected query. For a heartbeat that seemed to stretch endlessly, they stared at each other, mutual panic reflected in their expressions.

The silence stretched painfully as Kane's mind scrambled for a response to the proposal question. The room seemed to hold its collective breath, waiting for his response to the question. Just as Kane opened his mouth to attempt some deflection, a familiar voice cut through the tension from the back of the room.

"Interesting question about the proposal," Tony Alvarez called out, his voice carrying effortlessly over the crowd. "But shouldn't we first question whether they're actually dating, or if this is just an elaborate PR stunt?"

Kane's head snapped toward the sound, his body recognizing the threat before his mind fully processed the words. Tony stood at the back of the conference room, leaning against the wall, his smirk visible even from a distance.

"What exactly are you implying, Alvarez?" a reporter called out, the room suddenly electric with the promise of fresh controversy.

"I'm not implying anything," Tony replied with exaggerated innocence. "I'm asking what everyone's been whispering about. The timing just seems a little too convenient, doesn't it?"

Kane's back went rigid as rage bloomed hot and immediate in his chest. His hands gripped the podium edge so tightly his knuckles blanched white, the wood creaking under the pressure.

The press corps erupted, questions overlapping as they sensed the story evolving before them:

"Is there any truth to this allegation?"

"How did you two actually meet?"

"Kane, care to respond to Alvarez?"

"Ms. Wilson, were you hired as part of a reputation management strategy?"

Each question landed like a blow, threatening to shatter Kane's control. His breathing quickened as he fought against the surge of rage that had landed him in this predicament in the first place. The edges of his vision began to darken, his focus narrowing to Tony's smirking face at the back of the room. The rational part of Kane's mind recognized the trap even as his body prepared to spring forward to reach the man who kept trying to destroy his career.

A warm hand touched his forearm, and he shifted his head to find Daphne beside him. Her fingers pressed lightly against his skin, and her eyes briefly went wide.

Kane's eyes dropped to where her hand met his arm. Her simple touch, again, was anchoring him. His breath slowed to match Daphne's as the room's chaos continued around them.

Daphne leaned closer to the microphone, never moving her hand. "Mr. Alvarez is determined to create controversy where none exists," she stated simply. "It almost seems like he just keeps trying to create drama to keep his name relevant with the press."

Her words drew murmurs and nods from several of the reporters, and Tony's smirk faltered.

Daphne's fingers moved slightly against Kane's arm, and as he inhaled deeply, the red haze began to fade.

"Tony," Kane said, his voice lower and more controlled than he'd expected, "if you have legitimate questions about my upcoming fight, I'm happy to address them." The measured response clearly surprised Tony, and Kane felt a surge of satisfaction at denying him the confrontation he sought. "My relationship with Daphne is private," Kane continued. "Anyone who has spent time with us knows how strong our bond is, and, sadly, someone keeps trying to belittle our relationship." The words were honest.

More than that, they felt right.

Daphne's hand remained on his arm, her thumb tracing small circles against his skin. Without realizing it, he shifted his stance to angle his body towards her, his eyes meeting hers as he gave a small smile.

Daphne smiled back as she took a step closer. "I'm glad Kane is returning to competition, watching him prepare, his dedication, his process when facing an opponent like Elijah Carter, it's something I wish you all could see."

When a veteran reporter in the front row raised his hand with a question about Kane's strategy against Carter's ground game, Kane knew the worst was past. As Kane turned his attention to the technical aspects of the upcoming fight, he felt the tension in the room gradually ease.

Kane was very aware of Daphne beside him, her hand now resting lightly against the small of his back as he leaned forward to answer questions. The weight of her touch shifted everything inside of him. It suddenly struck him that instead of seeing her as a bother, he now saw her as a partner, something he hadn't really acknowledged before.

When he glanced at her between questions, the brief eye contact carried more meaning than the brief words they'd exchanged over the past week. Her slight smile warmed him and gave him the support he needed to stand there before the press and continue.

Kane turned back to the press; his focus sharpened with Daphne at his side. Tony remained at the back of the room; his eyes narrowed with calculation.

As the reporter finished asking about Kane's training regimen, Tony pushed himself away from the wall. A second later, all hell broke loose.

"Hey, Mitchell," Tony called out, waiting until Kane's eyes locked onto him before continuing. "When your contract with Ms. Wilson expires, will she be available for hire by the next champion? Because I'd like a piece of her myself."

The words lingered in the air for a fraction of a second before the audience responded. A female reporter gasped. Someone muttered "Jesus Christ" under their breath. The ECF public relations director stepped forward from the side of the room, his face tight with alarm.

But Kane didn't see any of it. The moment Tony's words registered, something broke loose inside him —something deeper than rage, something that obliterated thought. One instant, he was standing behind the podium, Daphne at his side; the next, he was in motion.

"Kane, don't!" Daphne's voice barely penetrated the roaring in his ears as he landed on the floor in front of the first row of reporters.

Chaos erupted immediately. Journalists scrambled from their seats as Kane carved a path through the center of the room. A security guard moved to intercept him but hesitated at the promise of violence in Kane's expression.

Tony stood at the back of the room, his smirk widening even as his body tensed in preparation. "That's it," he taunted as Kane closed the distance between them, "show everyone who you really are."

Kane didn't process the words; his vision had narrowed to a tunnel homed in on Tony's face. His only thought was to silence the man who had been so fucking crude about Daphne.

"Kane!" Daphne's voice cut through his rage, but not enough to halt his advance. She had pushed through the scattered reporters, moving with a determination that matched his own.

Just as Kane reached the midpoint of the room, Daphne caught up to him, her hand closing around his forearm with surprising strength. The feel of her hand —her fingers wrapped around his arm, the heat against his skin —made his jaw tense.

"Not like this," she said, her voice low enough that only he could hear it amid the continuing chaos. "He's not worth what would happen to you."

Kane's stride faltered. It was enough of an opening for Daphne to step in front of him, placing herself between his advance and Tony.

"Move," Kane growled, the single word scraped raw from his throat.

Instead, Daphne pressed her palm against his chest, directly over his pounding heart. The touch sent electricity surging through him as he met her determined gaze. The fire in them, paired with her concern for him, had rage and desire mixing, as her eyes stayed locked with his. "Don't," she whispered. Gently, never taking her eyes from his, she guided him toward a door at the side of the conference room.

Cameras continued to flash around them, recording the unfolding drama for the inevitable clips that would no doubt go viral within minutes. The ECF public relations team had swarmed Tony, physically blocking him from following or calling out further provocations. Security guards had finally moved into action, creating a barrier that separated the fighters while attempting to herd the press toward the main exits.

Through it all, Daphne kept her hand on Kane as she maneuvered him through the side door and into a narrow hallway beyond. The sudden absence of cameras and shouting voices didn't make Kane's rage fade; if anything, the silence only intensified the fury that still coursed through him.

"In here," Daphne pushed open a door to a small green room. The space had minimal furniture: a couch against one wall, a small table with bottled water, and a mirror mounted beside a bare countertop.

Kane stalked into the room; every muscle still coiled with anger. Daphne slid in behind him, the door closing behind her. The soft click of the lock echoed in the silence.

Kane turned, his breathing still heavy, adrenaline still flooding his system with nowhere to direct it. Daphne stood with her back against the door, her chest rising and falling rapidly from her own exertion, her eyes never leaving his as if maintaining visual contact was essential to preventing him from exploding.

For a long moment, they simply stared at each other, the small room charged with tension. With a snarl, he turned, not wanting her face to break through any more of the rage. He was used to being angry; he knew how to operate when he was, but he didn't know how to act with her. Not anymore.

Chapter Eighteen

"What the hell was that?" Daphne's hand pressed against the door as she stared at the man seething in front of her. Her composure had finally fractured. "Do you have any idea what you almost did out there? Everything you've worked for, all these months, and you nearly destroyed it all in five seconds of losing control."

Kane's back remained to her, his shoulders rising and falling with each deep breath. His fists clenched and unclenched at his sides, knuckles white with the effort of restraint.

"You know he was baiting you," Daphne continued, pushing away from the door to move closer. "And you nearly gave him what he wanted!"

Kane turned, his eyes nearly pitch black with anger. "You heard what he said about you." The words emerged as a low growl.

"Yes, I heard him," Daphne snapped, throwing her hands up in exasperation. "And it was disgusting and unprofessional. But that doesn't justify you nearly attacking him in front of two dozen reporters with cameras there to capture every second!"

She stepped closer, frustration evident in every line of her body. "The ECF board chose not to suspend you because they believed you'd changed. How do you think they'll react to you charging through a press conference like that?" The twitch of her eye told her he knew she was right. "What is your problem?" Daphne demanded as she stepped closer. "Why can't you just—"

"You." The word cut through her tirade, leaving her speechless. "You are my problem."

Daphne's eyes widened. "What?

Kane's eyes flared, and he took a step toward her as he continued. "You," he repeated, and Daphne found herself retreating as he continued to close the distance between them. "You won't leave my fucking head. Every night, every moment of the day, all I see is you."

Daphne continued backing up until her back hit the wall behind her, leaving her with nowhere to go as Kane closed the final distance between them.

"When Tony said that," Kane's voice dropped lower as he placed his hands against the wall on either side of her head, caging her with his body, "all I could think about was making him hurt for even thinking that way about you."

Kane's face was inches from hers, close enough that she could feel the heat radiating from his skin. His eyes searched hers, his gray irises darkened to the color of storm clouds. His gaze swirled with the same desire she'd been fighting since their kiss in the gym.

"Kane," Daphne whispered, her anger dissolving beneath the intensity of his gaze. Her pulse quickened as electricity seemed to arc between them.

"I can't sleep," Kane continued, and his rough tone sent shivers down Daphne's spine, heat coiling in her center. "When I do, I dream about you. About touching you. About how you felt against me when we kissed." His body shifted closer, not quite touching hers but close enough that she could feel the heat of him, and she had to fight not letting a small whimper of need escape. "I wake up hard and aching, your name on my lips, and then I have to face you across the breakfast table and pretend I'm not losing my fucking mind wanting you."

Her lips parted slightly as she struggled to find a response. "We can't—" she began, but the protest faded, the sound hollow even to her own ears, and her eyes dropped briefly to his lips before returning to meet his gaze as her breath quickened.

"Tell me you don't feel it too," Kane challenged, his face moving closer until she felt his breath against her ear. "Tell me you haven't thought about it—about us—and I'll back away right now."

Daphne's hands had somehow found their way to his chest, resting against the solid wall of muscle beneath his shirt. She could feel his heartbeat racing beneath her palm, the rhythm matching her own accelerated pulse. "Kane," she whispered again, her voice filled with the need that had enveloped her.

His eyes held hers, searching for permission. What he found must have provided the answer he sought, because the last thread of his restraint tore. "You won't leave my fucking head," he breathed, his tongue tasting just below her ear, and she couldn't hold back her gasp. "Every night, every moment of the day, all I see is fucking you."

The confession's honesty should have shocked her. Instead, it ignited the desire she'd been fighting for months. Daphne's fingers curled into the fabric of his shirt, and Kane's control snapped. His head closed the space between them to claim Daphne's lips with hunger. This was nothing like the kiss in the gym; this was raw, unfiltered need.

Daphne gasped against his lips, then the slight sound quickly dissolved into something closer to surrender. The parting of her lips was all the invitation Kane needed. His tongue swept into her mouth to tease hers. His taste, almost like whisky and chocolate, sent a surge of heat through her system.

His hand left the wall to wrap around the back of her throat as his fingers tangled in her hair, as he tilted her head, deepening the kiss. A whimper escaped her throat, and the sound broke the final barrier of distance between them. Kane pressed against her fully, his hips pinning hers to the wall, and she moaned as the feel of his sent a wave of heat to her core, and she could feel her panties growing damp.

"Fuck," he groaned against her mouth, the crude word transformed into something like reverence. Daphne moved her hands from his chest to his shoulders and let her fingers dig into the muscle there as her body undulated against his. Kane broke the kiss to trail his lips along the line of her jaw, down the column of her throat, teeth grazing the sensitive skin there in a gentle nip that drew another gasp from her lips.

"Kane," she breathed, his name emerging with desperation that matched his own need. Her head fell back against the wall, exposing more of her neck to his exploration, her body arching to press her breasts more firmly against his chest.

The outside world receded, and nothing existed beyond where their bodies connected. Kane's hand slid down the front of her blouse, his fingers working the button, and she could feel the tremor of desire that ran through him.

His palm cupped her breast through the thin fabric of her bra, and as his thumb brushed across the hardened peak of her nipple, Daphne arched at the pleasure it sent pouring through her. His eyes, when they met his, were almost black with desire, pupils dilated until only a thin ring of gray remained visible.

"Are you sure?" His words were rough-edged with need but genuine in their question. The fact that he would ask, that he needed confirmation, warmed her heart even as her body screamed for his with need.

Daphne's hands dropped to his belt, her fingers working the buckle as he groaned when her fingers brushed against his cock through his pants. "Yes," she whispered, and Kane growled.

Kane's mouth claimed hers again as his hands moved to help with the remaining clothing covering them. His pants fell open under her determined fingers, her skirt hiked up around her hips by his impatient hands, underwear pushed aside in their haste.

When his fingers finally found her center, the feel of his fingers as they stroked her clit nearly undid her. "Christ, Daphne," he groaned against her neck as he slid two fingers into her wetness, and she let out a moan at the feeling. Her body clenched around his fingers as her hips rocked forward, trying to take him deeper and ease the pressure as a soft cry escaped her lips.

"Please," she whispered, the word both plea and permission as her hand wrapped around his length, guiding him to replace his fingers. "Kane, please."

His nostrils flared at the words, his expression almost possessive as he watched her. He lifted her slightly, his hands gripping her ass as he positioned himself at her entrance. Their eyes locked as he began to push inside, both watching the other's reaction.

The fullness that she felt as he pressed into her sent sparks cascading through Daphne's body. The pleasure was so intense it bordered on pain as she gasped and writhed against him, desperate for him to fill her completely. He moved slowly, giving her time to adjust to his size, but she wanted none of that. She wanted him, raw, untamed. Her legs wrapped around his waist, drawing him deeper as her back arched, pressing her chest more firmly against his.

Kane rested his forehead against hers as he bottomed out in her, their breath mingling in the narrow space between them.

Then Daphne shifted her hips, and thought gave way to instinct as Kane began to move. His rhythm was desperate in its need, each thrust driving him deeper into her willing body. Her fingers dug into his shoulders, nails leaving half-moon impressions through the fabric of his shirt, marking him as surely as he was claiming her.

She couldn't hold back her sounds—small gasps, and broken moans echoed in the room. With a groan, Kane adjusted his angle, drawing even more from her as she let out a loud cry as the coil of heat tightened, and she knew she was close to shattering.

"Kane," she whispered against his ear, her voice breaking around his name as her body tightened around him. "I'm close—I'm—"

"Let go," he urged, one hand moving between them to find the sensitive bundle of nerves at her center, his fingers teasing it, and the heat grew even stronger, causing her to whimper as she shifted against him. "Fuck, I need to feel you come around me."

Her release shattered through her, and her lips parted in a silent cry as her body clenched rhythmically around his length. The sight of her completely undone pushed Kane over the edge. His hips stuttered against hers as she felt a pulse deep within as molten heat filled her.

Chapter Nineteen

Their ragged breathing gradually slowed in the quiet of the green room. Kane's forehead remained pressed against hers as his body pinned her to the wall. Neither moved, as if both were afraid to break the spell.

Several moments later, Kane slowly lowered Daphne until her feet touched the floor again, his hands lingering at her waist to steady her. The loss of intimate connection left him with a strange emptiness. She straightened her clothing with trembling fingers, her gaze on the floor, but it kept darting back to meet his, then away again. He was entranced by the slight flush that remained on her cheeks, the softness around her eyes, and the slight swelling of her lips.

Something protective unfurled in his chest at the sight of her. Without a thought, he turned her, gently drawing her back against his chest as his arms encircled her waist from behind. He buried his face in the curve where her neck met her shoulder and took a deep breath, letting her scent wash over him.

Daphne stiffened momentarily, then relaxed against him with a soft sigh. Her hands rested over his, where they were clasped around her middle, her fingers intertwining with his.

Kane let his lips brush against the sensitive skin of her neck. The gesture was gentle, and he felt both vulnerable and contented with the moment of quiet connection. "You know, I've never wanted to wake up next to anyone before," he murmured against her skin. His voice was soft despite its rough edges. Daphne's breath caught audibly in response, and Kane tightened his arms around her waist, drawing her more firmly against his chest. "In the past, after—" he hesitated, suddenly conscious of how this might sound, "—with other women, I always wanted space afterward. Sleeping next to them felt too...vulnerable." His nose nuzzled deeper into the curve of her neck, seeking more of her scent. "But with you...I want to hold you through the night. Want to wake up with you in the morning."

Daphne's fingers tightened, the only outward indication that his words had affected her. When she finally spoke, her voice was quiet but steady. "Kane," she began, the single syllable of his name carrying the weight of questions she didn't voice.

"I know," he soothed. Their arrangement had terms, and they suddenly felt like a looming shadow over his feelings. But now he wasn't sure he wanted it to be just pretend. He turned her gently in his arms, needing to see her face. Daphne's eyes met his, her brown gaze studying him, searching for answers to questions that he wasn't even sure she knew were being asked. "I don't know what this is," he admitted as one hand rose to cup her cheek, his thumb brushing across her cheekbone. "I just know that I want more than what we agreed to."

The confession's vulnerability left him reeling. His entire adult life had been defined by control. Yet there he stood, in to something that didn't make any sense, but felt right.

Daphne leaned into his touch, her eyes never leaving his. "It complicates everything," she said softly, not a rejection but an acknowledgment of the reality they faced.

"I know," Kane agreed, his thumb continuing its gentle path across her cheek. "But I think it was complicated from the beginning. We just didn't want to admit it."

A small smile curved Daphne's lips, and the expression caught at something profound in Kane's chest. "When did you get so insightful?" she teased.

"I have my moments," he replied, his own lips quirking in response. Then, more seriously: "Stay with me tonight. Not for the cameras, not for the contract. Just...stay."

The request contained all he couldn't articulate more directly. He didn't know how to express it; he just knew he wanted it more than anything else.

Daphne's hand rose to cover his, where it still rested against her cheek, her fingers warm against his skin. "Okay," she said simply.

Kane smiled as she lowered her head to his shoulder.

He bent to brush his lips against hers and knew that whatever happened next, their relationship had irrevocably transformed. The series of events that had brought them together now seemed insignificant.

He knew he wasn't going to be willing to let her walk away.

Chapter Twenty

A wkward.

That was the only way Daphne could describe how things had been at the condo. Waking up next to Kane, wrapped in his arms, had felt...amazing. Absolutely amazing. If she had thought Kane was hot before, seeing him in the morning light, the stubble on his jaw giving him a rugged look as those slate gray eyes met hers...

Oh, she was in trouble because she wouldn't mind seeing it every morning.

Which was precisely why she had fled back to her room when he had gotten up. That and she wanted to make sure she had taken her birth control pills.

It was a full retreat, and she was woman enough to admit it. The feeling she had made her nervous, and when you added the fact that she was technically paid to be there, it left a sour taste in her mouth.

It didn't stop her from wanting it, though.

Whenever Kane's gaze followed her through the condo, it sent heat through her body. Every accidental brush in the kitchen, every night spent in separate beds, especially when she heard his footsteps pause outside her closed door each evening, made her question her decision, which was more important, the job...or Kane.

"We're going to be late," Daphne called out as she checked her watch. She gathered her notebook for the sponsorship meeting that Gavin had scheduled; two new sponsors wanted to endorse Kane and had asked to meet with both of them for some reason. And then Kane emerged from his bedroom in a crisp button-down that stretched across his shoulders, and she almost forgot what she had been doing.

"Gavin can wait," Kane replied, his eyes tracking her movements, and she felt her skin warm beneath her blazer. "He's probably still setting up his PowerPoint with all those charts he loves."

The casualness of the moment, them preparing to leave together, sharing small jokes about Gavin, made her want to hold onto whatever it was with both hands. *'I've never wanted to wake up next to anyone before.'* The words had replayed in her mind countless times.

And that was why she had retreated. It wasn't rejection, it was self-preservation. Kane hadn't pressed, hadn't demanded an explanation, but she'd felt his disappointment when she had slowly closed her bedroom door the next night.

Now, as they rode the elevator down to the parking garage, Daphne was acutely conscious of Kane's body. His hand brushed hers, his fingers grazed her wrist in a touch too deliberate to be accidental, and she felt her pulse leap beneath his fingertips.

"Daphne," he began, his voice dropping, and she caught her breath.

The elevator doors slid open before he could continue. Whatever Kane had intended to say remained unspoken, with the driver able to listen in. As Kane groaned, Daphne turned her face to watch out the window. It was either that or give in to the temptation to kiss him again...or more.

If she were honest with herself, probably more.

The walk to Gavin's conference room was silent, but Daphne couldn't stop herself from sneaking glances at Kane, only to dart her eyes away when his met hers.

"Right on time," Gavin smiled as he gestured them in. He followed them to the open seats at the table before continuing. "We were just discussing the activation timeline for the campaign."

Daphne settled into her chair, opening her notebook with more confidence than she felt when Kane settled in next to her. The heat of his body warmed her, and her skin prickled every time he shifted in his seat. She looked at her notes, but for the life of her, she couldn't make any sense of them.

Kane's hand brushed hers as they both reached for the water pitcher at the center of the table. The contact lasted only seconds, but his fingers slid to her wrist, the pad of his thumb tracing a small circle against her pulse point before withdrawing. The simple touch sent electricity racing up her arm.

"Daphne, you know Kane. What are your thoughts on the social media requirements?" Gavin's voice cut through her distraction, his eyebrows raised in concern as he watched her.

She blinked, forcing her attention back to the meeting with effort. "I think the milestone bonuses make sense," she managed. "I've been helping him with them, but we should clarify the requirements. Ten posts per month seems excessive given Kane's training schedule."

Kane rested his hand on hers, making Daphne turn to meet his gaze. "Daphne understands my priorities," he said, the words sounding as though they were for the sponsors, but she knew his focus was on her. "Training comes first. Everything else has to work around that."

The intensity of his attention made her heart race. She knew without a doubt that what he was really saying was *You come first*. The unspoken message hung between them, and she felt the line she had tried to draw between them begin to dissolve. When he finally looked away, Daphne released her breath.

As the meeting continued, Daphne's distraction grew. When Kane's knee pressed against hers beneath the table, she lost her focus. When his hand dropped below the table and his fingers grazed her thigh, she couldn't pay attention to anything other than the soft pressure. Every time she managed to refocus on the discussion, Kane would shift beside her, and her attention would snap back to him.

Their eyes met during a discussion of media appearances, and the naked want in his gaze made her breath catch audibly. The sound drew Gavin's attention, his gaze narrowing as it moved between them.

"Perhaps we should take a five-minute break," Gavin suggested, his eyes never leaving them. "Kane, Daphne, may I have a word with you two in my office?"

He gestured them through the door into his private space, and it closed firmly behind them.

"Whatever is going on between you two," he said bluntly, "get it under control." His gaze moved between them. "The sexual tension is obvious enough that even the representatives are noticing. Either dial it back or get it out of your system before the next meeting."

Daphne felt heat climbing her neck. "We're fine," she insisted, but Gavin's eyebrows rose in disbelief.

"You haven't heard a word of the last fifteen minutes of discussion. Both of you keep getting lost in each other's eyes like teenagers." His tone softened slightly before he sighed. "Look, I'm not saying there's anything wrong with attraction developing. It might even help sell the relationship. But right now, you need to focus on this meeting."

Kane's hand found the small of Daphne's back as they followed Gavin back to the conference room. The contact sent a surge of awareness through her, but Gavin's warning was loud in her mind.

As the meeting resumed, she made a concerted effort to maintain focus on the sponsors. Yet even as Daphne discussed the schedule requests and how she could help Kane continue to keep up his social media, she remained hyperaware of Kane.

Whatever was developing between them should have frightened her, should have triggered all her professional caution. But Daphne found herself counting the minutes until they would be alone again. She needed to get a grip. She needed Melissa.

And she was going to try to pretend she also didn't need Kane.

Chapter Twenty-One

T he heavy bag swung on its hook as Kane drove another combination into its leather surface. Two hours into his training session at Warrior's Edge, his body moved with precision, leaving his thoughts to wander back to Daphne. The feel of her around him, her breath catching as he entered her, the small sounds that had escaped her throat as pleasure overtook her. Fuck if he didn't want that again with her...only her.

"Again!" Jackson barked from across the gym, his face set in lines of concentration as he assessed Kane's form. "Tighter on the hook, looser on the follow-through."

Kane reset his stance, drawing a deep breath before launching into the combination. The left jab, right cross, left hook, spinning elbow pattern flowed through his body with practiced fluidity. But as his muscles executed the movements, his mind slipped back to Daphne's fingers digging into his shoulders, the soft whimper just before she shattered.

The memory hit him with such intensity that he faltered on his final strike, his balance shifting awkwardly as heat pooled in his groin. It had been three days since their encounter in the green room, three nights since he had held her in his arms, and it still lingered.

"The hell was that?" Jackson called, crossing the mat with quick, purposeful strides. "You telegraphed that elbow so clearly that Carter's grandmother could counter it."

Kane wiped sweat from his brow with his forearm, frustration tightening his jaw. "Won't happen in the cage," he muttered, reaching for his water bottle to hide the evidence of his distraction. He knew the unmistakable tightening in his shorts that would be impossible to explain.

Jackson's eyes narrowed at the lie. "Again," he commanded, stepping back to observe. "Full speed, full focus."

Kane nodded, settling back into his stance. This time, he forced all thoughts of Daphne from his mind, channeling his energy into the sequence. The first three strikes landed with precision, power flowing from his core through each point of impact. But as he pivoted for the spinning elbow, his mind betrayed him again—Daphne's voice whispering his name as she came apart around him, the way her eyes had darkened with desire when he'd confessed to wanting more.

His cock hardened fully at the memory, the physical reaction throwing off his balance mid-rotation. The elbow connected, but with none of the power it should have carried, the technique was sloppy and ineffective.

"Enough," Jackson's voice cut through his thoughts. "Take a water break. Now."

Kane stalked to the edge of the mat, frustration and arousal mixing in him. He'd never experienced this level of distraction during training.

He drained half the water bottle in long gulps and willed his body to cool, his mind to clear. But even as he tried to redirect his thoughts to fight strategy, Daphne's presence lingered at the edge of his awareness.

"You're not here today," Jackson observed, joining him at the edge of the mat. The older man's voice had lowered, shifting from coach to something closer to mentor. "Your body's going through the motions, but your mind's somewhere else entirely."

Kane remained silent, unable to deny the observation but unwilling to confirm it. He'd never discussed his personal life with Jackson. The thought of explaining what was happening with Daphne —how their situation had evolved into something drastically different —felt impossible.

"You have two weeks until you face Carter," Jackson continued, his face impassive but his eyes sharp with concern. "Two weeks to prepare for a fighter who's been active while you've been sidelined. You need every second of training time, focused and present."

"I know," Kane acknowledged, crushing the empty water bottle in his fist. "I'm handling it."

Jackson snorted. "Sure looks like it." He paused, studying Kane with the experience of their many years working together. "This about the girlfriend, the PR thing?"

Kane's head snapped up at the description. "Daphne," he corrected, the defensiveness in his tone surprising even himself.

A knowing expression crossed Jackson's features, understanding dawning in his eyes. "Ah," he said, the single syllable containing volumes. "It's like that, then."

"Like what?" Kane challenged, though he knew exactly what his coach meant.

"You're not just playing the part anymore," Jackson observed, keeping his voice low enough that the other fighters couldn't overhear. "That press conference wasn't an act. The way you went after Alvarez when he disrespected her—that was real."

Kane remained silent, neither confirming nor denying the statement.

"You need to get your priorities," Jackson said bluntly. "This comeback fight or whatever's happening with her. Because right now, you're half-present in both, and that gets you nowhere."

The oversimplification irritated Kane. "It's not that simple," he growled, crushing the plastic bottle further. "I can handle both."

"Doesn't look that way to me," Jackson replied, gesturing toward the heavy bag. "You're distracted. Sloppy. Making mistakes a rookie wouldn't make. And Carter won't be as forgiving as that bag."

Kane clenched his jaw, but honestly, he knew it was true. His performance today had been subpar, his technique compromised by thoughts of Daphne that seemed to intrude with increasing frequency.

"She's only here to do a job," Jackson continued. "To play the supportive girlfriend for the cameras. But yours is to be prepared for this fight. To prove to the ECF board that you deserve this second chance." He paused, his expression softening slightly. "Don't let this PR stunt derail what you've spent years building. I know it's helped, but when a relationship, Hell, a fake one at that, starts to affect your work here..."

Something snapped inside Kane. "Don't call it that," he snarled. Jackson's eyebrows rose at the reaction. "It's not fake," Kane continued, his voice dropping to ensure no one else could hear the admission. "Not anymore."

Concern dawned in Jackson's eyes. "That complicates things," he observed.

"Yeah," Kane agreed, the fight draining from him as quickly as it had erupted. "It does." It was why he avoided relationships in the first place; he had seen too many fighters stop once someone else came into the picture.

Jackson studied him for a long moment. "Then find a way to channel it," he said finally. "Use it instead of letting it use you." He gestured toward the mat they'd abandoned. "You think you're the first fighter to get caught up in a relationship during training? Find a way to compartmentalize or separate. For two hours in this gym, she doesn't exist. Outside, do what you need to do."

The practical advice was exactly what Kane needed. Jackson wasn't dismissing what was happening with Daphne; he was pointing out the need to control its impact on his preparation.

"Two hours," Kane repeated, nodding as renewed determination settled into his features. "She doesn't exist here."

"Good," Jackson approved, already turning back toward the training area. "Now show me that combination again. Full speed, full focus."

As Kane returned to his stance, he forced all thoughts of Daphne from his mind. For the next two hours, he would be only a fighter preparing for combat.

But even as his body executed the combination with perfect precision, earning a grunt of approval from Jackson, Kane knew that Daphne was far from his thoughts. Outside these walls, she waited, her presence in his life something he was unwilling to give up.

Ever.

Chapter Twenty-Two

D aphne hid in the corner booth at Hideaway Café as she traced the rim of her untouched latte with one finger, avoiding Melissa's amused gaze. Five days after the green room, she still hadn't found equilibrium. Her thoughts kept circling back to the shifting dynamic between them. She'd sought out Melissa's counsel before regarding Kane, but this conversation felt like...more. It wasn't just confusion about attraction but something deeper.

"Okay, you've been staring at that coffee for ten minutes," Melissa said, leaning forward across the table. "Either it's done something personally offensive, or you're avoiding whatever you want to discuss."

Daphne managed a weak smile as she shifted her head to meet her friend's gaze. "It happened," she admitted, her voice barely above a whisper. "With Kane."

Melissa's eyebrows shot up. "The fact that you're whispering and blushing suggests we're not talking about a chaste goodnight kiss for the paparazzi..." She observed. "I'm going to need details. Now."

Daphne's cheeks warmed at the memory of Kane's body pressing her against the wall, his hands possessive yet gentle, his eyes raw with need. "After the press conference," she began, forcing herself to maintain eye contact despite her embarrassment. "Tony provoked him, said crude things about me. Kane nearly attacked him in front of everyone."

"I saw the video clips," Melissa nodded, her expression sobering. "It looked bad."

"I managed to get him into a side room before he could reach Tony," Daphne continued, the memory of those tense moments still vivid. "He was so angry, but it wasn't just rage. It was..." She trailed off, searching for words to describe the intensity she'd witnessed in Kane's eyes.

"Passion," Melissa supplied.

Daphne nodded, grateful for her friend's perceptiveness. "One moment we were arguing about his reaction, the next..." She gestured vaguely, heat crawling up her neck as explicit images flooded her mind. "It just happened. Against the wall. It was intense and desperate and nothing like I'd imagined it would be."

"Better or worse?" Melissa's eyes danced with curiosity.

"Better," Daphne admitted without hesitation. "So much better. Like nothing I've experienced before." She took a sip of her cooling latte to buy time to collect her thoughts. "It wasn't just the physical aspect, though that was..." She paused, her words trailing off as her cheeks warmed. "It was what happened afterward. The way he looked at me. The things he said."

Melissa's expression shifted from curiosity to concern. "What things?"

"That he couldn't stop thinking about me. That he wanted to wake up with me." Daphne's voice dropped even lower. Saying it almost felt like a betrayal, but she needed advice. "He said he'd never wanted that before with anyone."

Understanding dawned in Melissa's eyes. "And that meant something to you, more than just sex."

"Yes." Relief flooded Daphne at finally being able to say what had been consuming her thoughts. "It shouldn't have happened, I know that. It complicates everything. But Mel, I..."

"You've developed real feelings for him," Melissa interrupted.

Daphne nodded. "I see him differently now," she confessed. "Not just because of that, but because of everything else. The man I met months ago, or thought I met, is not who he really is." Warmth colored her voice as she continued. "He's disciplined and dedicated and god, so focused when he trains. He cares deeply about his craft, about being the best he can be. And he's loyal—to Jackson, to the people who've stuck by him. He just doesn't know how to express it without it sounding angry or aloof. And he's vulnerable in ways I never expected," Daphne's voice softened. "He hides it well, but there's an insecurity there—a fear of not being good enough, of being dismissed or discarded. I think that's why he pushes people away before they can reject him."

"You've put a lot of thought into understanding him."

Daphne let out a wry laugh. "I've spent months with him. And despite his initial resistance, he's really trying, Mel. He's putting in the work to prove he deserves this second chance."

"Sounds like you admire him," Melissa noted, and her eyes were knowing.

"I do," Daphne acknowledged with a smile, surprised by how easily the acknowledgment came. "He's trying to prove something, and I want people to see that he has value beyond his ability to fight." She paused, realizing how personal her assessment had become. "And I want him to succeed."

Melissa studied her for a long moment, the silence stretching between them as the words hung in the air. When she finally spoke, her voice was gentle but direct. "Daphne, do you realize you sound like you're in love with him?"

Daphne froze, her eyes going wide. "What?" she managed, the single word emerging strangled and uncertain.

"In love," Melissa repeated. "The way you talk about him—seeing past his defenses, recognizing his struggles, being proud of his growth—that's not just physical attraction or professional respect. That's deeper."

Daphne's heart began to race. Love? The possibility had never consciously entered her mind. Attraction, yes. Growing affection, certainly.

But love? That wasn't what she had been looking for at all; it was just supposed to be a job.

"I can't be, I can't be Julia Roberts in this..." she whispered, the denial automatic, yet even as she said it, her thoughts were on the lingering touches, the heated glances, the way he made her laugh, her ease when they were just in the same room, sitting quietly. "It's too complicated. There's an expiration date, Mel. He isn't Richard Gere coming to find me at the end."

"Do you really believe that?" Melissa challenged gently. "After everything you've just described?"

Did she still believe their relationship would simply dissolve when the year was up and the contract was over? Once, she'd been sure of it, but now, the idea of walking away seemed impossible.

"I'm scared," she admitted, the confession emerging in a whisper. "If this is real, I'm setting myself up for heartbreak. Kane has never had a serious relationship. He's built his entire life around avoiding emotional vulnerability."

Melissa reached across the table, covering Daphne's hand with her own. "Have you talked to him about any of this?"

Daphne shook her head, shame coloring her admission. "We've been circling each other since it happened, and that's on me. I freaked out and retreated." She sighed, frustration evident in the sound. "We nearly got called out by Gavin during a sponsorship meeting because we couldn't keep our eyes off each other."

A small smile curved Melissa's lip. "That doesn't sound like someone who just wanted sex without strings, Daph. It sounds like Kane might be just as confused by this as you are."

Daphne thought that through for a moment. Could Kane be experiencing the chaos she was? "What do I do?" she begged. "How do I navigate this without risking everything?"

"Maybe you start by being honest," Melissa suggested gently. "Not with me, but with Kane. And with yourself." She squeezed Daphne's hand reassuringly. "Because from where I'm sitting, you've already crossed the line from arrangement to something real. The question isn't whether to take the risk—you already have. It's whether you're brave enough to acknowledge it and see where it leads."

Daphne's heart continued its rapid rhythm as she absorbed her friend's words. The possibility that she had fallen in love with Kane was both terrifying and exhilarating.

Chapter Twenty-Three

The ECF fundraiser had transformed the hotel ballroom into a glittering showcase of the fighting world's elite. Daphne adjusted the strap of her midnight blue gown as she navigated the crowd. She felt restless tonight. Though she and Kane had arrived together, they had been drawn apart almost immediately, he to a conversation with an ECF board member, and she to a potential sponsor who wanted to discuss Kane's change and her role in it. Yet despite the physical distance between them, Daphne remained acutely aware of Kane's presence across the room.

The gala represented everything she had come to know about the Elite Combat Federation. It was sophisticated, elegant, and a far cry from the reality of the fighting world. The fighters were something discussed as if they were merely commodities, not men and women who put their blood, sweat, and tears into their efforts. Here, men in tailored tuxedos and women in designer gowns moved through the space with practiced ease, the occasional flash of cameras documenting the carefully curated elegance for social media. Charity auction items lined the perimeter of the room: signed gloves, exclusive training packages, VIP fight experiences, all designed to raise money for the ECF's youth development programs. Yet Daphne had never seen any of these people at the events she and Kane had helped with.

Daphne smiled and nodded as a marketing executive from a major sports drink company detailed their interest in Kane's "redemption narrative," her mask firmly in place, even though she knew exactly where Kane stood in the room. She'd felt his gaze on her several times, brief moments of connection across the crowded space that sent heat coursing through her.

"His comeback fight gives a unique opportunity to align our brand with him; we are drawn to his perseverance and comeback," the executive whose name Daphne couldn't even remember continued, despite Daphne's lack of focus. "We'd like to discuss the possibility of featuring both of you in our next campaign. You know, your standing with him and helping him really resonates strongly with our female demographic."

"I'll speak with Kane's agent about trying to get a meeting," Daphne murmured automatically. "Gavin handles all endorsement negotiations for us."

Her gaze drifted toward the far side of the room where Kane stood in conversation with two ECF board members, his powerful frame accentuated by the formal black tuxedo. He moved differently in these settings, more restrained than she was used to. The sight of him, composed, controlled, yet unmistakably dangerous beneath the veneer of civilized attire, sent a flutter of awareness through Daphne's body at the memory of those strong hands on her skin, those arms holding her against the wall as pleasure had overwhelmed them both. Melissa's suggestion that she might be in love with Kane haunted her for days, the possibility too frightening to fully examine yet impossible to dismiss.

As if sensing her thoughts, Kane's head turned, his gaze finding hers across the crowded ballroom. The contact, even from a distance, hit Daphne with physical force. His expression remained composed, but his eyes held heat that inflamed her.

Daphne felt her breath catch. Even across the room, with dozens of people between them, the connection felt as intimate as a physical touch. Kane's gaze remained locked with hers, and the ambient noise of the gala receded as Daphne found herself caught in his focus. The slight darkening of his eyes, the almost imperceptible tension in his jaw—subtle tells that only she could read, told her that he was affected as she was.

When his tongue briefly touched his lower lip, Daphne's knees nearly buckled beneath her. The memory of his mouth on hers flooded her thoughts, and she had to grip her champagne flute tighter to prevent it from slipping through her fingers.

She wanted him. Even though it had been several weeks, she still thought about it daily. She wanted his hands on her body, his weight pressing her into the mattress, his voice rough with need as he whispered her name. But more than that, she wanted his trust, his willingness to let her see beyond the armor he presented to the world.

And therein lay the danger, the fear that while he might desire her body, might even care for her in his way, he might never be capable of offering what she wanted. Kane had built his life around avoiding the kind of vulnerability that genuine love demanded. What if she surrendered completely to these feelings, only to discover that he couldn't—or wouldn't—meet her there?

Across the room, Kane's attention was drawn back to the board members, his gaze reluctantly breaking from hers as he nodded in response to some question. The loss left Daphne feeling strangely bereft. She inhaled deeply, forcing her attention back to the marketing executive who had, thankfully, been too engaged in detailing his thoughts to notice her slip of attention.

"I should find Kane," Daphne said, offering an apologetic smile as she excused herself from the conversation. "There are several people he said he wanted me to meet."

She moved through the crowd with grace, the blue silk of her gown flowing around her legs as she navigated toward Kane. Her heart accelerated with each step closer, anticipation and anxiety churning in her chest. They hadn't really been alone and in the same place since that day, and they hadn't discussed what had happened. If they had to make plans, they did so by text message rather than being in the same room. Part of that was her fault, she knew that, but he had also withdrawn, then retreated.

As she approached, Kane turned as if sensing her presence. His eyes found hers again, something softening in his expression as she drew near and the board member excused himself.

"The Morrison Foundation representatives were asking for you," Daphne said, her voice steady despite the flutter in her chest as Kane's hand came to rest at the small of her back. "They're interested in having you participate in their youth outreach program."

Kane nodded as his fingers spread against the silk covering her lower back, his touch possessive as they moved through the crowd. "Lead the way," he murmured. After a moment, his voice dropped, his words only for her. "I've been watching you all night."

The simple admission sent another wave of heat through Daphne. This was what she found herself craving, the moments of raw honesty and glimpses of genuine feeling.

As they navigated toward the foundation representatives, Daphne leaned slightly into Kane's touch, allowing herself the small pleasure despite the uncertainty between them. Sooner or later, they would have to discuss the change between them and what it meant. Until then, she would treasure these moments of contact, these heated glances across crowded rooms. And she would try not to think about what would happen when the year ended.

***

The digital clock on Daphne's nightstand taunted her with the time, 2:17 AM. She couldn't sleep; her mind was too crowded to rest. The gala had left her wound tight; every glance with Kane across the ballroom had compounded her feelings of denied desire. She stared at the ceiling, trying to trace invisible patterns as her body remembered the heat of his hand at the small of her back, the brief moments when his fingers had spread possessively against her spine through the silk of her gown.

Their ride home had been torture. They were both in the backseat of the car, separated by inches, but at the same time felt like a chasm. Even now, hours later, she could feel the weight of things she had wanted to say but bit back.

With a frustrated sigh, Daphne threw back the covers and swung her legs over the edge of the bed. Sleep clearly wasn't coming, and lying here with her thoughts offered no relief. Some tea might help, or at the very least provide a distraction.

The hardwood floor was cool beneath her bare feet as she padded toward the kitchen in the soft cotton of her sleep shorts and tank top. As she passed Kane's room, she noticed his door ajar, and she frowned. Usually, he had the door shut the moment he disappeared into his room. A glance revealed rumpled sheets but no Kane.

Concern ran through her as she continued through the darkened apartment, checking the kitchen and living room without finding any sign of him. It wasn't like Kane to wander at night. She could count on one hand the number of times she had heard him after he went to his room. The possibility that he might have left sent a pang through her.

Something told her to look outside, and following that, she moved to the large windows overlooking the street below. Her eyes scanned the sidewalk until they landed on a familiar figure standing alone, a silhouette in the soft glow of the street light. Kane's broad shoulders were unmistakable even from this distance, his face tilted upward toward the night sky.

Before she could question the wisdom of her actions, Daphne found herself slipping on her shoes and grabbing her keys. All she knew was that in that moment, she just needed to be near him.

The night air carried a hint of chill as she pushed through the building's front door. Kane didn't turn at the sound of her approach, though the slight tensing of his shoulders suggested he was aware of her presence.

"Couldn't sleep either?" Daphne asked softly, coming to stand beside him without touching.

Kane's profile was striking in the muted light, the strong lines of his jaw and cheekbones cast in shadow, his sweatpants and a thin t-shirt the only barrier to the night's chill.

"No," he admitted, his gaze still fixed on the sky. "Too much noise in my head."

His honesty made her bite her lips. This was the Kane few people ever saw, and she held it all the more precious for its rarity. "Me too," she said, following his gaze upward. "The gala was...intense."

Kane's mouth curved in what might have been a smile under different circumstances. "That's one word for it." He fell silent for a moment before adding, "One week until the fight."

The change in topic didn't surprise Daphne; Kane's thoughts were never far from his upcoming return to competition. What did surprise her was the undercurrent in his voice. That made it sound like he was questioning the fight.

"You're ready," she said with quiet certainty. "I've watched you train. Carter doesn't stand a chance."

Kane turned toward her then, his eyes drifting to hers. "I used to think that was all that mattered," he said, his voice lower, rougher than before. "Winning. Proving myself in the cage."

The subtle shift in his expression sent Daphne's heart racing. It had nothing to do with their physical attraction, but everything to do with the moment.

"And now?" she prompted gently when he didn't continue.

Kane's gaze dropped briefly before returning to her face. "Now I find myself thinking about things that never mattered before. Things I never wanted." His hand lifted, hesitated, then returned to his side without completing whatever gesture he'd intended. "A life outside fighting. Someone to come home with after a match." He exhaled sharply, his eyes closing for a moment before snapping open. "You make me want those things, Daphne. And it scares the hell out of me."

The confession hung in the air between them. This wasn't desire speaking, this was Kane laying bare parts of himself he'd kept carefully guarded from everyone. "Why does it scare you?" Daphne asked, her voice barely above a whisper, afraid that speaking too loudly might break the fragile openness of the moment.

Kane's jaw tightened, a muscle jumping beneath the skin, a sign she had come to realize meant he was struggling. "Because I've never had it. And I have never seen it work." His eyes held hers. "My father left when I was four. My mother cycled through men who showed her exactly why trusting someone is a mistake. Then, when I was eighteen, she kicked me out." He shook his head slightly. "I never got to see what a real relationship looked like. Then I met Coach and learned from him that fighting made sense. It was simple, you win or you lose. You can see pain coming, and you learn to expect it."

The pieces of Kane's emotional armor —his defensiveness —made painful sense. It had become the coping mechanism of a child who'd learned early that attachment only led to abandonment.

"This," he continued, gesturing vaguely between them, "wasn't supposed to happen. It was a contract. A business arrangement with set terms and responsibilities. Clean, annoying, yeah, but carefully outlined with clear parameters. I wasn't supposed to start wanting mornings with you. Evenings. A fucking future."

Daphne's breath caught. The thoughts that had kept her awake tonight —the confusion of emotions, the uncertainty about what existed between them—were all reflected in Kane's confession.

"I know," she said softly, allowing her own barriers to lower in response to his honesty. "I've been lying awake thinking the same things." Her hand reached for his, and her fingers trembled slightly as they interlaced with his larger ones. "When we started this, you were exactly what I expected: difficult, defensive, someone I could distance myself from. But now..."

She drew a steadying breath. "Now I find myself thinking about you all the time. Wanting to be near you. Wondering what happens when our contract ends." Her voice dropped lower, vulnerability threading through each word. "I'm scared too, Kane. Because I never expected to feel this way about you."

Kane's fingers tightened around hers. The air felt charged with electricity. Kane's eyes never left hers as he reached for her, his hand rising to cup her cheek. His fingers shook as he ran his thumb over her skin, and Daphne knew he was as overwhelmed as she was.

Daphne hesitated briefly. Crossing this line again would change everything.

The moment of hesitation passed and she leaned into his touch, knowing that her decision had been made. Kane's thumb traced the curve of her cheekbone, his gaze holding an intensity that made her breath catch in her throat.

"Daphne," he whispered, her name emerging as both question and answer before he leaned down to claim her lips.

Unlike the heat of their first few kisses, this began with exquisite gentleness. His mouth brushed against hers with tenderness, and Daphne's hands rose to rest against his chest. She could feel the steady rhythm of his heart beneath her palm as the kiss deepened slowly, heat building between them with deliberate patience rather than desperate urgency.

Kane released her hand to circle her waist, pulling her closer. The solid wall of his chest against hers felt like coming home. Her arms wound around his neck, fingers threading through the short hair at his nape as their mouths continued to explore with unhurried thoroughness.

When they finally separated, Kane's forehead rested against hers, their breath mingling in the narrow space between them. "We should go inside," he murmured, voice rough with restrained desire.

Daphne nodded, not trusting her voice as he took her hand and led her back toward the building's entrance. Their hands remained linked as they moved through the lobby. Once they were inside the elevator, Kane drew her against him again, his kiss deeper now but still controlled. She could tell from the way his hands clutched her that he wanted more, but was holding himself back.

The soft ping of the elevator reaching their floor barely registered as Daphne found herself pressed against the wall beside the doors, Kane's body a warm weight against hers. Their first time was a desperate coupling driven by frustration and a little bit of anger. This felt different, so very different.

They made their way down the hallway, pausing occasionally when the need to taste became too great to resist. Kane's hand remained at the small of her back, and she relished the heat of his skin through her thin shirt. At his door, he fumbled with the key, refusing to remove his hand even to get the door open. Finally, with a soft click, the door slid open, and he pulled her inside and into privacy.

Kane paused just inside the doorway and turned to face her.

"Are you sure?" he asked, and the echo of the question from their first time together carried more weight now. She knew he wasn't just asking about sex, but everything...about them.

Daphne answered by rising on her toes to press her lips to his. Kane made a sound deep in his throat as his arms circled her, and together, they stumbled to his bedroom. When her legs hit the edge of his bed, she smiled.

Kane drew back to look at her, his eyes dark with desire and a need she was hesitant to name but desperately wanted. His hands found the hem of her tank top, and his fingers skimmed the skin beneath as he lifted the fabric. Daphne raised her arms, allowing him to pull the garment over her head before it was discarded beside the bed. The shiver that went through her had nothing to do with temperature and everything to do with Kane.

"You're beautiful," he murmured, his words raw with their honesty.

Daphne's hands reached for him in turn, tugging his T-shirt until he helped her remove it, revealing his sculpted chest to her. Her fingers traced the definition of muscle, exploring him with the same deliberate care he had shown her. When she leaned forward to press her lips against the steady beat of his heart, Kane's breath caught.

Their remaining clothing was removed between kisses that ranged from gentle to desperate. When they finally stood before each other, Kane guided her onto the bed with gentle hands, hovering above her with his weight supported on his forearms.

He looked directly into her eyes as his body lowered to hers, the feel of skin meeting skin drawing soft sounds from both their throats. Daphne's hands traced the contours of his back, her fingers tracing the corded muscles, and she felt him quiver beneath her touch.

"Kane," she whispered, the single syllable carrying all she couldn't say.

He still understood. His head lowered to capture her lips as his hand traveled the length of her body, leaving sparks in its wake. When his fingers found the heat between her thighs, Daphne arched against him, a soft gasp escaping into his lips. Kane's touch was hesitant at first as he learned her responses —what made her gasp and what had her quivering. Each caress built upon the last, drawing her into a world of heat and need for him...only him.

Daphne's hands explored his body with equal curiosity, eager to discover the places that made his breath stutter. When her fingers encircled him, Kane's forehead dropped to rest against hers, his eyes closing briefly as pleasure overtook his features.

"Daphne," he breathed, and the plea in his voice made her pant. "I need—"

"Yes," she whispered. She felt the same.

Her legs parted further in invitation, hands guiding him to where she wanted him most. His eyes captured hers as he moved, entering her slowly. The sensation of fullness drew a soft cry from Daphne's throat as Kane echoed the sound with his own deep groan. For a moment, they remained motionless, the feeling of being so intimately connected nearly overwhelming them. Then Kane began to move. Each thrust made her keen, and it felt as though his attention was entirely focused on her responses. Daphne's body rose to meet his with increasing urgency.

"Kane," she gasped as pleasure built within her, her fingers digging into the solid muscle of his shoulders. "Please—"

His hips stuttered before surging into her with a groan, the movements deeper now. He slid one hand between their bodies, his fingers teasing the center of her pleasure as he continued to pound into her. The sensation of his body filling her, and his fingers thrumming against her, sent Daphne spiraling toward release with startling speed.

When it claimed her, the intensity stole her breath. Her body arched beneath his as waves of pleasure coursed through her. Kane's name fell from her lips in broken syllables; she wasn't capable of more than that as her entire world was focused on him. He followed moments later, his own release triggered by the sight of her undone beneath him. His body shuddered as he buried his face against her neck with a groan that vibrated through both their bodies as she felt heat spread through her.

They remained entwined, neither wanting to move, as their breathing gradually slowed. Kane eventually shifted to lie beside her, drawing her against his chest with an arm that curved protectively around her waist. It was the first time they had lain like this, but it just felt...right.

Daphne lay her head on his chest and listened to the rhythm of his heart beneath her ear as it slowly returned to normal. The silence between them should have felt awkward, but it wasn't. It felt comfortable and natural.

Kane's fingers traced a pattern along her spine. In the dim light of his bedroom, with the city quiet beyond the windows, they both knew they had crossed a line, but they also knew that neither of them regretted it. Whatever came next, this moment would remain between them, perfect.

Chapter Twenty-Four

The digital clock on Kane's nightstand read 4:36 AM, its soft glow the only light in the dark room. He should have been exhausted after the emotional confession and the pure fucking bliss and peace that had followed. Yet sleep was the last thing on his mind as he lay propped on one elbow, watching Daphne's peaceful form beside him. Her breathing was slow, and the way her features softened in slumber made him smile.

Yeah, he'd shared his bed with women before, but always briefly, and only if he had passed out. The moment he woke up, though, he was always sure to ask them to leave immediately. But this was different; there was no urge to flee, no shutting down of any connection. It was so foreign that it had kept him awake for hours.

In the past, the moments after sex, he had always felt the walls closing in, and he was desperate to be alone. Those women had accepted the limitations he always placed on sex, and none had ever really been invited to stay.

Yet here he lay, watching Daphne's chest rise and fall, and felt something dangerously close to contentment. Her dark hair spilled across his pillow in a way that should have panicked him, and in the past, he knew it would have, but it didn't, not with her. One of her hands lay near her face, her fingers slightly curled, and Kane resisted the urge to trace the lines of her wrist, not wanting to disturb her.

There were fewer than six months left in their agreement. The thought had once brought relief, knowing there was an end date to sharing his life. Now, though, those six months suddenly seemed so short.

He watched Daphne's sleeping face, his lips curving as he scanned the slight asymmetry of her features and the tiny freckle near her left eyebrow, which he had only recently become obsessed with. Each detail drew him to her, captured him.

In the cage, Kane understood exactly who he was. He was a fighter. His reputation had been forged through years of training, of pushing his body to its limits, of channeling his anger into something that earned respect rather than rejection. Fighting had always made sense to him, as people had a way of both irritating and boring him.

Until Daphne. She saw him, not just the fighter, but the man under his armor. She had seen him at some of his worst, but still stood by his side, her hand clutched around his

He was falling in love with her.

Kane, who had never allowed anyone close enough to bother with affection, was falling in love with a woman whom he had only met because of a contract and one of his own fuck ups. The irony wasn't lost on him, yet it felt as if all paths had been leading to him being there, with her at his side.

Daphne stirred beside him, her body shifting toward his warmth without waking. Kane held himself still, his arm lifting automatically to accommodate her movement as she settled against his side. Her head rested against his shoulder as she draped one arm across his chest, holding him close even in her sleep. God, it felt so right. She felt so right.

Yeah, fighting had given him purpose, but never this sense of having found something he didn't want to be without.

Kane had no illusions about the challenges that they faced; Hell, their arrangement had a fucking expiration date. But as Daphne's breath

165

warmed his skin, they seemed unimportant against the truth he was letting himself acknowledge.

He was falling in love with Daphne Wilson. Hell, if he was honest, he was probably already long past 'falling.' And somehow, despite everything he'd believed about himself, that didn't cause panic.

His arm curved more securely around her as he rested his head against hers. Whatever came next, he would face the challenges and pass them. Because what he had with Daphne was worth fighting for.

Chapter Twenty-Five

K ane knelt to talk to a young boy at the gym, and Daphne bit back her smile. It was so different from the first awkward time she had accompanied him to a children's event, where he had stood in the back of the room. He had looked both irritated and terrified of the hyper kids as they had called out questions to him and the others at the event, letting anyone else do the talking. Now, he was in the thick of it, answering questions honestly about his journey, about the ECF.

Then he turned to catch her eye, a smile curving his lips as he watched her for a moment before turning back to the inquisitive boy.

That was also different, but she couldn't deny it made her happy.

It had been two weeks since the night under the stars, or what she now considered them officially becoming a couple. Two weeks spent with him, waking in his arms, talking as they lay, their limbs entwined, each night.

If she thought she cared for Kane before, it was now set in stone. The anger had melted away, and the man that had emerged captivated her.

Kane's hand came to the little boy's shoulder as the boy nodded enthusiastically, a broad smile crossing his face as he did. A minute later, the boy scampered off to his mother, and Kane stood, watching the boy as he hugged his mother's waist. Daphne made her way to his side, and his hand slid around her waist as he held her, nodding to the boy when he turned and waved goodbye.

"Ready to get out of here?" Kane squeezed her hip as he turned to meet her gaze, a question in his eyes as she nodded in response. "Come on, let's go eat."

It was funny; she had been with Kane for months now, but not really *with* him. She had seen him at the fancy events, the set appearances, where he had to perform, to act a certain way. She giggled as he ripped open his McDonald's Quarter Pounder, his eyes closing with the first bite.

There was no pretense with him anymore. It was just them against the world. Sure, people still pointed as they walked down the street, Kane was stopped for autographs, and there were the occasional sneers slung at them, but her hand would tighten around Kane's, and none of it mattered.

"You want some of my fries?"

Daphne glanced at Kane as he held out the container and smiled as she reached out to take one, but only one. She had come to learn that fries were Kane's favorite food, McDonald's fries in particular, and he was very wary of sharing his food. She would not take it for granted that he offered her some.

Part of her saw it as more than just the fries; by offering her some, he was offering her a piece of him, and she would never turn that down. She would take each piece he shared and treasure it.

When she offered him a sip of her chocolate shake, he hesitated, his eyes on her, before he slowly leaned down to take a sip.

Almost as if he knew she was offering part of her with that as well.

As they stepped out of the McDonald's, he held her close, making sure she wasn't near the street. Even though he hadn't said the words, she wondered if he knew his actions shared everything.

"You want to head home?" Kane's brow rose as he asked, but she shook her head.

"Is it ok if we walk for a bit?"

Kane placed a kiss on the top of her head. "Sure, Daph."

Her head rested against his chest as they walked, tucked safely under his arm as they navigated through the sidewalks of Philadelphia. They shared a laugh at the tourists who were snapping wacky pictures at the Franklin Memorial as they made their way towards Love Park in the center of the city.

"You know, even though I live here, I don't think I've ever done the whole tourist thing." Kane mused as he shifted his arm to take her hand. "The Liberty Bell, the Franklin Institute, Carpenter's Hall, none of it."

"Do you want to?" Her brow raised as Kane seemed to think for a second before giving a small laugh.

"Nah, not today. Those guys taking photos at the memorial made me realize it, though. How you can live in an area and not really appreciate what's around you."

"I would have pictured you more in the Mütter Museum than the Franklin Institute." Daphne teased, knocking her shoulder into his side as he laughed.

"I know enough about the human body, so I'll pass."

Her eyes drifted to his face as they stopped by the fountain in Love Park. There was a wariness in his gaze as it slid around the park, taking note of everyone that he could see. Before she accepted this job, she didn't quite understand the constant pressure public figures faced from paparazzi and fans, the constant pictures, always wondering if someone would jump out at you to get a shot or ask for a quote. It had been the most significant adjustment to being part of his life, but it seemed to weigh on him less than it had when she first met him.

And she hoped that in some way, she was the reason for that.

There was so much to him that people didn't see, didn't care to look at. They didn't see the man who woke every day at 6 am to keep himself disciplined. They didn't look at the pain in his eyes when someone said he was all bluster and no skill. They didn't see the set of his jaw when people would talk about how she was only with him because she was being paid.

But she did. She also saw the man who would watch the Great British Bake Off, commenting on each item as if he were a judge. She saw the man who kept his workout clothes carefully separate from his everyday clothes, as if he were trying to keep both parts of his life separate. The man who struggled with his own insecurities every day but stood with his chin high as he stepped out of his condo into a new minefield of reporters and Tony Alvarez.

And that was the man who had drawn her so deeply to him.

He turned to meet her eyes, giving her a small half smile as he squeezed her hand.

Her free hand rose to stroke his cheek, and he tugged her to close the space between them before lowering his head to hers for a soft kiss.

They didn't see his intelligence, his humor, his wicked side, but she did. She was the only one who saw the true Kane Mitchell. The man beneath his armor, beneath his fighting prowess. She longed for the world to see him as she did, to understand the complexities they tried to hide away by focusing on only one side of him.

He shifted to wrap his arm around her waist as the kiss deepened, and her hand slid around the back of his neck to hold him in place.

As they drew apart, Kane's forehead came to rest against hers for several seconds as he let out a deep sigh. Some may have said it sounded like disappointment, but she knew better. She knew *him*, knew how to read him, and to understand everything he didn't say. When his gray eyes opened and met hers, she gave a small nod. His smile grew as his hand around her waist tightened slightly before he drew back, taking her hand in his again.

Yes, she wished that others could see the man that she knew, but at the same time, she was glad they hadn't. If they had, she would likely have never met him, and she couldn't imagine a life without him in it. Their hands never parted as they turned and slowly made their way through the streets back to the condo.

Chapter Twenty-Six

Tony Alvarez was a fucking asshole.

Kane's jaw tightened as he watched Tony's most recent interview. His eye twitched as he heard the shit the man was saying about Daphne. Kane was angry, fucking livid, but this time his anger ran cold. Tony had crossed a fucking line.

"Daphne Wilson? Mitchell's supposed girlfriend?" Tony sneered. "Everyone in the industry knows that's just a PR setup. But I'll give Mitchell credit—if you're going to hire someone to pretend to be your girlfriend, it helps if they are hot like her. I'd like to see what else that mouth can do besides defend him to the media."

Kane set the phone down, even though he wanted to hurl it across the room. How could the fucker say shit like that? His fingers trembled with the effort of containing the cold rage that filled him.

He glanced toward the bedroom door, grateful that Daphne had left early for breakfast with Melissa. She didn't need to see this shit. Kane knew she would eventually; in the social media age, nothing remained hidden, especially when it was designed to go viral, which was probably exactly why Tony had done it.

Well, this time Kane wasn't going to stand by and try to just brush it off. This time, he would give the fucker exactly what he wanted, and God help the man when they squared off.

He took a deep breath, retrieved his phone, and immediately called Gavin.

"Kane, I was just about to call you. I assume you've seen Alvarez's interview?"

"Set up the fight," Kane replied, his voice low and controlled. "Call whoever you need to call, but make it happen."

There was a moment of silence before Gavin sighed heavily. "Kane, think about this. You just beat Carter and are returning to the top of your game. Everything you've done hangs in the balance if you make this personal."

"It's already personal," Kane bit out as he paced through the room, too restless to stay still. "He made it personal the moment he opened his mouth about Daphne."

"This is what he wants, though," Gavin argued. "Alvarez is baiting you. He knows your history, and he's been paying attention. It's not a secret that going after Daphne is the quickest way to get a reaction from you, so he's using it to try and get your title without having to earn it."

"Well, he fucking is getting a reaction." Kane paused by the window, looking out at the city skyline as morning light glinted off glass and steel. Six months ago, he would have already been in his car, going to find Tony and shut his mouth, whatever the consequences. Now, he knew it was a desperate attempt to derail him. "I'm not going to attack him in a parking lot, if that's what you're worried about," Kane scoffed, "I want to face him where it counts—in the cage, with rules, with everything legitimate. He thinks he can say shit like that and get away with it? No."

"Kane—"

"Listen to me, Gavin." Kane cut him off, his voice firm but not aggressive. "Yes, it's personal. But I don't care. This is about standing up for someone I care about."

The admission hung between them, and Kane knew Gavin was reading everything he hadn't said. He could almost see Gavin connecting dots and reassessing the situation.

"You're in a real relationship with Daphne," Gavin said, not a question but a realization. "Well, that complicates things."

Kane released a breath. "Yeah."

"You need to be even more careful then," Gavin murmured. "Your career is one thing, but dragging her further into this mess with Alvarez is another. Have you considered what this will mean for her? Right now, Alvarez's comments are irritating, but they aren't getting much traction. You challenge him, and it blows up. We are talking media attention, public scrutiny, and the ugly comments that will inevitably follow. Are you sure you want to do that?"

The question forced Kane to stop for a moment. He had been focused on defending Daphne, but Gavin raised a valid point about whether that defense would expose her to more harm.

"She's stronger than you think," Kane said after a moment, knowing full well she was, and that she could handle any storm that blew their way. "But I'll talk to her, then call you back. Thanks."

"That's...surprisingly mature of you," Gavin noted, the faint surprise in his voice almost amusing.

Kane moved to the kitchen, grabbing a glass of water from the counter. "I've changed, Gavin. She's changed me. I'm not just talking about changing in front of the Board." He took a sip of water as he thought. "Six months ago, I wanted to fight Alvarez because I was pissed at what the guy was trying to take from me. Now, I want to fight him because one, he's an asshole, and two, it's the right thing to do. There are consequences for going after someone I love."

The word slipped out before Kane could stop it. It was the first time he had said it to another; he knew he should have told the words to Daphne first, but it felt natural to say it, and to show *why* this fight needed to happen.

Silence stretched across the line before Gavin spoke again, and this time his tone was softer. "I'll make some calls, see what can be arranged. But Kane—this must be by the book. There can't be any confrontations outside the cage, no engaging with him on social media. Don't do anything that gives the ECF a reason to question your stability."

"Understood," Kane agreed, relief ringing in the word. "Thank you."

"Don't thank me yet," Gavin warned. "If this goes sideways, you could lose everything." A pause, then: "And Kane? Talk to Daphne first. She deserves to have a say in this. I can start calling tomorrow."

After the call, Kane stood in the kitchen, his unseeing gaze focused out the window. When his phone dinged, it pulled him out of his thoughts. A glance at the screen had him smiling despite everything when he saw Daphne's name at the top.

"Breakfast finished early. Heading back now. Miss you."

Those words would have terrified him months ago. Now they filled his chest with warmth even though his anger still lingered. He typed a reply, then set his phone aside, his mind spinning on how to discuss his conversation with Gavin with her. He knew Gavin was right; it was a choice they needed to make together, but still, he wanted to shield her from it.

He let out a chuckle. His entire life, he had only needed himself, no one else to discuss or plan things with. Now he found himself wanting to include her, to get her perspective on things. Somehow, she was the reason he had found something worth fighting for.

And he would make sure everyone knew it.

Chapter Twenty-Seven

T he heavy punching bag swayed with each impact of Kane's fist as he threw himself into another training session. Sweat gleamed on his shoulders as he executed a combination, each strike landing with punishing intensity. Kane moved with an intensity that was more focused, more determined than his previous training as Jackson watched with narrowed eyes.

Three weeks had passed since Kane issued the formal challenge to Tony, and something had changed with his approach. The anger that had once fueled his movements had given way to something colder, more planned, and methodical. Every movement Kane made flowed with purpose, as Kane sought to conserve his energy rather than expend it in quick and violent outbursts.

"Two more rounds," Jackson barked, his face revealing nothing as Kane nodded and reset his stance.

Gavin pushed through the gym's doors, pausing near the entrance as he watched Kane's movements. Kane launched into another combination, the familiar jab, cross, and weaving slip, and the uppercut was executed cleanly. Where before he was sharp and powerful, now he moved with economy, each strike flowing into the next with minimalist precision.

"Impressive," Gavin murmured.

Jackson made his way to Gavin, his arms crossed over his broad chest as he continued to monitor Kane's work. "He's different," the older man stated, his voice pitched low to remain between them. "Been at this game thirty years, I've seen fighters change their technique. But it's rare that they one change their entire approach."

They watched as Kane finished his bag work and moved toward the sparring area where a middleweight spar partner waited. The younger fighter bounced on the balls of his feet as Kane stalked to the cage.

"This should be interesting," Jackson said, a hint of anticipation in his tone. "Kid's been talking all week about how he's going to push the pace on Mitchell."

The session began with the younger fighter pressing forward, throwing heavy combinations designed to overwhelm an opponent. In prior matches, Kane would have met that aggression with his own. Now, however, he retreated strategically, his eyes calculating as he studied his opponent's patterns.

"He's reading him," Gavin observed, surprise evident in his tone.

Jackson nodded. "Used to be Kane would just wade through punches to deliver his own. Now he's looking for openings. He's making the other guy work while he conserves his energy."

It became more apparent as the match progressed. The younger fighter grew frustrated by Kane's evasions, and as he did, his combinations grew wilder. Kane remained calm, absorbing information, his breathing controlled.

"Two minutes in and the kid's already breathing hard," Jackson noted with professional satisfaction. "Meanwhile, Kane's barely winded."

Near the end of the round, Kane shifted. The young fighter launched another aggressive combination, but when he overextended himself on his right hand on a punch, Kane ducked it, then countered with a short left hook to the jaw. The younger fighter staggered, momentarily dazed.

"Damn," Gavin whispered, impressed despite his familiarity with Kane's abilities. "He set that up."

"He was setting it up the whole round," Jackson confirmed. "He saw early on that the kid drops his left when he throws the right cross. Kane fed him opportunities, made him confident, then struck when it wasn't expected." He shook his head slightly. "That's not the Kane Mitchell I've been training for years. This is someone much more dangerous."

The buzzer sounded, ending the round. Kane immediately stepped back, nodding respectfully to his partner before stepping forward to offer suggestions on how to tighten the man's defense. The action drew a thoughtful hum from Jackson.

"He told me about Alvarez," Gavin said after a moment, watching as Kane took a water break. "That's why I'm here. I wanted to see for myself if he's really ready for that so quickly after his match with Carter."

Jackson turned to study Gavin's expression, reading beneath the man's careful expression. "You're worried he'll lose control again."

It wasn't a question, but Gavin answered anyway. "Alvarez knows exactly which buttons to push. He's already started with comments about Daphne that should have sent Kane into a blind rage."

They watched as Kane returned to the mat for another match, this time facing a different sparring partner who had a more technical style. The contrast in Kane's approach was obvious—where he had been patient and defensive with the aggressive fighter, now he pressed forward with even pressure against the more methodical opponent.

"Look at that," Jackson said, gesturing subtly. "Complete strategic shift based on who he's facing. Used to be Kane had one mode: toy with his opponent until bored, then forward pressure until something broke. Now he's like water, he'll adapt to whatever you throw at him."

Gavin's eyebrows rose as Kane transitioned from striking into a takedown as his opponent overcommitted on a move. "That's new," he noted.

"He started working his ground game more seriously about three weeks ago," Jackson confirmed. "Said something about wanting to be prepared for all scenarios." He paused, a rare smile touching his features.

"First time in ten years he's admitted there might be something he didn't already know."

They fell silent as Kane worked methodically, his strikes measured and controlled. When the round ended, he helped his sparring partner up, the two exchanging words again as Kane offered tips and pointers and gave the other fighter some suggestions.

"It's because of her, isn't it?" Jackson asked as Kane moved toward the heavy bags for a cooldown. "Daphne?"

Gavin's head tilted as he watched Kane. "Apparently."

"Figured as much," Jackson nodded, amused. "I noticed the change as they happened gradually, but its sped up these past few weeks. The way he moves, how he's now thinking in there. He's fighting for something beyond himself now." He turned to face Gavin directly. "Makes him more dangerous than he's ever been."

"Dangerous enough to handle Alvarez without losing his composure?" Gavin pressed, the real question finally emerging.

Jackson watched as Kane did a final combination on the heavy bag, his every movement controlled but devastating. "This Kane," He gestured toward Kane as the man gulped his bottle, "he's fighting with purpose. His head is clearer than I've ever seen it, and he's calculating." He met Gavin's gaze steadily. "To me, that's a hell of a lot scarier than his anger ever was."

Kane unwrapped his hands as he spoke with another fighter. The easy camaraderie they were seeing, so unlike his former distance, was yet another sign of the change in him.

"I've got the date for the Alvarez fight," Gavin stated. "Six weeks from now, they started promoting it today."

"He'll be ready," Jackson's eyes narrowed as Kane shook hands with he man he was speaking to. "And Alvarez won't know what hit him."

Chapter Twenty-Eight

D aphne absently stirred her iced tea as she checked her watch for the third time in five minutes. Her brother Aaron was usually annoyingly punctual, which meant being late was likely deliberate. Either that or he was dreading the conversation as much as she was, but that was likely wishful thinking. She'd been avoiding her brother's questions about Kane for weeks. But Aaron's text this morning had left no room for evasion: "We need to talk about your fighter boyfriend. Lunch at Meridian, 1 pm." Considering every text with her brother ended with an exclamation point, the lack of one made her even more nervous for what was going to follow.

The café hummed with lunchtime conversations among business professionals and college students who lingered over their food. Daphne had chosen a corner table, one that offered privacy but was still public enough to hopefully dissuade the kind of heated exchange that she and Aaron could get into.

"Sorry, I'm late." Aaron's voice cut through her thoughts as he appeared beside the table. She looked up to the familiar face and found herself smiling despite her nerves. His hair had always been a shade darker than hers, closer to black, and it was offset nicely by the light charcoal suit he wore. His hazel eyes saw right through her when he raised a brow, and she squirmed in her seat, suddenly uncomfortable again. A lock of his hair fell into his eyes as he bent to kiss her cheek. "Conference call ran long." He shrugged as he slid across from her in the booth, his eyes watching her carefully.

Daphne doubted the excuse but smiled anyway. "I ordered you an iced coffee. Still black, right?"

"Some things never change," Aaron smiled, but the expression did little to calm Daphne.

Daphne could feel her brother's impatience building as they placed their order. Sure enough, as soon as the waiter stepped away, Aaron's expression shifted to what she called his "boardroom face," serious and slightly concerned.

"So," he began, leaning forward slightly. "Kane Mitchell."

Daphne met his gaze steadily. "Yes?"

"What exactly are you doing, Daph?" The question was direct and laced with concern. "This guy is a ticking time bomb. Everyone in the sports world knows it."

"Everyone doesn't know him." She countered, her voice calmer than she felt.

Aaron pulled out his phone, tapped the screen several times, then slid it across the table. "This is who he is," he said as the video of Kane and Tony in the parking lot began to play. "The man is violent, uncontrolled, and dangerous. I've been doing a lot of research on him, and there's a pattern of violence."

Daphne watched the familiar fight, but now she saw it through new eyes. So much had changed since that moment.

"That was eight months ago," she said, pushing the phone back toward her brother. "People can change, Aaron."

"Violent men don't change," he countered, the certainty in his voice triggering a flare of irritation within her. "They just get better at hiding it. I've seen it before, too many times. Guys like Mitchell don't suddenly lose tempers like that."

The waiter's arrival with their food provided a brief pause that Daphne was grateful for, but Aaron continued the moment they were alone again. "I told you I did some digging. Come on, the sudden girl-friend after years of being notoriously single?. Is this even real, or is it some kind of PR stunt that you got involved with somehow?"

The question struck close to the truth of how things had started, but it missed what it had become. Daphne set down her fork, her appetite fading beneath the weight of her brother's scrutiny.

"It started that way," she admitted softly. "I was hired to act as his girlfriend, to be the hands-on PR person to help fix his image."

Aaron swore as he pushed his food aside. "Jesus, Daphne. You've lived your entire life preaching about integrity, and now you're participating in some fake relationship scheme?"

"It's not fake." The words emerged quietly as her fingers curled around her napkin. "Not anymore."

"Come on," Aaron scoffed, the disbelief evident on his face. "I've seen the kinds of guys you date; you go for guys who are educated, stable, and professional. You really expect me to believe you're genuinely involved with someone who attacks people in parking lots?"

Her brother's dismissal irritated her; she thought he was someone who wanted to find out all the facts before making a decision. Instead, he disappointed her.

"You don't know him," she repeated, her voice strengthening. "You've seen thirty seconds of the worst moment of his career and decided that defines him. You haven't seen his dedication to training, how he mentors younger fighters at his gym, how he respects his coach even when they disagree."

Aaron's eyebrows rose, but Daphne continued before he could inter-rupt. "You haven't seen how he fights to control his temper now, how he's working every day to be better. How he makes me coffee exactly the way I like it without being asked. How he listens, and I mean really listens, when I talk about my day."

"Daph—"

"No, you are going to shut up and let me finish." She leaned forward, meeting her brother's concerned gaze directly. "The man in that video was responding to pain the only way he knew how. The man I know is fighting to become a better person. And he's doing it not just to try and save a career, but because he genuinely wants to be more than what everyone expects of him. And if you had issues with me working and being with him, no offense, but you are eight months too late, Aaron."

Aaron studied her for a long moment, and some of the judgment in his expression changed to confusion. "You care about him," he said finally, the realization evident in his tone.

"I do," she confirmed, but the simple words were inadequate for what she felt.

Their food was forgotten as Aaron leaned back, his brow furrowed as he thought. "I saw the announcement about the upcoming fight." He said after a pause, "That's the same guy from the parking lot video. Doesn't that concern you?"

The question wasn't entirely unfair. She'd had concerns, too, when Kane first told her he wanted to challenge Tony, but she also knew the reason.

"He's different now," she said with quiet certainty. "The fight isn't about pride." She hesitated, then said quietly, "He's doing it to defend me."

Aaron's head tilted slightly. "Defend you? What the hell, Daph..."

"Tony said some..." She paused, trying to think of a polite way to describe what Tony had said. "He's been saying disrespectful things about me to whoever would listen, but the final straw for Kane was a live interview that Tony did, where he said some extremely inappropriate things about me. They were crude, sexual comments, and we know it was done to provoke Kane."

"And that didn't send him on another rampage?" Aaron asked, genuine surprise in his question.

"No," Daphne answered, unable to stop her smile. "Of course, he was pissed, but he handled it differently. We talked about it, and he made sure I was comfortable with it before they issued the challenge." Her eyes lifted to meet her brother's. "Given what you thought when you walked in today, you can't tell me that's the same man that you thought he was from that one video and articles written to put him in a bad light."

Her brother's expression shifted to thoughtful concern, though she could see it linger in his eyes. "You keep talking about him like..."

"Like I love him," Daphne finished when Aaron trailed off. The words were surprisingly easy, considering what they meant. "Because I do."

The words hung in the air between them, Aaron's expression giving way to astonishment.

"Wow," Aaron said finally. "I've never heard you say that about anyone you've been with before. This is really serious for you."

"Because I haven't," she confirmed, relief washing through her as Aaron's hostility eased. "I didn't expect it, but as we spent time together and got to see each other for who we were, what started as a business arrangement became something..." She paused, searching for words. "Something I've never felt before."

Aaron reached across the table to cover her hand with his. The simple movement reminded her of how protective and supportive Aaron was. "I'm still concerned," he admitted. "His history, his outbursts, if you were me, you would feel the same."

"I know," Daphne acknowledged. "But I've seen who he is beneath all that. Aaron, he's terrified of wanting a family because he never had a stable one. He pushes himself because he's afraid failure means he's worthless. But he's someone who struggles every day to be more than what people expect."

Her brother studied her face carefully. He gave a small nod when her expression reassured him. "You've always been a good judge of character," he conceded with a slight smile. "Better than me, if we're being honest.

If you see something in him that's worth loving, then maybe I need to reserve judgment until I've met him properly."

Daphne squeezed his hand, gratitude warming her. "Thank you. That's all I'm asking."

"But," Aaron added, his protective instinct reasserting itself, "if he ever hurts you—"

"He won't," Daphne interrupted with quiet confidence. "That's not who he is." She smiled, "I've never seen any sign of violence or anger at home or with me. In many ways, he's a lot like you."

Aaron chuckled. "Not going to lie, that's kind of ironic." He picked up his fork to point it at her. "I guess I should start preparing myself to meet the man my sister loves. Somewhere without cameras in case I deck him just on principle."

Daphne laughed. "I think that can be arranged," she agreed. She felt lighter after the conversation. She hadn't fully realized it until she said it out loud, but there was no denying it.

She was completely and irrevocably in love with Kane Mitchell.

Chapter Twenty-Nine

T he ECF's media center hummed as technicians adjusted the lighting and sound levels for the pre-fight interview. Kane sat beside Daphne on a small leather couch with his arm around her shoulder. He was relaxed in a way that would have been unimaginable before Daphne. From the edge of the room, Gavin watched him, taking note of the changes in Kane. He no longer saw the barely contained temper or the impatience he was used to dealing with at Kane's previous media appearances. In its place was a focused calm.

"We're live in thirty seconds," the producer announced, and Alicia Chen, a respected sports journalist who would be running the interview, settled into her chair. The lights reflected off her porcelain skin, making her black hair shimmer. She soothed the skirt of her royal blue dress before nodding to Kane and Daphne.

"Remember," Gavin had cautioned them earlier, "they will ask about Alvarez's comments. Don't let it get personal, stay focused on the fight itself."

Now, as the red light on the camera blinked to life, Gavin found himself less concerned about Kane than he expected. He couldn't deny that Kane was different.

"I'm here with Kane Mitchell and Daphne Wilson," Alicia began, her smile warm as she turned to them. "Kane, you're just three weeks away from your highly anticipated match with Tony Alvarez. How are you feeling?"

185

R. KATZE

Kane leaned forward slightly, his hand trailing across Daphne's shoulder to drop to his side. "Training's been excellent. My coach has pushed me to refine my technique and focus on efficiency rather than just power. I feel sharper than I've been in any other match."

"Your last encounter with Alvarez ended, some would say, controversially," Alicia noted, and her black brow rose as Kane smiled.

"I'll admit, not my greatest moment." He chuckled. "That situation taught me valuable lessons about reacting before thinking," Kane acknowledged, his hand finding Daphne's between them on the couch, and she gave his hand a light squeeze. "I'm a different person now. And this match will show that."

Gavin's eyebrows rose slightly at the response. Kane was never that open in interviews; it was part of why the media had focused on his temper and uncontrolled behavior. He wanted to say that some of the media training had gotten through, but he knew that there was more to it than that.

"Daphne," Alicia turned her attention to the woman beside Kane. "Many have attributed Kane's resurgence to your influence. What are your thoughts on it?"

Daphne smiled as she leaned into Kane's side. "Kane's journey has been entirely his own," she said, her tone warm with pride. "I've been lucky enough to be by him to witness it, to support the work he's been doing. The dedication he brings to fighting has always been there."

"The two of you have become one of the sport's most visible and talked about couples," Alicia continued. "How has that affected your relationship, if it has?"

Kane and Daphne's eyes met, and for a moment, it seemed they forgot they weren't alone. It shocked Gavin when Kane answered.

"The public sees only what we choose to share," he said, his voice softer as he smiled at Daphne. "And we are grateful for their support, but honestly, the best moments are the private ones, laughing over coffee, being there for each other, even just being in the same room without saying anything."

Daphne drew their joined hands into her lap. "We've separated the public from our private lives," she added. "We know that it doesn't really matter what people think they know about us, but what we share."

Gavin shifted his weight as it really began to hit him. The affection between them wasn't pretend; it really had become genuine. He had heard Kane say it, but seeing it, really seeing it, was something different.

"I have to address the elephant in the room," Alicia said, her expression growing more serious. "Tony Alvarez has made some particularly crude comments about your relationship and has specifically targeted Daphne. How has that affected you heading into this fight?"

Kane's jaw tightened momentarily, the only visible sign that she had struck a nerve, before he exhaled slowly. "Tony's trying to make this personal because he knows he can't beat me at my best," he responded. "He wants me off-balance in the ring, and I hate to break it to him, that's not going to happen." He paused for a moment before continuing. "I respect Tony as a fighter. But I don't respect how he's approached trying to increase his rank without really earning it. There's a line between competitive trash talk and disrespect, and he crossed it."

"Daphne, how do you feel about being drawn into this situation ?" Alicia asked, turning to address her directly.

"It upsets me if I'm being honest," Daphne replied with a sniff. "It isn't so much what Tony said about me, it's more about how women should be treated. I'm more than just 'Kane's girlfriend'—I'm a woman with my own interests, career, and identity." She smirked before adding, "And I'll be front row to watch Kane win."

"Final question," Alicia said warmly. "What happens after this fight? I know there have been people wondering about Kane's future, and a lot of curiosity about you two."

Kane slid his arm around Daphne as she looked up at him. "You know," he said with a wry smile, "I used to just think about the next fight, the next title I could compete for." He drew Daphne close to rest her head against his shoulder. "But now, there's something I want more than being in the cage. " Whatever comes next," he continued, returning his attention to Alicia while keeping Daphne's hand in his, "it will be together." Sure, the fight with Tony is important both professionally and to shut him up finally, but really it's just one chapter in the story."

Alicia was momentarily stunned by the simple honesty before she recovered to wrap up the segment.

"Thank you both, it's been great speaking with you." She turned to face the camera directly. "I know we and our viewers are looking forward to what we are sure will be an exciting match in three weeks."

As the red light on the camera blinked off, Gavin approached the couch, taking in the way Kane and Daphne remained connected even after the cameras stopped rolling. Kane's arm stayed around Daphne's shoulders as he shook Alicia's hand, thanking her for the opportunity to give the interview.

"That," Gavin said quietly as Alicia walked away, "was not what I expected."

Kane glanced up, a question in his expression. "Problem?"

"The opposite," Gavin clarified. "That was..." He paused. "That was amazing."

Kane pressed his lips to Daphne's hair, and she smiled. "Yeah," he agreed, meeting Gavin's gaze. "It is." With the simple agreement, Kane rose from the couch, turning to offer his hand to Daphne. As she rose, she stepped closer, placing a gentle kiss on his lips, his chasing hers as she drew back.

Gavin watched them as they turned to leave the studio, their hands linking as they walked. He knew Kane would go into the match with a clear mind, and the methodical processing Gavin had seen at Warriors Edge.

And that, he knew, would make Kane even more of a threat in the ring.

Chapter Thirty

"Yeah, I'm watching his socials....No, I don't think we need to respond, just let it play out...Gavin..."

Kane smirked at the half of the conversation he could hear between Gavin and Daphne. He hadn't warned her about how Gavin was after an interview; maybe he should have, but it was amusing listening to her. Gavin was a control freak when it came to his clients, wanting to control every aspect of the story.

Realistically, that shouldn't have surprised her, given how she entered his life in the first place. If you looked up OCD in the dictionary, Kane was sure that a photo of Gavin would be next to it, with the caption 'example A, Gavin Richards.'

The interview had gone well, and that was one of the first times that he could say that. In the past, he had always come away from interviews and press conferences with his stomach churning and pressure in his chest.

"Gavin, I swear to God if you don't..."

Kane could not hold back his laugh at Daphne's exasperated tone. She turned to glare at him for a second before her eyes rolled and her lips twitched into a smile.

"Gavin, you need to chill out..."

"Good luck with that," Kane called out, and Daphne laughed at whatever Gavin had said in response.

"Don't mind Kane, he was just...yeah, you know how he is." Her lips quirked as she raised a brow at him. "Snarky is his default."

"Yeah, yeah, go ahead, make fun of me." Kane groused as he fell back onto the couch with his arms crossed. Daphne let out a small laugh as she moved to his side, placing a kiss against his hair before moving down the hall, continuing the conversation with Gavin.

Kane watched her as she disappeared from view, and his throat went dry. She was the reason it was different. The things that had always terrified him, made him sweat, were easier with her there at his side.

He knew why they were talking; he had seen some of the comments before Gavin had called. While most people were supportive of them, there were a few who seemed to have bought into Tony's bullshit and were trying to rip their interview apart.

Staged. Scripted. Fake.

It wasn't the first time he had seen messages like that, and he knew it wouldn't be the last. There would always be people critical just because of his success, who wanted to try and bring him down to make them feel better about their own shitty existence.

He just hated that they had targeted Daphne too, just because she was with him.

Kane let his head drop to the back of the couch as he took a deep breath. There wasn't anything he could do about the idiots; all he could do was make sure that Daphne knew just how much he cared about her, how much he loved her.

Even though he couldn't make himself say the words.

She was the one good thing in his life, the only thing that was there for him. Sure, he knew Gavin would throw a fit if he heard that and would insist that he was there for Kane, but Gavin made money off of him, so it was different. Even Jackson, the one steady force in his life, was there for business. If Kane walked away from fighting, he doubted he would ever see Jackson again. He hoped he would, because he had come to appreciate his coach's insight and wisdom truly, but there would really be no reason for their paths to cross.

With Daphne, though, he felt...lighter. There was someone to stand with him, to help him when he struggled, to cheer for him when he succeeded because she wanted to, not because she had to. He had meant it in the interview; the best moments were when they were at home, just them, sitting in silence, or sharing a meal and talking about their day. He had never had that before, someone to just *be* with, who didn't want more from him, didn't have expectations that he had to meet.

He could just be Kane.

Sitting on the couch with her snuggled into his side, her sable hair down as they watched whatever show they chose, were perfect moments that he was coming to treasure. Even when they would argue, the spark in her eyes would draw him in, and god help him, but she was hot when she was pissed. Every time her cheeks would flush in anger, he just wanted to grab her and show her.

They had ended a lot of disagreements that way, naked in bed, their bodies entwined. And he wouldn't have it any other way.

He grabbed the remote to turn on the television, wanting to distract himself from the thoughts that had started to run through him.

And one second later, he wished he hadn't, as Tony's smirking face filled his screen. The subtitles on the screen told Kane that Tony was talking bullshit about him again, calling him old as if twenty-eight were ancient.

But when the captions caught Daphne's name, Kane's muscles tightened. He sat rigid as he read Tony's words, saying Daphne looked uncomfortable, that Kane was probably forcing her to be there, when it was clear she didn't want to be.

That one day, Daphne would wake up and realize she was being fed a lie.

Kane felt a block of ice settle in his stomach at the words.

Because in some way, he worried Tony was right.

Yes, Daphne had come into his life because of a PR thing, but that wasn't the reason she stayed. At least, he hoped.

Though part of him did wonder, which was why he hadn't been able to say the three words that would change everything. Not until he was sure.

He knew that he was a lot to deal with. He had learned that early on as a child, first with his dad leaving, and then his mother throwing him out the moment she couldn't get in trouble anymore for it. Jackson was the first person to stay for more than a few years, and that was only because Kane brought money into the gym. Gavin was there because Kane had hired him.

And then Gavin had hired Daphne.

Kane swallowed as bile began to rise in his throat. The tiny seed of doubt, nurtured by his experiences in his childhood, never seemed to fade. The worry that he had done something to push everyone away, that he was so defective that no one wanted to stay with him long term, was so ingrained in him that he didn't know how to stop it.

He had survived his father's leaving. He had survived his mother's leaving. He had made sure that he didn't let anyone else close enough to have that kind of power over him until he had met Daphne. Until he had gotten to know her, to see her, to understand her.

His eyes drifted to the hallway where she had gone, her voice barely audible through the closed door.

He wouldn't survive her leaving, too.

Kane had spent the past ten years making sure he didn't need anyone, making sure he was safe from the pain wanting someone who didn't want you back could cause. And then one girl with her sable hair and brown eyes had shattered that.

He wanted her —wanted to keep her —and that terrified him. Because even though she had said she wanted him, that she thought about him all the time, they hadn't made any promises. He couldn't be sure she would still be there after the one-year term ended in a few short months.

No, he told himself, she would be. She would not leave him —walk away at the end —not now. She wouldn't listen to the shit that Tony was saying and realise that he was right...

He would make sure of it.

Chapter Thirty-One

T he changes were subtle at first, a slight distance during conversations, a distant look in his eyes in the morning. But Daphne couldn't deny that as the fight grew closer, Kane was withdrawing. His entire focus was on the fight, watching videos of Tony's matches to identify tells, hints of his motions. His gray eyes now reminded her of ice when they met hers, but she thought it wasn't her he was withdrawing from, that he was just going into focus mode even more than he had with Carter.

At least, she hoped...

While most would say he was in game mode, she could see the stress on his face. The tightening around his eyes and jaw gave it away. While he wasn't worried about the fight, really, she knew it also mattered more to him than any in the past.

Two weeks before the fight, Daphne woke to find Kane's side of the bed empty, the sheets already cool to the touch. When she stumbled into the kitchen, she saw him there, looking absentmindedly out the window, a protein shake in his hand.

"Morning," she said, keeping her voice light as she moved to pour herself coffee from the brewed pot. "Did you sleep okay?"

Kane took a moment to pull himself out of his thoughts before turning to her. "Fine," he replied, but didn't say any more.

Daphne leaned against the counter as she studied his profile. "I thought we could grab dinner at that Italian place tonight," she suggested, giving him a light grin. "The one with that handmade pasta you liked."

Kane took a long swallow of his shake before frowning. "Can't. I've got an extra training session with Jackson." He finally turned toward her, and she saw the effort he made to soften. "Maybe tomorrow."

But she knew tomorrow would bring another training session. The pattern had established over the past week, and Kane's world was slowly contracting to focus solely on the fight.

She knew...but it still hurt.

"Why are you pulling away," she asked softly. "I know it means a lot to you, but you're disappearing a little more each day."

Kane's eyes met hers, his gaze steady but also troubled. "I need to focus. There's too much at stake."

"I know that," she responded, taking a step closer. "But let me help you. You are only doing this because of me. Let me understand what you're thinking."

He stepped close, physically near her, but she still felt the chasm between them growing.. His hand reached out to brush her cheek before he bent to press his lips against her forehead.

"I need to do this my way," he murmured against her skin, and she could hear the apology in his voice. "I need to be ready."

Before Daphne could respond, he'd stepped past her, heading toward the bedroom to get ready for another day of preparation. She frowned as she watched him disappear, in no way settled by the conversation.

The next morning, Daphne woke to find Kane not just drinking his shake but already dressed and zipping his gym bag. "Kane, it's not even six yet," she murmured groggily as she pushed herself up on one elbow.

Kane glanced at her, his gaze holding hers for a moment as he took her in, but then it was gone. "Sorry, I was trying not to wake you. I'm meeting Jackson at six-thirty. We have a new strategy to refine."

"Will I see you tonight?" she asked, hating that it was now an honest question.

Kane paused at the bedroom door, and she could see his shoulders tense. "Don't wait up," he finally admitted, "I don't know what time I will be back."

After he left, Daphne lay back down on the bed, unable to go back to sleep. This wasn't like Kane—at least, not the Kane she'd come to know. Needing to speak with someone more familiar with him, she reached for her phone. There was only one person she could call.

"Daphne?" Gavin's voice held surprise as he answered after one ring, even that early in the day. "Everything okay?"

"I'm not sure," she admitted as she pushed herself up to sit against the headboard. "I wanted to ask you about Kane. He's...different, and honestly, I'm getting worried about him."

A pause, then Gavin asked cautiously. "Different how, exactly?"

"It's like he's pulling away from everything, including me." She sighed. "The fight seems to be the only thing he thinks of." She realized she was biting her nail and shook her head; it was a nervous habit she thought she had long outgrown, but she still had to force her hand to the side. "Is it normal for him? He wasn't like this when he fought Carter."

Gavin's sigh worried her even more. "Honestly, no," he said after a moment. "That's not Kane's usual pre-fight pattern at all. You saw him with Carter, even though that was slightly different, too. He's confident, at ease. Yes, he's prepping, but remember, he didn't have anyone around him but Jackson before."

"So, this is unusual," Daphne confirmed as a hollow feeling opened in her stomach.

"Yeah," Gavin agreed. "Daphne, I've managed him through every professional fight of his career, and I've never seen him like that."

The confirmation did nothing to ease her nerves. "What do you think it means?"

"I don't know," Gavin admitted. "This isn't just another fight for him, you know that. Alvarez hit him where it hurts, expecting him to come out swinging. But this response..."

196

"It's like he's carrying weight I can't see," Daphne said softly.

"Keep an eye on him," Gavin advised. "He can't afford to burn himself out before he steps foot into the cage."

After ending the call, Daphne curled back onto the bed, her hand resting on the empty side where Kane should have been. Maybe it was naïve, but it bothered her that when you would think Kane would want *more* support, he backed away. Instead, Kane seemed to prefer her not being around, rather than being there to support him.

What worried her, though, wasn't just his withdrawal, but that the fight with Tony had somehow become an obsession, going beyond any personal or professional reasons. There was something in Kane's eyes when he spoke of it, when they went cold, yet they were also seething, that reminded her of why he was so formidable in the cage, and why her brother had concerns.

For the first time, Daphne felt afraid. She wasn't scared of Kane, but *for* him. If he wasn't going to open up to her, she was going to talk to him in his space...make him acknowledge her.

And that meant she was heading to Warriors Edge.

***

The heavy bag swayed violently under the impact of Kane's combination as Daphne stood in the doorway. Sweat poured down his face and soaked through his shirt as he reset his stance without pause, his muscles trembling with fatigue as he launched another pattern of strikes. Jackson watched from the edge of the mat, arms crossed over his broad chest, growing as he took in Kane's movements.

"Enough," Jackson called out as Kane completed the set. "You've done enough for today."

Kane didn't even glance in his direction, just reset his stance and drove another series of strikes into the bag. His breathing was ragged, but he still pushed himself.

"Mitchell!" Jackson's voice sharpened as he stepped closer. "I said that's enough."

Kane paused, one hand coming to rest against the bag to steady himself. For a moment, it looked as though he would listen, but then Kane straightened and resumed his position.

"Again," Kane bit out, and Daphne knew he was commanding his own body.

Jackson moved to position himself between Kane and the bag. "I said enough. You keep going like this, you won't make it to the fight. You'll be too broken down to even step into the cage."

"I need to be ready." Kane's words were low as Daphne crossed to them.

"Ready doesn't mean destroying yourself before you even face Alvarez," Jackson argued. "Fuck, you're training like someone who's trying to punish themselves."

Kane's jaw tightened as his eyes drifted to her. Without uttering a word, he stepped around Jackson and moved to the speed bag in the corner.

"How long has he been at it?" Daphne asked quietly, stopping beside Jackson as they watched Kane begin a sequence of punches against the speed bag.

"Too long," Jackson replied, his voice pitched low so Kane wouldn't hear. "He's been at this today for four hours without any breaks. We were supposed to be technique refinement, not this...whatever this is."

Daphne's eyes never left Kane as she frowned. She could see the fatigue in his movements, but he never stopped. "Has he been like this all week?"

Jackson grunted in response. "It's been getting worse each day this week. He keeps pushing harder, demanding more reps from himself, pushing to the brink. But trying to talk sense into him is like talking to the heavy bag."

The speed bag's rhythm faltered momentarily as Kane faltered slightly, breaking his flow. Frustration flashed across his features before he reset and resumed, forcing his trembling arms into motion.

"Again," he muttered to himself. "Again."

Daphne bit her lip. This wasn't the disciplined training she'd seen with him before, and, beyond his emotional distance, she was worried about him.

"Has he eaten anything since he got here?" she asked as she noticed the way his training shorts seemed to hang looser than usual. The last time she had seen him with anything other than a protein shake had been over a week before, when they had eaten dinner together.

Jackson shook his head. "Protein shake this morning is all I've seen. Says that food slows him down." He sighed, running a hand over his face. "I've been doing this long enough to know when a fighter's pushing toward injury, and he's right on that edge."

Daphne watched as Kane abandoned the speed bag and moved to the pull-up bar. His arms shook as he pulled his body upward through sheer will. Each repetition looked like his arms would give out, yet he continued.

"Kane," Jackson barked, trying to snap him out, "that's it for today. I'm telling you you're done."

"Not done," Kane replied without pausing, his voice flat. "Not ready yet."

"You'll be ready for a hospital bed if you don't," Jackson countered, frustration edging into his voice.

Kane completed one final pull-up, hanging for a moment before reluctantly dropping to the floor with less grace than usual. He stood motionless for a second before visibly forcing his spine straight, his shoulders back.

"Thirty minutes on the treadmill," he said, already moving toward the machines. "Then I'm done."

Jackson stepped into his path again. "No. You're done now. You need food, rest, recovery, or everything you've done so far is wasted." He gestured toward Daphne. "Go with Daphne. Eat something. Be a human being instead of a machine for a few hours."

Kane's gaze finally met Daphne's, and for a moment she knew he really saw her before the curtain drew back over his eyes.

"Fine," he conceded, the word clipped. "I'll be back tomorrow morning at five am."

Jackson nodded in relief. "Six. And we're doing recovery work only, not this Superman thing you concocted."

Kane didn't argue further; he just moved toward the locker room, his steps laced with exhaustion. Daphne exchanged a worried glance with Jackson before following. She stood outside the door, giving Kane a few minutes alone before she entered.

He was seated on a bench, staring at his taped hands as if they belonged to someone else. The sweat still dripped from his hair, but his breathing had slowed to where it sounded almost normal. He didn't look up at her entrance, but she knew he was aware by the slight tensing of his shoulders.

"You know you don't have to follow through with this fight," Daphne said softly as she stood in the doorway.

Kane's head lifted slowly, his gaze finding hers with an intensity that took her breath away. "I do," he replied, his voice low but certain. "It's something I need to do."

"Need to? Or want to?" she pressed, taking a single step forward. "There's a difference."

He rose from the bench then, his movements slow. She could tell how much effort it took him just to stand. When he finally spoke, his tone had lost all its warmth, the sound almost glacial. It was the tightening around his eyes that gave away how he really felt.

"It's both," he said as his eyes met hers. "Both need to and want to." He paused as his eyes closed and his head tipped back. "This means more than any other fight has."

The simple statement lingered in the silence that followed. Before she could ask what, Kane had moved past her toward the showers. The sound of running water followed moments later, and Daphne sighed. She knew why he had entered the fight initially, but she could tell it now went well beyond just defending her honor. She didn't need him to go to this length to do that.

She just needed to know what that 'more' was.

Chapter Thirty-Two

The apartment was quiet except for the sound of Kane's knife against the cutting board. He kept his focus on making sure that every piece of chicken was the right size...mostly to try and distract himself from Daphne's presence. She stood in the doorway as he worked, and it took everything he had to keep his focus on what he was making. He knew she was frustrated, and Hell, even he could tell that they were drifting apart, but he knew that he had a good reason for it.

He just wasn't sure she would feel the same way. But it didn't matter; he knew what he had to do.

What he had to prove.

After he had been forced to leave the gym, he had driven them home in silence. Now he moved through the kitchen the same way, deep in his own head. His muscles protested each movement, but he pushed it aside, just as he had been the past week. It just meant he was getting stronger.

"Can I help?" Daphne asked, and he wanted to say yes, he really did. He had missed just being with her, but she was who he was fighting for, in more ways than one.

Kane shook his head without looking up, his attention never wavering from the cutting board. "I'm almost done."

He knew she was moving through the kitchen, but didn't let himself turn to watch her. He wanted to, he really did, but he also knew if he did, he would be lost. When a bottle of water appeared at his elbow, he forced himself not to glance at her, only letting himself nod in response.

"Kane," Daphne began, and he briefly closed his eyes as he let her voice wash over him. Until she continued, that was. "Why is this fight so important to you?"

He stilled for a moment before finishing the chopping. He knew what she was asking, but he wasn't ready to go there, not then. "It's my comeback," he finally replied, giving her the media answer, even though he knew she would probably see through it.

"That's not it," he was right, she had, "you already proved that with the fight against Carter. Something's driving you, and it's pushing you toward a breakdown."

Kane's jaw tightened, the muscle jumping beneath his skin. He didn't want to go there. Instead, he turned his focus to transferring the chicken to a heated pan, letting the resulting sizzle fill the silence between them.

"What did you mean at the gym?" Daphne continued when he didn't respond. "When you said it meant more than any other fight?"

His eyes remained fixed on the stove rather than turning to look at her. He wasn't sure how to make her understand, how to tell her what was going through his mind. The *fear* wasn't of the fight; he wasn't scared to face Tony and knew he would beat the man easily, but that didn't mean he wasn't scared.

He knew there was tension between him and Daphne now, and that he was the reason it was there. He didn't know how to navigate the feelings he had for her; it was all new to him, and he was probably fucking it all up.

And that was when it struck him. By going to his go-to response, pulling away from others, he was going to push her away, and she would walk away. His heart stuttered at the thought. There was no way he could let that happen, not if he could do something to let her in, to let her see the turmoil that he was fighting.

"At first," he began, before grabbing a bottle of water, needing to wet his suddenly dry throat. "At first, when this arrangement started, did you know that I resented you?" He heard a soft laugh behind him, yeah, he hadn't been subtle about it, had he? "You represented everything I hated about what was happening, because I hate feeling like I am being handled." He flipped the chicken in the pan as he gathered his thoughts. "When I couldn't chase you away, I was just going to get through the year, get my life back on track, and walk away."

He adjusted the heat beneath the pan as he tossed in some broccoli and added garlic. The activity helped keep him from shaking. "Then things changed, or more my view of you did. You became..." he paused, searching for the words as his head tilted to the ceiling, "...real in a way. You weren't just a PR babysitter there to scold me. You were someone who somehow saw past all the defenses to see me."

When he didn't hear any sound from Daphne behind him, he let out his breath and continued. "Then you became the bright point of my life, the good that came after all the struggling, all the fighting." And God had been there, and there had been a lot of fighting. One of his first memories was of his parents screaming at each other before his dad had walked out of their lives for good.

Then, every one of his mother's boyfriends had an issue with him for some reason, and he had grown up trying to avoid beatings or being told he was nothing. "When Tony started making those comments about you, about us—" His voice hardened slightly. "He wasn't just insulting you. He was attacking the one genuinely good thing in my life. The one thing I needed, just for me —not for my rankings or a title, but for me. Something that made my life brighter just by being part of it."

He turned off the burner and transferred the chicken to two plates. The rice cooker beeped, but he made no move to open it, his hands coming to rest on the counter. This was the part he was worried about. He knew Daphne would be supportive, but for twenty-eight years, he had never had anyone to care about his feelings, his vulnerabilities, before. Talking about them made him nervous, but he knew she needed the truth.

"I'm afraid," he admitted finally. "Not of losing the fight, hell I've lost before, I know how to come back from that. I'm afraid of losing everything else." He exhaled slowly before lifting his head to meet her stunned eyes. "Most of all, I'm afraid of losing *you*."

He ran his hand over his face as he let out a groan. "Tony said what I'm sure others think: that this is just a setup, that you're just paid to pretend to care about me in public. Hell, some of them may think you are being paid to sleep with me, which you fucking aren't, at all. Yeah, in the beginning, maybe that was true." His voice trailed off, and he closed his eyes. "...not the paid to sleep with me shit but the being paid to be near me as a babysitter. But now? Now it's so much more than that, you are so much more than that, and I need to show that what we have together isn't something he can tarnish with crude comments or slurs."

He took a half step forward, but then stopped, needing to get it all out now that he had started. "I wasn't expecting you," he continued, "Hell, I tried like Hell to chase you away, but thank God you are more stubborn than I am. Because now I can't imagine what my life would be like without you."

This was the part that was going to hurt. It hurt him to think about it, but he knew she needed to know. It would be better to get it out in the open so she can either confirm or condemn his feelings. The three words lodged in his throat; he couldn't say them until he knew she felt the same. He wasn't that strong.

"I don't want people thinking what Tony was saying is true. Because if enough people believe it..." He paused, swallowing visibly. "Maybe you'd start believing it too."

And there it was, the reason he had pulled away. He needed to show her that he was worthy, that he could stand at her side. If he lost, he was terrified she would look at him with disappointment, as if he were walking away like everyone else in his life. He was for them, fighting to protect the person he cared about the most.

"Every time I step into that cage, I know why I'm fighting." He swallowed. "I fought for rankings, for championship titles. But this time..." He shook his head slightly, struggling to articulate his thoughts. "This time it's about something I never thought I'd have, something I'm not sure I honestly deserve."

His eyes met hers, taking in her wide stare and her partially opened lips. "I'm fighting because you mean more than any of those fights ever did. I'm not fighting because you need defending from an asshole like Tony, but because what we have matters to me more than anything ever has. So, I want to win to show the world how strong we are together. But I *need* to win because it's the only way I know how to protect what we have."

The rice steamer continued to beep softly in the background, their meal forgotten as they stood facing each other across the kitchen.

He had laid it all out for her; he just hoped he hadn't lost her in the process.

Daphne's mouth opened and closed several times, but she didn't say a word in response. Her chocolate eyes were damp, and it made him nervous, unable to handle her tears. When she started to move towards him, her steps were stilted, her eyes never leaving his.

He just needed something from her, something to let him know that she felt the same. He watched her with guarded hope blooming in his chest as she slowly drew closer until she stood before him, tears beginning to fall from her beautiful eyes.

When her arms wrapped around his waist, his eyes closed, his own eyes suspiciously moist as she rested her head against his chest and just held him.

"Kane," she whispered as her fingers spread across the breadth of his back, as if she were anchoring him to her.

For a moment, he remained motionless, frozen by both the hope and the fear that surged through him. Hope that she would stay, fear that she was saying goodbye. When she didn't move, his arms slowly encircled her, and when she pressed herself closer, he let himself tighten his grip as his head dropped to rest against her hair.

"I'm not going anywhere," Daphne's voice was muffled against his chest.

Kane's breath stopped as emotion flashed through him, and his arms tightened even more as he tried to process what she was saying. The fears she was alleviating. Daphne pulled back just enough to look up at him, her damp eyes locking onto him but never leaving his embrace.

"It may have started as a business thing," she acknowledged, her hands moving to rest against his chest. "I won't pretend otherwise. But that's not why I fall asleep in your arms each night."

His eyes searched hers, frantically looking for any sign of...what he wasn't sure, he just knew he hoped he didn't find it.

"When Gavin first told me about this...situation," she smiled, "I was hesitant, sure. I came in to interview for one job and was offered something completely different with more requirements and, yeah, more money, but it would be a lot more intense than anything I could imagine. Then I met you, and honestly, I almost said no." She gave a small laugh as Kane clutched her shirt tighter, not wanting her to pull away. "I knew from how you were acting that day that you were going to be difficult, more than I thought I could handle. I mean, I was just trying to get into the public relations business, and now I was being told it was a hands-on 24/7 thing?" Her hand fell from his chest as she shook her head. "Then you were so adamantly against it, and my temper got the best of me."

A ghost of a smile touched Kane's lips at her honesty. He remembered that meeting, and the one before it when he had bumped into her. There was no question about it; he had been a grade-A prick, but somehow she had stayed.

"But somewhere along the way," Daphne said, her voice softening, "you became more than a client, and it stopped being just a job." Her hand rose to his cheek, and he pressed his face against it, needing the connection as her words calmed the fear that had taken hold of him. "You don't understand how much I care for you. So, people like Tony can say whatever they want," she continued, "we know the truth. You are my choice; one I will choose every day."

Kane turned his head to press a kiss against her palm, his eyes never leaving hers.

"I would tear up the contract right now if you asked me to," she said, and he could hear the sincerity in her voice. "Walk away from the money, the offer, just to be here as the woman who loves you, so don't be scared, I'm not going anywhere."

Her words sent a rush of relief through Kane, followed by the warmth of how much he felt for her. Her words, the honesty in her face, wrapped around him so tightly that he felt surrounded by her. All he knew was that she was the one thing he had never sought, never knew was missing from his life, but now that she was there, his life would be hollow without her.

"Daphne," he breathed, and the single word contained everything he was feeling. In that moment, his focus shifted from the fight with Tony. No matter the outcome, she would be by his side. He didn't need to prove to her that he was worthy; she already knew he was.

Kane moved, one hand lifting to thread gently into her hair as he lowered his head towards hers, and he cherished the way she shifted to meet him halfway. His lips moved against hers with exquisite tenderness, pouring everything he wasn't ready to say into his kiss. Daphne's hands shifted to curl around his shoulders, and he held her closer as the kiss deepened by degrees. The kiss was slow, both desperate for the connection it brought.

When the need to breathe was too strong, Kane reluctantly pulled away, resting his forehead against hers.

"Daphne," he whispered again, and felt her arms wrap around his waist. His lips found hers again, needing to feel her against him, to taste her.

They moved together toward the living room, their dinner forgotten. When Kane reached the couch, he lowered her onto the cushions, his body hovering above hers. He rested his arms next to her head, lowering himself to press against her as she made a soft sound of contentment.

His lips left hers to trace the line of her jaw and to sample the taste of her skin at her neck. He lingered at each point until she was shifting beneath him, small whimpers accompanying the movement. He cherished every sound she made and sought to draw more from her as she gasped and writhed against him. Daphne's hands slid beneath his T-shirt, and in one move, he grabbed the back of the neck and drew it over his head, tossing it to the side. When her fingers began to trace his chest, he groaned. He loved the way her soft touch made him feel and the look of awe in her eyes as she traced the muscles of his torso.

Kane used one hand to undo the buttons of her blouse slowly. As the fabric parted, his lips followed the path of skin that was being revealed to him, worshiping her as he knew she deserved to be. He would spend all night, Hell, the rest of his life if she let him, showing her how much she meant to him.

"You're everything," he murmured to her, glancing up to capture her gaze, his words barely audible. "Everything I never thought I would find."

Their remaining clothing was slowly removed, each item forgotten the moment it was dropped. Kane's hands and lips mapped her body as each part was revealed, touching and tasting as if he wanted to commit her to memory. Daphne arched against him, her arms holding him close as she panted beneath him.

When they were bare, Kane settled between her thighs. He entered her slowly, wanting to feel every moment with her, to always remember how it felt, how *she* felt. His eyes held hers as their bodies connected, and when he was fully seated inside her, he paused. There was no feeling like being wrapped in Daphne's body, feeling her heat, and squeezing his. Daphne's hand rose to his cheek as she smiled at him.

"I'm not going anywhere." She promised, and her words set him free.

He began to move, his hips shifting, responding to the feel of her nails clutching at his back and the way her eyes fluttered shut at the pleasure she was feeling. This wasn't about chasing their release; this was him basking in the knowledge that this amazing woman had chosen him.

Loved him.

Daphne's eyes opened to meet his as she bit her lip, her body tightening around him. The feeling cracked Kane's control, his movements growing faster as need took over. Daphne gasped against his shoulder as her fingers dug into his back.

"Kane...Kane...oh God." She arched in a gasp. "I..."

Kane knew what she needed, even though she hadn't said it. His hand slid between their joined bodies to flick against her clit, and Daphne cried out as he plucked his fingers against her. A moment later, she shattered, her body arching as a soft cry escaped her throat. Kane followed only a second later, whispering her name against her neck. His body shuddered as wave after wave of pleasure pulsed through him, and Daphne cried out again as he felt her shake against him.

He shifted himself to the side, not breaking their connection as he drew her leg across his hip. He held her close as their breathing slowly calmed and their hearts returned to a. Normal rhythm. Kane buried his face against her neck, and Daphne traced idle patterns along his spine. He was okay with not moving; in fact, he never wanted to leave the haven that she presented again.

When Kane finally stirred, he pressed a kiss against her temple before reluctantly withdrawing from her body. Her murmur of protest faded as he gathered her into his arms to lift her from the couch. Her arms wound around his neck as her head fell against his shoulder while he carried her to their bedroom.

The sheets were cool as Kane lowered her onto the bed before joining her, immediately drawing her back against the solid warmth of his chest. His arm curved possessively around her waist, his body curled around hers.

"Sleep," he murmured against her hair, his voice heavy with the physical and emotional exhaustion of the day. "I've got you."

Daphne nestled closer to him, and it struck him once again how much she fit next to him, how right she was. The tension that he had been carrying had drained away completely, leaving only her and his love for her in its place. Whatever tomorrow might bring, this would always be there.

As sleep finally claimed him, Kane's arm tightened around Daphne's sleeping form, drawing her closer against his chest. He finally understood what it meant to have something beyond victory worth returning to.

Chapter Thirty-Three

D usk settled over Philadelphia, the fading light casting long shadows across Kane's living room. He stood at the window motionless, his shoulders both relaxed and tense. In less than twenty-four hours, he would be in the cage with Tony Alvarez.

Behind him, Daphne moved quietly through the apartment, double-checking his gear for the next day. She knew that Kane had entered a mental space where he needed to be left alone to process and prepare.

In the two weeks since their heart-to-heart and reconnection, he had shifted the focus of his training. Rather than push himself to exhaustion, he had been more strategic, working with Jackson on weaknesses and increasing his speed, but never spending the entire day there training.

And every night, he came home to her.

The doorbell's chime cut through the silence, and Daphne flicked her eyes towards Kane. He didn't react; the sound didn't pull his attention from the darkening skyline. She moved to answer the door, but she had a feeling she knew who would be coming to see them this close to a fight.

When the door opened to show Gavin, she knew she had been right. He stepped into the apartment and immediately found Kane at the window. Gavin stopped in the entryway as he assessed the fighter before turning to Daphne.

"How long has he been like that?" he asked, voice low enough not to disturb Kane.

Daphne laughed softly as she closed the door behind him. "He's fine, Gavin. Just focused."

Gavin nodded, though she could see tension in his shoulders that said he wasn't really convinced. He moved toward Kane, opening a leather portfolio that Daphne knew would contain notes on media strategy, post-fight scenarios, sponsor expectations for the match, and all the business needs surrounding a title fight.

"Kane," Gavin began. "We need to go over a few things for tomorrow."

Kane didn't respond, but Daphne saw his shoulders shift and knew that he was listening.

Gavin took out one of the portfolio pages, scanning it before speaking. "The press has been running with the redemption angle, which, while not true, does work in our favor. The official ECF marketing has positioned this as your comeback story, saying that while you have already faced Carter, he is still new. Tony, as an established fighter, is your true return to the ring. They are avoiding the personal aspect altogether in the coverage, but I have to tell you, people are still talking about it." He glanced up to gauge Kane's reaction, but Kane still stood silent.

Gavin let out a little huff before continuing. "I've prepared responses for the post-fight interview, one for if you win, one for if you lose. We need to make sure we don't give them anything that could be interpreted as a setback in your growth." Gavin continued his briefing. He was accustomed to Kane's typical nods in response, but not so much the silence.

"The sponsorship representatives will be ringside," Gavin pressed on. "You will need to acknowledge them briefly during your walkout. It can just be a nod toward their section, but it gives them attention from the coverage, and trust me, there will be a lot of coverage."

Kane remained motionless at the window, his calm visible now that darkness had settled over the city.

Gavin moved to stand beside Kane at the window, close enough to speak directly but not so close as to invade the fighter's space. "I know what this means to you personally," he continued, voice dropping lower. "But you need to remember what it means professionally as well."

For the first time, Kane reacted with a slight turn of his head as his eyes shifted to meet Gavin's gaze. The look lasted only a second, a brief acknowledgment that he had heard, before Kane returned his attention to the view of the city skyline.

Gavin turned toward Daphne, a silent question in his expression, and she responded with a small shake of her head. Kane would emerge from it in his own time; it wasn't something to force.

Gavin collected his portfolio from the coffee table, tucking the papers back into it. As he moved towards the door, Daphne followed, sensing from his glances towards her that he wanted to speak with her.

"He'll be ready," she said quietly as they reached the entryway.

Gavin studied her face before glancing back to the man standing stoically by the window. "You know, I've worked with him for years, I've never seen him like this."

"Were you ever there with him the night before the fight?" Daphne countered softly. "You need to trust him, Gavin. He'll be ready to face Tony."

After a moment's hesitation, Gavin nodded. "Call me if anything changes," he said, hand already on the door handle. "Otherwise, I'll see you both at the venue tomorrow."

As the door closed behind him, Daphne remained in the entryway for a moment with her thoughts before returning to the living room. Kane hadn't moved, his silhouette outlined against the window. She crossed the room with quiet steps, joining him by the darkened glass. For a moment, she simply stood beside him, sharing his view of the city spread below them.

She shifted to place her fingers against the small of his back, the touch just a connection with him. Kane didn't turn immediately, but she felt him lean into her touch, and she moved closer to him to slip her arm around his waist.

"You don't have to talk," she said softly. " I'm here. Whatever you need tonight, space, silence, conversation, it's yours."

He stayed quiet, but his arm lifted to curve around her shoulders, drawing her more securely against his side, the simple gesture an acknowledgment of her place beside him.

When Kane finally spoke, his voice was roughened by hours of silence. "I used to do this alone," he admitted. "Before every fight, I'd be standing somewhere, looking out at the city, reminding myself that beyond the cage there's a world that continues regardless of whether I win or lose."

Daphne remained quiet as she listened.

"It used to help me get everything into perspective," he continued after a moment. "The reminder that while a loss could end my career, it wasn't the end of the world." His arm tightened around her shoulders. "It's different this time."

He turned to face her fully, and his eyes found hers.

"This time, for the first time in my life, what happens in that cage tomorrow matters less than what's waiting for me after," Kane told her. "This time, I know that win or lose, you'll still be here. And that's..." He paused, searching for words adequate to the feeling. "That's something I never had before. Someone to be there with me." His hands moved to her cheeks, and the feel of his calloused fingers against her skin made her smile. His lips parted as if preparing to say more, but the words didn't come. Instead, a shadow passed across Kane's face. His hands dropped from her face to rest at her waist as his gaze lowered momentarily.

Daphne understood. He had spent his life avoiding being vulnerable and never had anyone he could truly rely on to be there just for him. Everyone in his life was tied to his fighting career and had that first in mind, so having someone on his side was new. She could only imagine how uncomfortable it was for him.

Before she could respond, Kane pulled her against him, his arms coiling around her waist to eliminate the space between them. His face dropped to her hair as he held her, letting it say the words he couldn't.

Daphne's arms wrapped around him in return. A slight tremor went through him at her touch. And she knew he was drawing strength from her.

"I know," she whispered against his shoulder, answering the unspoken emotion in his embrace.

His arms tightened around her, the brief increase in pressure acknowledging her understanding. He continued to hold her as her hand ran up and down his spine.

Their embrace was broken by a sudden spike of noise from the television Daphne had forgotten was on. The sports network logo flashed across the screen as the broadcaster's voice boomed. "And now, just hours before tomorrow's highly anticipated matchup, we are joined live by Tony Alvarez." Kane's body tensed as Tony's face filled the screen. He sat in what appeared to be a luxury hotel suite, the ECF logo strategically visible on the wall behind him.

"Tony, you're just hours away from facing Kane Mitchell in what many are calling the most anticipated comeback fight of the year. How are you feeling?" the interviewer asked.

Tony leaned back in his chair; his arms spread across its back. "I'm feeling great, man. Ready to show everyone that Mitchell's career should have stayed buried." His smile widened, and it almost reminded Daphne of a shark. "You know, a lot of people forget that before the girlfriend makeover, Mitchell was just a hothead with little skill, inside or outside the cage."

Kane's breathing changed, becoming more measured even as she felt his heart begin to pound. His arms remained around her, but his attention was now on the screen.

"Speaking of Mitchell's girlfriend," the interviewer continued, eager for something controversial that would get him more views, with that lead-in. "You've made some comments about Daphne Wilson that have raised eyebrows and received disapproval across the fighting community. Would you care to address those remarks?"

Tony's laugh made Daphne's skin crawl. "Look, I just call things how I see them. Everyone knows their relationship started as damage control after Mitchell lost his shit in that parking lot." He shrugged, but Daphne could see it was strategic nonchalance. Whichever PR rep worked with Tony had trained him well. "If he wants to hire someone to play at being his girlfriend to convince everyone he's somehow changed, that's his business. But tomorrow night in that cage, there's no one to manage him. It will be just him and me, and the world will see who's really the better fighter and who deserves that championship belt."

Daphne pulled back slightly from their embrace, needing to see Kane's face. His jaw was tight, the muscle beneath the skin jumping slightly, but his eyes remained steady, focused as he watched Tony continue speaking.

"Kane," she said softly, and his eyes shifted to meet hers. Without breaking that gaze, he reached for the remote on the nearby end table and silenced the television with a single press of his thumb. Tony's face continued to smirk from the screen, but neither paid it any more attention.

"Forget him," she said quietly.

Kane's hand trailed down her neck. "Don't worry," he assured her.

Daphne nodded, pride warming her chest. "Tomorrow you'll kick his ass," she said, absolute faith in her voice. "And after the fight, whatever happens, we'll come back here, and Tony Alvarez won't matter."

Kane's arm tightened around her waist as he swallowed. "After the parking lot fight, and how that blew up," he whispered, "I honestly thought my career might be over, that there was no coming back from it as sponsors walked away and the ECF considered suspending or even releasing me. I know that's what Tony was gunning for, get the stronger fighters taken out, no matter what it took."

"Maybe Tony will learn something tomorrow," Daphne murmured, a slight smile curving her lips. "About the risk of underestimating you."

Kane's answering smile held a predator's confidence. "Maybe," he agreed, though his tone suggested he cared less about that than defeating Tony in the cage.

Without another word, he drew her back into his embrace, and her hands slid up to link behind his neck. The television continued its silent broadcast, and fight promos and analyst predictions eventually replaced Tony's face, but all they focused on was each other.

Daphne closed her eyes, settling deeper into Kane's embrace. The city might buzz with anticipation, but couldn't touch them.

And tomorrow Kane would show them all that he was truly the better fighter.

Chapter Thirty-Four

T he early morning light filtered through the high windows of Warrior's Edge Gym, casting long rectangles across the blue mats where Kane moved through a series of warm-ups, each one flowing into the next. Anticipation seethed through him, but he kept it contained. Fight day had arrived, and he let out a breath as he finished stretching. Where once his mind had been a roaring chaos of emotion, the pressure of expectations, and the desperate need to prove himself, now there seemed to be whatever he could only imagine was peace.

This calm had not come easily. When he had woken at dawn, Daphne was still asleep. He had spent thirty minutes in meditation before slipping from the apartment with only a gentle kiss to her forehead.

Across the gym, Jackson checked his watch, then approached with determined steps. His face revealed nothing as he stopped a few feet from Kane, arms crossed over his broad chest as he studied his fighter.

"How's the weight?" he asked, his gruff voice pitched low for privacy.

"On point," Kane replied, the words emerging with none of the tension that had once characterized his fight-day communications. "One eighty-one point five this morning."

Jackson nodded once, satisfied. "Hydration?"

"Following the protocol exactly. Electrolytes at six, water intake measured."

Jackson's eyes narrowed slightly as he searched Kane's face for signs of any pre-fight jitters. When he found none, he exhaled slowly.

"Your timing on the combinations yesterday was perfect," Jackson said, shifting to a technical assessment. "Remember what we discussed about Alvarez's tendency to drop his right when he circles left. He'll be looking for your counter hook, so your feint when you use it needs to be convincing."

Kane nodded, his eyes sharpening. "His tell before the right uppercut is more pronounced when he's tired. The shoulder dips about two centimeters lower than his normal guard."

"Good, I was hoping you'd noticed that," Jackson acknowledged.

"I watched his fight against Garcia sixteen times," Kane replied, "plus his last three training videos. It's been consistent in all of them."

A half-smile touched the corner of Jackson's mouth before disappearing. This approach —the cold, methodical breakdown of an opponent —was something Jackson had been trying to get Kane to do for years. Now, instead of just relying on a combination of skill, rage, and luck, Kane was bringing his intelligence to the prep, and in Jackson's mind, that was far more dangerous to an opponent.

The door at the gym's entrance swung open, and Kane turned as Gavin entered first, a leather portfolio tucked beneath one arm and a phone pressed to his ear as he conducted last-minute business.

But behind him was Daphne, and he straightened. The dark jeans and a deep blue blouse she was wearing emphasized her curves, and her hair was pulled back in a simple style that highlighted her face. She didn't have any of the flashy fight-night attire that some of the fighter groupies would wear, and she looked perfect.

Kane's eyes found hers across the gym, and his chest loosened at the sight of her. Her lips curved into a small smile, the expression conveying her confidence without words.

Gavin ended his call as they approached, tucking the phone into his jacket pocket with practiced efficiency. "Car's waiting outside," he announced, glancing at his watch. "Media check-in is at four, walkout preparation starts at six-thirty. Everything's on schedule."

Kane nodded once, acknowledging the information without shifting his attention from Daphne. She stepped closer, careful not to touch him. She had been warned about his need to focus before the match, but she was still letting him know she was by his side.

"Ready?" she asked simply.

The question carried layers of meaning. At one time, Kane might have responded with bravado, but now he just held her gaze, allowing her to see his quiet confidence. "Yes," he replied, and the single syllable rang with certainty.

Jackson cleared his throat, and Kane finally looked away from Daphne. "Gear's already packed. Final check on tape and wraps at the arena." He gestured toward the door with a tilt of his head. "Let's move."

Kane gathered his hoodie from a nearby bench, slipping it on as they moved toward the exit. Daphne fell into step beside him, close enough that he could sense her presence without looking. Gavin led the way, his phone already back at his ear while Jackson brought up the rear.

At the door, Kane paused briefly, glancing back at the gym. This place had witnessed some of his worst moments of uncontrolled rage, and now his growth into something more. The blue mats and the hanging bags had seen countless hours of preparation, yet it all felt different now. Now, the gym wasn't his sanctuary, and it made him see it differently.

Daphne waited beside him, patiently. When he turned back to her, something in his expression softened. "Let's go," he said quietly, and together they stepped through the door into the bright afternoon light.

Chapter Thirty-Five

T he locker room at 2300 Arena had its own rhythm, the snap of athletic tape, the squeak of shoes against the concrete, and the murmured instructions between coaches and fighters. Kane sat motionless on a bench in the corner, his back straight, hands resting palm-up on his thighs. Unlike the other fighters who paced or bounced or chattered with nervous energy, he was still.

Jackson knelt before him, wrapping Kane's hands. It was a ritual they had performed together before every professional fight. The white tape spiraled around Kane's wrists, wrapping around his fingers and across his knuckles. Neither man spoke during this process.

Around them, the arena support team moved with quiet efficiency, arranging gear, checking equipment, and coordinating with event staff through their crackling radios. Gavin had disappeared fifteen minutes earlier, needing to work the media. His final instructions to Kane were brief: "Be yourself out there. Not who they expect, but who you've become."

As Jackson pressed the final piece of tape into place, Kane flexed his fingers, testing the wrap's tension and support. Perfect. Jackson's eyes met his, the older man's face revealing a subtle pride.

Jackson stood, rolling his shoulders as he prepared to give his traditional pre-fight talk. Kane had heard versions of this speech before every match. Today, however, something gave the older man pause.

"You don't need the speech today, do you?" Jackson asked, and Kane could hear the amusement in his gruff voice.

Kane's lips curved slightly in acknowledgment. "I know what I need to do."

Jackson nodded. "Alvarez throws wild when he's frustrated. Hooks get sloppy, chin comes up."

"Third round against Mendez," Kane confirmed. "Left himself open after missing the combination."

"His ground defense favors—"

"The right side," Kane finished. "Protects the liver but exposes the ribs on the left. Transitions telegraph when he's setting up submissions."

Jackson's eyebrows rose slightly, impressed. "You've done your homework."

"I always do," Kane replied, his voice steady. "The difference is now I'm using it."

The observation drew another nod from Jackson. He extended his hand, palm up, offering a container of petroleum jelly that Kane accepted. As Kane applied it to his face, focusing on areas prone to cuts, his mind catalogued Tony's patterns.

Tony relied on explosive movement in the first round to tire his opponent, then tended to conserve energy in the second before pushing for a finish in the third. His right cross followed a slight shift of weight to his back foot; his takedown attempts were predictable when his striking failed to land cleanly. Most importantly, Kane knew Tony fought with ego and the need to dominate. It was this that Kane intended to exploit.

A production assistant appeared at the doorway, clipboard in hand. "Five minutes to walk out, Mr. Mitchell."

Kane stood, rolling his neck in a final release of tension. Jackson moved around him, checking him over one last time as Kane put on his gloves, stretching his fingers to test the fit. They both knew that championships could be won or lost in the gear and how it fit.

"Remember," Jackson said as he finished and handed Kane his mouthguard. "Control the pace. You make him fight your fight, not his."

Kane nodded once. The corridor outside the locker room stretched before him as they stepped out of the locker room, and he put his mouthguard into place. The crowd's energy reached him in waves as he began the walk.

Kane felt himself settle the closer he moved. The commentary from the broadcast booth, crowd reactions to the video packages playing on the massive screens, and the heavy bass of his walkout music barely registered.

As the tunnel widened into the arena proper, a wall of sound and light hit him. His name erupted from the announcer's booth, carried through speakers that surrounded the venue, and the response from the crowd vibrated through the concrete beneath his feet. Kane moved forward at a measured pace, nodding briefly towards where his sponsors sat. Unlike previous fights where he had played to the audience as he entered, trying to hype up the crowd even more, tonight he was focused on the center of the arena.

The octagon stood illuminated, its chain-link walls containing the space where it would all end, one way or another. As Kane approached, his eyes scanned the first rows surrounding the cage, seeking the one face he cared about among the thousands.

He found her right where she had promised to be, in the third row, directly behind his corner. Unlike the screaming fans around her, Daphne offered no dramatic gesture of support for cameras to capture. Instead, when their eyes met across the distance, she simply held his gaze with unwavering confidence. Kane felt that confidence settle around him like the final piece of armor sliding into place.

As he climbed the steps into the cage, he carried with him the clarity that had come from understanding what truly mattered beyond victory or defeat, Jackson following close behind.

The fight official checked him one final time to make sure his gloves, mouthguard, and shorts were in order before opening the gate for him. Kane stepped through, his focus narrowing as he entered the space. This cage was where he had always felt most comfortable. But tonight, he knew he was defined by the life he was building, not just what happened in the arena.

Across the cage, Tony bounced on the balls of his feet, his expression filled with aggressive confidence as he performed for the cameras, tracking his every move. Kane simply moved to his corner, a stark contrast to his opponent. The difference between them went far beyond fighting styles or techniques. He and Tony had fundamentally different understandings of what the night truly represented.

For Tony, this was about dominance, about public vindication.

For Kane, it was a demonstration of growth beyond the limitations that had once defined him.

The referee gestured both fighters to the center of the octagon, his expression stern. Kane moved forward, his focus absolute as he took his position opposite Tony. The space between them hummed with tension. It went beyond the normal adrenaline of a fight, fueled by months of insults and provocations. Tony's eyes burned with hatred, his body language designed to intimidate. But Kane just met the other man's gaze with detachment.

"I want a clean fight," the referee instructed. "Obey my commands at all times. Protect yourselves at all times. Touch gloves if you want."

Tony extended his gloves with a smirk that promised punishment, leaning close enough to whisper: "Is your girlfriend watching? I hope she enjoys seeing what a real fighter looks like."

Once, the taunt would have triggered an immediate response, and Kane's technique would have been compromised as he retreated to rely on punishing power. Now, he simply touched gloves with Tony, his expression unchanged as he stepped back to his corner. The lack of any reaction seemed to disturb Tony, and Kane saw a flicker of uncertainty pass through Tony's eyes before his confidence reasserted itself.

The bell rang, and Tony exploded forward immediately, throwing a high kick that whistled past Kane's ear as he slipped to the side with millimeters to spare. The attack continued with a flurry of punches aimed at overwhelming. Kane's defense was tight as he evaluated every move rather than reacting.

A right hook slipped through his guard, the blow connecting with his temple with enough force to momentarily daze him. The crowd erupted as Tony pressed his advantage, following the hit with a combination that drove Kane toward the cage wall. Each impact of Tony's gloves only registered as data as Kane took in the angle of Tony's shoulders, the slight drop in his shoulder before his left uppercut, and noted the momentary overextension after his cross.

"That's one, Mitchell!" Tony taunted between strikes, his voice carrying over the crowd's excitement. "I guess you're getting slow in your old age!"

Kane's breathing was controlled despite the hits. When Tony paused to reset his position, Kane countered with a precise jab that snapped his opponent's head back, creating just enough space to circle away from the wall. That set a pattern that continued through the first round—Tony attacking with combinations that occasionally broke through Kane's defense, while Kane adapted, landing fewer but more precise counters.

By the round's end, Kane had a cut above his right eye, and Tony's confidence had grown visibly with each successful hit. As Kane returned to his corner, he could see the concern in Jackson's face as he immediately wiped off the blood.

"He's faster than his footage showed," Kane said, his breathing already returning to normal as Jackson worked on the cut.

"He's putting everything into this round," Jackson replied, pressing the metal enswell against Kane's swelling eye, the cold helping to ease it. "He's burning through trying to make a statement. You see it?"

Kane nodded once. "His left shoulder drops before the hook, and he leaves his right side open after the combination."

Jackson's eyes narrowed as he applied petroleum jelly to the cut. "He expects you to fight angry. He's waiting for you to lose control."

"I know," Kane replied, a cold certainty in his voice. "He won't get what he's looking for."

The bell signaled the end of the break, and Kane rose, his mind already working out adjustments. Across the cage, Tony was again bouncing, playing to the crowd with raised arms, inviting their cheers with the confidence of a man who believed victory was already within his grasp.

As the second round began, the subtle shift in Kane's approach was invisible to casual observers but immediately apparent to those who understood the technical aspects of fighting. He adjusted his stance slightly, inviting specific attacks by presenting carefully crafted openings, then countered them with strikes that targeted the weaknesses he knew Tony had.

Tony landed a heavy leg kick that Kane absorbed, following it with the left hook that had been effective earlier. This time, though, Kane slipped it and countered with a right cross that connected with Tony's jaw. The impact stopped Tony's forward momentum, surprise registering in his eyes.

"That's all you got?" Tony taunted, but his voice lacked conviction, and his breathing was noticeably heavier.

Kane didn't respond; he only pressed forward with a combination that forced Tony to retreat. The audience could see that the dynamic had shifted. Kane now controlled the center of the octagon as Tony could only circle the perimeter. When Tony attempted a takedown out of desperation, Kane grabbed Tony's legs, sending the man crashing to the floor.

The crowd's energy went crazy as the round progressed. Tony's attacks grew increasingly wild, his movements now driven by frustration.

Each failed attack drained him further, while Kane maintained the same measured pace.

With forty seconds remaining in the round, Kane saw the pattern he had been waiting for. Tony was overextending on a right cross, his left hand dropping to compensate. Kane feinted a jab then slipped to the outside of the punch, delivering a left hook that connected with Tony's exposed jaw.

The impact reverberated through the arena, a clean connection that snapped Tony's head to the side. His eyes glazed as they rolled into he back of his head. A second later, Tony hit the mat, his body limp against the canvas—the referee dove between them, waving off the fight with emphatic gestures that signaled a clean knockout.

The official announcement echoed through the arena. "WINNER BY KNOCKOUT, KANE MITCHELL." The stadium erupted, thousands of voices filling the arena. The fight officials swarmed around Kane, attempting to guide him through the customary post-fight events, but his eyes scanned the crowd to meet Daphne's gaze straight on.

The victory, sweet as it was, paled in comparison to what awaited him outside the cage. The thrill that had once been his primary motivation now felt hollow compared to the anticipation of returning to Daphne, to the life they were building together. In defeating Tony, he had proven something important about his evolution as a fighter. As necessary as the fight had felt, it was merely a milestone. For the first time in his career, Kane stood victorious in the cage and understood that what made the win meaningful wasn't the professional accolade, but the person waiting for him when the cameras stopped rolling.

Daphne stood, her eyes never leaving his, even as the crowd celebrated around her. An ECF official appeared at Kane's elbow, clipboard in hand, to get Kane to the interview room. "Sir, we need you for the post-fight interview first, then medical, then the press conference in thirty—"

"Not now," Kane interrupted, his voice calm as he moved toward the cage door. The referee was still raising his hand, the ceremonial acknowledgment of victory, but his mind had already moved beyond it. Jackson intercepted him at the cage door, his face split by an uncharacteristic grin. "Beautiful work," he began, reaching for Kane's shoulder. "That counter in the second round was exactly what we—"

Kane met his coach's eyes. "I need to go to her," he said simply, and Jackson's expression morphed from professional pride to personal understanding.

The older man studied him for a moment, then nodded once, stepping aside. "Go," he said.

Kane descended the cage steps, moving through the security personnel and officials who were approaching. Several reached for him to try and direct him towards the media room, but something in his expression caused them to pause just long enough for him to pass.

The crowd's energy shifted as he entered the audience. Phones appeared in dozens of hands, cameras swiveling to capture him, but Kane registered none of it. His focus was narrowed to one person.

Daphne watched his approach with widening eyes. Around her, a ripple of awareness spread as people realized where he was heading. The man beside her nudged his companion, pointing, his words lost beneath the arena's persistent roar, but it could have only been one thing. Kane Mitchell, who had just delivered one of the most technically impressive knockouts of his career, was ignoring every post-fight protocol to make his way to his girlfriend.

Security personnel materialized at the barrier separating the floor from the audience seating, their expressions conflicted as they debated whether they should stop him. Kane didn't slow down, vaulting over the barricade with ease.

As he landed on the other side, he found himself surrounded by fans, their hands reaching to touch him, as voices calling his name, and he was vaguely aware of the phones capturing the moment. Kane ignored them all as he prowled through them, his gaze locked onto his target.

Daphne stood motionless as he approached, her chest rising and falling more rapidly with every step he took. When he reached her, the surrounding crowd receded, creating a small pocket of space around them. Kane wasn't sure if it was because of his energy or desire to watch what unfolded, but right then, he didn't care. For a moment, they stood amid the chaos, neither speaking.

Then Kane moved, closing the distance with a single step, his hands coming to frame her face. His eyes held hers with an intensity that communicated everything before words could form. Without hesitation, he pulled her into a kiss that tried to tell her everything. It was raw, a declaration of his emotions. Daphne responded instantly, her arms circling his neck as she rose slightly on her toes to meet him fully, her body fitting against his.

The crowd's reaction washed over them as cheers, whistles, and the electronic clicks of countless phones captured the moment, but neither gave any notice to the people around them; they were lost in each other. Kane's arms encased her waist, lifting her as the kiss deepened.

Kane didn't release her when they finally separated, wanting to keep her close as he lowered his head until his lips were beside her ear. His breath was warm against her skin, his words pitched low enough that only she could hear.

"I love you."

Daphne stiffened momentarily in surprise; her jaw dropping before her eyes began to tear up. She drew back just enough to see his face, her hands rising to his hair as she searched his eyes.

"I love you too," she whispered, her voice steady despite the emotion that was tightening her throat.

At her words, Kane's face lost all tension as he broke into a large smile. For a man accustomed to fighting alone, used to having to stand firm, admitting he was in love should have been terrifying. But all he felt was strength knowing that this amazing woman chose to love him back.

Kane claimed her lips with another kiss, this one softer, but it carried no less meaning. Around them, camera flashes erupted, capturing the moment from dozens of angles. He was sure that videos would soon be played on every sports website and social media platform. The triumph of his knockout victory over Tony Alvarez, paired with the confession, would dominate attention. Yes, Daphne had entered his life for a job, as part of an attempt to fix his image. But that was just fate bringing them together.

When they finally separated enough to acknowledge their surroundings, the chaos was immediate. Reporters who had abandoned their assigned positions pressed forward, shouting questions that overlapped into the cacophony.

"Kane! Was this planned or spontaneous?"

"Daphne! Was there any truth to the claims that this was just a PR arrangement?"

"Are you two officially together now?"

"Kane! What about the post-fight interview?"

Kane's arm remained firmly around Daphne's waist, anchoring her against him as if she might disappear if he loosened his hold. His other hand rose in a gesture indicating his disinterest in engaging with the media frenzy. He had no desire to be part of the typical post-fight spin and media frenzy. He did not need to grow his reputation or try to give himself a bigger name. All he needed was right there in his arms.

His dismissal stunned the reporters into silence.

Daphne's hand rested against his chest, feeling the steady rhythm of his heart beneath her palm. For once, she wasn't trying to direct him to the press. She was just there, in the moment with him. And that was what he needed.

From the edge of the crowd, Gavin watched with an amused expression. Beside him, Jackson stood with arms crossed over his broad chest, a rare smile softening his features.

"I should be having a heart attack right now," Gavin chuckled. He knew there would be some fallout from Kane's abandoning protocol. "His sponsors will have questions, and the ECF board will want explanations. The media circuit is completely derailed."

Jackson's laugh had a warmth rarely heard from the coach. "And yet you're standing here looking like a proud father instead of a panicked agent."

Gavin's lips twitched toward a smile he couldn't quite suppress. "Because that," he said, nodding toward Kane and Daphne, "isn't the performance we arranged months ago. That's something real." He shook his head slightly, wonder creeping into his tone. "In twenty years of public relations, I've never seen someone actually find themselves through one of these arrangements. They've always. been temporary solutions, not..." He gestured vaguely, searching for words.

"Not real growth," Jackson finished for him, understanding evident in his tone. His eyes remained on Kane as he watched his fighter draw Daphne in for another kiss. "He's fought better tonight than I've ever seen him fight, and now I understand why. He wasn't just fighting for himself anymore."

The crowd around Kane and Daphne began to part slightly as security personnel finally established a semblance of order, creating a path for the two to exit. Kane noticed the opening immediately, and with his arm still securely around Daphne's waist, he guided her down the cleared path, never moving his arm from around her waist.

The questions continued to follow them as reporters called for statements, fans cried for acknowledgment, and fight officials tried — and failed — to get Kane to speak to reporters. It was all background noise; his attention focused on the woman beside him.

Kane drew Daphne to a halt as he lowered his forehead to rest against hers, needing the contact. His thumb traced a gentle path along her back as they stayed still.

"I meant it," he said quietly, his voice only for her despite the dozens of microphones that strained to capture their words. "It wasn't adrenaline, and a heat-of-the-moment thing. I love you."

Daphne smiled. "I know," she replied, certainty in her voice. "You've been saying it every day with your actions."

A slight smile touched the corner of Kane's mouth at how thoroughly she had come to understand him. "Let's go home," he breathed.

Home. The thought had always just been a place to sleep between training sessions, serving his professional needs without any emotional significance. But somewhere in the months since Daphne had entered his life, the meaning had shifted. Home was no longer defined by walls but by her. She was his home.

Security personnel established a clear corridor to the backstage area, allowing Kane and Daphne to leave the press of the crowd. Gavin and Jackson fell into step behind them, creating a buffer between the couple and the crowd. Kane kept his arm around Daphne's waist. She was his, and he was going to hold onto her for as long as she let him.

On another day, the chaos would continue. Interviews would need to be rescheduled, and he would need to explain why he had done what he did. Tomorrow would bring its own challenges, but for now, Kane had found something he'd never expected, not just victory in the cage, but a home in the truest sense, and a woman who had seen beyond the fighter to the man he was.

EPILOGUE

T he polished maple floor of Warrior's Edge Gym gleamed under the bright overhead lights, a far cry from the worn mats and peeling paint it used to have. Kane moved with grace across the octagon, his body still carrying the powerful build of his fighting days, but now he moved with a different kind of confidence. He circled the young fighter before him, eyes narrowed in assessment only, his hands raising to demonstrate the proper defensive stance to the man.

"Again," Kane instructed. "Your weight is still shifting too early. You're telegraphing the kick before you throw it."

He studied the young fighter that he was working with. Andrew Winters was one to watch. At nineteen, his 6'2" frame was already built with contained power. His blond hair dusted into his blue eyes. If the kid got the technique down, he could go far. He was raw talent wrapped in frustration. Andrew nodded once before resetting his stance. Sweat darkened his shirt and plastered blond hair against his forehead, evidence of the work they'd already spent working on the same sequence. Andrew's eyes burned with an intensity that Kane recognized. This kid wanted it, and Kane would help him get it.

"I almost had it that time," Andrew bit out with a defensive edge that made Kane's lips twitch.

"Almost isn't enough in the cage," Kane replied. "Almost gets you knocked out." He stepped closer, adjusting the younger man's elbow.

"The difference between victory and defeat isn't just power or speed. It's control. Discipline."

The gym hummed with afternoon activity around them: fighters working heavy bags, the rhythmic slap of jump ropes against the floor, and the sound of sparring sessions supervised by assistant trainers Kane and Jackson, who had carefully selected them.

What had once been a gritty, underground training facility had transformed into one of Philadelphia's premier fighting academies. In the past five years, its walls had become adorned with championship belts and framed photographs that chronicled not just Kane's career but the successes of fighters who had come after him.

Kane's own championship belt from the fight against Tony hung in a place of honor near the entrance as a reminder of the moment everything had changed for him.

"Watch," Kane instructed, stepping back to demonstrate the combination again. Despite having retired from competition two years ago after successfully defending his title twice, his body still moved with precision, each strike flowing into the next.

"See how my weight stays balanced until the last possible moment?" he explained, slowing the movement to highlight the subtle shift of his body. "Nothing is wasted; nothing is revealed until it's too late for your opponent to counter."

Andrew observed, his frustration forgotten as he absorbed the demonstration. Kane recognized himself in Andrew's gaze and remembered the desperate need to prove himself as he watched the raw talent not yet fully harnessed by discipline and took in the simmering aggression that could either fuel greatness or destroy the kid.

"You fight like you've got something to prove to everyone watching," Kane stepped back to give Andrew space as he reset to try the combination again. "That was me once. Fighting angry. Fighting scared if I'm honest, though I'd never have admitted it at the time."

Andrew's eyes flashed. "I'm not scared of anyone in that cage."

"Maybe not," Kane acknowledged with a slight nod. "But there are worse things to fear than your opponent. Failure. Meaninglessness. The possibility that all your sacrifice might mean nothing." He held Andrew's gaze, his own expression reflective. "It took me years to realize those were my real opponents."

From the edge of the training area, Daphne watched the exchange with one hand resting lightly on the pronounced curve of her seven-month pregnant belly. The afternoon sunlight streaming through the high windows caught the diamonds on her left hand. Kane had placed the emerald-cut engagement ring on her finger four years ago, and the platinum wedding band two weeks later, as neither had wanted to wait. Her brown hair was gathered in a simple ponytail, and she had her suit jacket hanging over one arm. She had just come from Richards PR Management, where she now worked as a partner..

She smiled as Kane demonstrated another combination; the patience in his instruction would have been unimaginable when they met. Their journey had been filled with challenges and adjustments as they both learned to balance their own ambitions with each other. Their connection had only deepened through the years.

Kane caught her eye across the gym, his expression warming instantly. The look still sent a flutter through her. He nodded once before returning his attention to his student.

"Try again," Kane instructed Andrew. "This time, I want you to concentrate on the transition between movements. Fighting isn't just about stringing techniques together. It's about flow, you need to move from one position to the next with purpose."

Andrew nodded as determination replaced frustration as he reran the combination. This time, the execution came closer to Kane's demonstration. It still wasn't perfect, but it showed the first hint of understanding rather than just imitating.

"Better," Kane acknowledged. "But we're not done. Give me twenty more repetitions and focus on that weight transfer we talked about."

As Andrew began the drills, Kane stepped back slightly, his stance shifting from instructor to observer. Jackson approached from the other side of the gym.

"He reminds me of someone," Jackson commented dryly, coming to stand beside Kane as they both watched Andrew.

Kane's mouth curved. "Stubborn. Talented. Convinced he already knows everything."

"Sound familiar?" Jackson chuckled.

"Every day," Kane admitted, his gaze drifting briefly back to Daphne before returning to Andrew. "But he's got potential, if he can learn to channel that energy instead of being consumed by it."

Jackson nodded. "Then it's a good thing he's got someone who understands that journey firsthand." He clapped Kane once on the shoulder before moving toward another area of the gym where a trainer was signaling for him.

Kane returned his focus to Andrew, his careful gaze noting improvements while identifying adjustments still needed. Kane knew how difficult the transition would be, and if the kid weren't ready, it would be harder. But he would be there to help Andrew shift from being a fighter defined purely by aggression to a man who had discovered greater strength in relying on others.

"That's enough for today," Kane said with a nod of dismissal. "Go get some rest and ice that shoulder. We can pick up tomorrow morning." Andrew exhaled heavily, his fatigue finally showing. Kane watched him for a moment, seeing not just the raw talent that could be shaped into greatness but also the reflection of a younger version of him. Andrew was hungry, driven, searching for identity through victory. With a slight shake of his head, Kane turned away from his past.

Daphne straightened slightly as he approached, her hand still resting protectively over the swell of their child. Kane felt the familiar shift in his chest that had once terrified him but now served as a constant reminder of how completely his life had transformed.

"Hey," he said softly as he reached her, his hand coming to rest at the small of her back while he placed a gentle kiss on her forehead.

"Hey, yourself," Daphne replied, her free hand finding its way to his chest. "Andrew looks exhausted."

Kane's arms slid around her waist, hands coming to rest beside hers on the curve of her belly. His chin dropped to her shoulder as he breathed in the familiar scent of her perfume. "He's learning," Kane murmured against her skin. "Slowly. Stubbornly."

"Sounds like someone else I know," she teased, her fingers tracing small circles against his shoulder blade.

Kane chuckled, the sound rumbling through his chest. "Took me long enough," he acknowledged, pulling back just enough to meet her eyes. "But I got there eventually."

The journey from championship fighter to coach and mentor unfolded gradually after the fight against Tony. Kane had defended his time there more times after that, approaching each one with disciplined focus. When Kane had finally decided to retire, it had been on his own terms.

"You hungry?" Kane asked, his thumb tracing gentle patterns against the side of her belly, hoping to feel their child press a foot or elbow against his hand.

She smiled. "Always," she replied, the simple answer carrying their private joke about her pregnancy appetite.

Kane's hand moved to the small of her back again as they turned toward the gym's exit. Fighters and trainers acknowledged them with respectful nods or brief greetings, some out of reverence for Kane's fighting legacy, others to the partnership that had become something of a legend in the fighting community.

The story had evolved over the years, details embellished or simplified in the retelling, but the essential truth remained: Kane Mitchell, once known for his volatile temper and aggressive fighting style, had found something beyond victory that transformed him both in and out of the cage.

"Lopez is looking sharp for his bout next month," Daphne observed as they passed one of the gym's promising competitors working with an assistant coach. She watched his movements, taking in her client as he prepared. Her marketing experience had become integral to the gym's growing success, her professional eye for promotion helping elevate Warrior's Edge from a local training facility to a nationally recognized academy.

"He's ready," Kane agreed. "Making weight shouldn't be an issue this time."

They paused at the office Kane shared with Jackson long enough to collect Daphne's purse and his keys before continuing toward the exit. Kane knew the gym would remain open for hours still, the evening training sessions already underway with the coaching staff Kane and Jackson had carefully assembled. Kane's hand found Daphne's, their fingers intertwining as they stepped out of the gym.

He squeezed her hand gently, and she leaned against his shoulder as they walked toward the parking lot. Kane lifted her hand to press a kiss on the back of it.

"I was thinking Italian for dinner," he suggested as they reached his car, the flashy sports vehicle of his early career had been exchanged for an SUV, and he felt no regrets at that; it meant their family was only growing. "That place on Walnut you liked last week."

Daphne hummed appreciatively, her free hand resting on her belly as their child shifted position. "The one with the gnocchi that made me consider proposing marriage all over again?" Her smile carried a playful edge as she glanced at him from the corner of her eye.

"That's the one," Kane laughed.

As Daphne settled into her seat, she caught his hand before he could close the door, her expression shifting to something more serious. "I saw you watching him today," she said quietly. "Andrew. It looked like you were seeing yourself in him."

Kane paused. It amazed him how well she could read him, but he never took it for granted. "He's got the same demons," he acknowledged. "The same need to prove himself."

"And the same potential," Daphne added, her fingers tightening around his. "With the right guidance, he'll get from you."

The simple faith in her words settled into Kane with profound warmth. "I love you," he said, the declaration emerging with the same certainty as the first time he had spoken the words to her.

Daphne's smile lit the entire sky with its brilliance. "I love you too."

As Kane closed her door and moved around to the driver's side, he thought back to his journey and how he had gotten where he was. The high he had once chased from fighting was calmer now, but no less meaningful to him. Now, he found his joy in the morning light across Daphne's face, the movement of their child beneath his palm, and the progress of the fighters he worked with. He slipped behind the wheel, casting one final glance at the gym before turning to Daphne.

"Ready?" he asked, the simple question carrying echoes of countless others they had answered together over the years.

Daphne's hand found his once more, her fingers lacing through his with perfect familiarity. "Always," she replied.

Want to see more of Kane and Daphne's relationship? Get a special chapter of their proposal here or scan the QR code!

Author Note

T hank you so much for reading my book! It has taken me a year to bring this book to you, and I am so excited to be able to share it. This story is inspired by a boy that I tutored in High School who fought in the underground circuit in our area. I used to hear the stories he would tell, the way he would laugh at the antics of the fighters, and knew that one day I wanted to write a book to capture that energy.

If you have enjoyed reading this book please consider writing a review on Amazon, Goodreads or wherever you hang out online, to help others decide if they would like it.

You can find out the latest news, find bonus scenes and background information, and sign up for my newsletter at http://www.rkatze-books.com. Subscribers get access to early chapters, giveaways, and updates on upcoming stories to add to your reading list.

Thank you again for reading Challenging the Heart!

About the Author

R. Katze is a fan of all genres of novels. She began reading at a young age, and her most treasured possession was her library card because it gave her access to new worlds to explore. She began writing in grade school, when she realized that you can create and shape your own worlds, and she hasn't stopped. In high school R. Katze wrote and published poetry, and began writing full novels in 2020 during the Covid-19 pandemic.

R. Katze has a particular love of Romance Novels, and is drawn to all genres. She loves stories with a happily ever after, and will never write a story that doesn't end with one, even if it takes the characters time to achieve it. There is enough chaos in the world, and if a book can transport you for even a few moments to another place, then keep reading!

Other books by R. Katze
Of Sense and Sensibility
Hearts on the Line (Coming Soon)